Praise for *Constance Harding's (Rather) Startling Year*

"Wildly entertaining and amusing."   —*Publishers Weekly*

"Radford's alternate persona as a middle-aged housewife was clearly successful in her earlier blog and remains as witty and outrageous in her first novel."   —*Library Journal*

"Wonderfully amusing. A comic gem."

—Alexander McCall Smith

"Warning: unintended snorts of laughter may occur in public places. Comic satire erupts when modern mores and reality TV invade the comfortable confines of Constance Harding's cozy upper-crust world. I loved every dizzy, delightful page."

—Helen Simonson, bestselling author of
Major Pettigrew's Last Stand

"Ceri Radford has perfectly rendered the inner monologue of a clueless but loveable Everywoman. Comforting, witty, poignant, and delicious."   —Beth Harbison, *New York Times* bestselling
author of *Thin, Rich, Pretty* and
Always Something There to Remind Me

"With a heroine as sweet and naive as Constance, there is bound to be trouble. And there is. Hugely enjoyable, this is an unusual and sparkling debut. . . . *The Diary of an English Provincial Lady* de nos jours."

—Elizabeth Buchan, author of *Revenge* _____ *Woman*
and *Separate Beds*

PENGUIN BOOKS

CONSTANCE HARDING'S (RATHER) STARTLING YEAR

Ceri Radford is a journalist and author who lives near Geneva, Switzerland. *Constance Harding's (Rather) Startling Year* is her first novel.

To access Penguin Readers Guides online,
visit our Web site at www.penguin.com.

Constance Harding's (Rather) Startling Year

Ceri Radford

PENGUIN BOOKS

Previously published as *A Surrey State of Affairs*

PENGUIN BOOKS
Published by the Penguin Group
Penguin Group (USA) Inc., 375 Hudson Street, New York, New York 10014, U.S.A.

USA | Canada | Ireland | Australia | New Zealand | India | South Africa | China
Penguin Books Ltd, Registered Offices: 80 Strand, London WC2R 0RL, England
For more information about the Penguin Group visit penguin.com

First published in Great Britain as *A Surrey State of Affairs* by Abacus,
an imprint of Little Brown Book Group 2011
First published in the United States of America by Viking Penguin,
a member of Penguin Group (USA) Inc. 2012
Published in Penguin Books 2013

A Pamela Dorman / Penguin Book

THE LIBRARY OF CONGRESS HAS CATALOGED THE HARDCOVER EDITION AS FOLLOWS:
Radford, Ceri.
A Surrey state of affairs / Ceri Radford.
p. cm.
ISBN 978-0-670-02342-4 (hc.)
ISBN 978-0-14-312286-9 (pbk.)
1. Middle-aged women—Fiction. 2. Family secrets—Fiction. 3. Self-actualization (Psychology)
in women—Fiction. 4. Surrey (England)—Fiction. I. Title.
PR6118.A333S87 2012
823'.92—dc23
2011037624

Printed in the United States of America
10 9 8 7 6 5 4 3 2 1

Designed by Carla Bolte

ALWAYS LEARNING   PEARSON

To my husband, Chris.

*And to Constance's loyal online friends on
the original Telegraph.co.uk blog:
Expat in the US, Dolores Doolittle, and Canary Islander.*

ACKNOWLEDGMENTS

I would like to thank my mum for providing the occasional inspiration for the character of Constance, but without running away to Argentina; and Bev for her constructive badgering.

A huge thank-you to Pamela Dorman for delicately transplanting Constance to American soil. I'm also indebted to Julie Miesionczek, Grainne Fox, and Peter Robinson for their enthusiasm and support.

For reading my manuscript and helping to put Constance on the right track, thank you to my talented friend Sophie Hardach.

At the *Telegraph*, thanks to Marcus Warren, Shane Richmond, Kate Day, and Lucy Jones for their input, ideas, and humor while I was writing the blog.

Constance Harding's
(Rather) Startling Year

I suppose that this, my inaugural "blog," represents at least one new element to the New Year. If my son, Rupert, is to be believed, it may be read anywhere from Milton Keynes to Mauritius. This would certainly be a marked expansion from the usual audience for my reflections, which consists mostly of Darcy, my Eclectus parrot. He is a magnificent specimen who has been a great source of comfort since the children left home, but his attention span is not unwavering. Occasionally he punctuates my stories—on Natalia, the housekeeper's, blunders, or Miss Hughes, the bell ringer's, bunions—by breaking open a Brazil nut with a resonant crack. At that point I usually try calling my daughter, Sophie, or Rupert, who suggested last time that I might like to tell the World Wide Web all about it, rather than him. He is such a thoughtful boy.

In any case, now that Sophie has got me all set up—she also seemed to think that a blog would be a wonderful idea—and kindly shut herself away in her room to give me some privacy, I had better find something to tell you about. I may as well start with last night's little gathering. Now, I don't know how you feel about New Year's Eve, but, at the age of fifty-three, I have come to greet the passing of one year and the beginning of the next with a certain sense of jaded déjà vu. Party poppers and the like are best left to excitable eighteen-year-olds like Sophie.

And yet, for my husband, Jeffrey's, sake, I decided to rouse myself and organize a Murder Mystery evening. As he is a lawyer, I thought it would appeal to his professional powers of deduction. He may be specialized in mergers and acquisitions rather than homicide, but I imagine there are underlying similarities. And seeing as he has been a little cranky recently, I thought the distraction would do him good.

The evening began well. I wore an elegant old velvet dress of Mother's, several strands of pearls, and a fox stole—which blended nicely into my bobbed auburn hair—to play the countess. Jeffrey was the count, which suited his dignified manner. His brother, Edward, wore a stethoscope to play the physician, while my sister-in-law, Harriet, was a nun. Mother played an exiled French aristocrat with impeccable haughtiness. Reginald, our vicar, gamely took the part of the butler. Sophie avoided the proceedings entirely by staying at a friend's house for the evening. This was just as well, given that the last time she saw my fox stole she screamed.

Natalia played herself. I doubt whether the housekeeper of the original tale was a surly Lithuanian with a tenuous grasp of the Queen's English, but one must make do with the materials at hand. To her credit, she topped up Jeffrey's wineglass very diligently, although the girl really should sort out some sturdier buttons for the front of her blouse. Perhaps I should have given her a new one for Christmas, instead of the flashy ostrich feather earrings that Jeffrey had given me seven years ago.

After dinner, I paced in the drawing room, as the instructions recommended, while the other dramatis personae scattered themselves throughout the house. Then the lights went out. There was a brief, manly gasp, which was almost immediately drowned out by the shrill, theatrical screech of my sister-in-law, Harriet. The nun was dead.

The ensuing investigations were quite good fun, with Reginald blushing lest he should cause offense to anyone by implying even fictitious guilt, and the corpse rising from the dead to demand a glass of port. Jeffrey was the only one shrewd enough to guess that Natalia, who had remained impassive throughout, had committed the dastardly deed. He has a fine legal brain. Mother slapped him on the back so hard that he nearly choked on his brandy. At midnight, there was a cheerful ambience as we clinked our crystal champagne flutes. Harriet threw off her wimple, and Reginald attempted to dance, with the same jerky motion of a shot crow plummeting to the ground. Even Mother managed to smile.

The evening may have been a success, but I went to bed for the first time this year with the memory of that curious, masculine gasp ringing in my ears long after "Auld Lang Syne" had faded.

WEDNESDAY, JANUARY 2

Forgive me for going on a bit yesterday. I don't know what got into me. The ease of tip-tapping away on this new Lap-Top must have gone to my head. I haven't even introduced myself yet.

My name is Constance Harding. I am wife to Jeffrey, a senior partner at Alpha & Omega; mother to Rupert, a twenty-five-year-old IT consultant, and to Sophie, a slightly directionless adolescent who will shortly be returning to her gap-year project counting stickleback at an eco lodge in the Ardèche.

I am currently sitting in my favorite cream Regency-style chair in the drawing room, typing on the computer that Jeffrey gave me for Christmas and Rupert obligingly set up with the necessary "software." While I write, I am attempting to peel off a small, obstinate Alpha & Omega sticker, which Jeffrey must have affixed to my gift in an absentminded moment of corporate loyalty.

Our home is a comfortable five-bedroom Georgian house located on the outskirts of a pleasant village in Surrey. Our community has a green, a pub called The Plucked Pheasant, a church called St. Mary's, a florist, a restaurant, and a post office: in short it is quintessentially English, with the exception of the tea shop, which has unfortunately been converted into a faux-Italian, chrome-furnished café selling biscotti and lattes.

This information will have to suffice for now. I will not be more specific lest rampaging hordes of Internet users trample my snowdrops, smash the French windows, and steal the candlesticks. Such things occur. I have read about them in the *Daily Telegraph*.

THURSDAY, JANUARY 3

Jeffrey was in a funny mood this morning. He hardly paused to kiss me good-bye as he hurried off for the 7:22 to Waterloo, leaving behind two toast crusts smeared with marmalade and half a tepid cup of Earl Grey.

Perhaps he is sad that it is time to return to work after the Christmas break, and that Sophie will be leaving for France soon. Or perhaps he is simply irritated by Natalia's increasing slovenliness. Despite my reprimands, she keeps leaving her underwear to dry in his study, eschewing the foldaway rack I put in her room expressly for this purpose. Cluttered house, cluttered mind, I have always said. No wonder he looked so distracted. To make matters worse, the undergarments in question are made of some sort of unpleasant, black polyester material. I worry that they might melt and mark the radiators, which I had the handyman regloss only last autumn. I will have to have words with her again.

Anyway, after Jeffrey had left I put the dishes to one side for Natalia, poured myself a coffee, and went to sit in the conservatory to read a magazine. I'm not the idle type, but I don't believe in denying myself life's little luxuries either.

I had just finished a good article on the resurgence of floral wallpaper, of which I approve, when I spotted an advertisement in the classified section that shocked me to the core. It was for something called Illicit Encounters. "Married, but want some excitement back?" it queried, offering "free gold membership for women" and "complete confidentiality."

Now, I'm not saying we should go back to the days of horse-whipping adulterers, but I do think there's something very wrong with our society if a service that explicitly promotes infidelity can advertise in a magazine aimed at respectable women.

I felt a little sordid just reading it. But mainly grateful that Jeffrey and I have such a stable, trusting marriage.

FRIDAY, JANUARY 4

Why is it that no sooner has Jeffrey taken the Christmas tree down each year than newspapers start haranguing us to lose the weight we presumably gained by following their festive recipes? The newspaper today carried a "New Year, New You" diet feature, which advocated cabbage soup as the means of transformation.

I find the modern attitude to food most alarming. It is all Belgian chocolate torte with panna cotta one day, "detox" diets of hot water and coal the next. Stuff and nonsense, I say. Women of my generation know the simple truth: if you want to lose weight, eat less and move more. I may not be quite the lithe young wraith that I was on my wedding day, but I am still more hour-glass than port glass, so Jeffrey has no cause to complain. I do hope Sophie doesn't succumb to all the mumbo jumbo. She is as thin as a reed—as I was at her age—so certainly doesn't need to, but, then, she is at a delicate and impressionable age.

Earlier, as she was sprawled across the sofa reading a trashy-looking magazine, I attempted to talk to her about how important it is to keep a healthy attitude toward her figure. Just as

I was getting into my stride on the benefits of light, regular exercise such as brisk walking or gardening, she rolled her eyes, popped a mince pie into her mouth, and turned the television on.

Nine days until she returns to France.

SATURDAY, JANUARY 5

Once again I have been lured by the ease of this "blog" writing into saying more than I should. I do not want you to conclude that I am earnestly counting down the days until my daughter's departure. It is just as well that I changed the title of my blog as soon as Sophie had set me up ("Silver Ringer" has a nice, yet anonymous, ring to it): I certainly would not want her to read it and conclude the same. I shall miss her. The days after she has left always drag; the clock ticks more loudly, Natalia's singed omelet chafes the palate, I find myself pacing the hallway as I wait for Jeffrey to get home. And yet, as any mother of teenagers will realize, affection and frustration are not mutually exclusive. I can only hope that a year of counting sticklebacks will add some much-needed patience and poise to her character. And that should she happen to meet a respectable young man, he won't be put off by the sight of her in Wellington boots.

SUNDAY, JANUARY 6

The usual activities today: church and a visit to Mother at The Copse. I imagine the name of her retirement home is supposed to evoke a pleasant image of a small group of trees, possibly waving in the breeze, but unfortunately some reprobate keeps spray painting in an extraneous *r.*

Much of the day was spent listening to monologues of a moralistic bent, which Reginald delivers as a vocational duty, and

Mother, a hobby. The contrast in their approaches is marked. Whenever our dear vicar speaks, he assumes a look of mild physical pain, as if one of the pins from the parish notice board had been slipped into his vestment, and seeks to involve others as quickly as possible. He insisted on asking each member of the congregation in turn how we would renew our faith this year. I only just managed to elbow Jeffrey awake in time for his turn.

Mother does not share Reginald's pluralistic zeal. A light goes on in her eyes when she begins to speak, which intensifies to a laserlike fury should anyone interrupt. My small initial question—about how best to stop Natalia from drying her underwear on the radiators—prompted a lengthy discourse on the role of the servant, the decline of morals, the decline of girdles, the importance of hierarchies, the empire, and the penal code. It culminated in the recommendation that I lock Natalia in the larder for two days. This is certainly a tempting prospect, but Jeffrey tells me it would contravene modern employment legislation.

MONDAY, JANUARY 7

Today I took Sophie shopping. I had hoped to find her some warm, practical, yet elegant clothing for the winter, which despite global warming is quite chilly this year in the south of France. I had also hoped, perhaps optimistically, for an opportunity to impart a little valuable advice before she leaves. To these ends, I was prepared to undertake the ultimate maternal sacrifice—much like a lioness hurling herself in the path of a stampeding elephant to save her cubs—and endure both the London Underground and the January sales.

The day did not begin auspiciously. As soon as we sat down on the train into town, Sophie plugged herself into the tiny pink iPod that I had reluctantly given her for Christmas, making conversation impossible. If only I had not succumbed to her hunger strike and bought her the accursed thing.

When we finally arrived in central London, having been pitched into a roiling bath of malodorous humanity on the Underground, I immediately craved the safe haven of John Lewis. Sophie favored H&M, a shop that resembles a jumble sale held in a hurricane-struck brothel. She prevailed.

A similar conflict ensued at lunchtime. I wanted to go to the tearoom in the Victoria and Albert Museum, where they do lovely open sandwiches and scones, and Sophie wanted to go to a cramped canteen with an incomprehensible menu called Wagawama. Once again, I complied, in the hope of putting her in the right mood for a nice chat, but the wretched din and clatter of our fellow diners ruled this out. I muttered into my misbegotten noodles that one should never trust boys who don't own cuff links. Then I requested a knife and fork.

Things did not improve after lunch. My offer to buy her a smart pair of shoes with a low, practical heel was rebuffed. My offer to buy her a cashmere cardigan was rebuffed. In fact, throughout the course of the entire day, our tastes coincided on one single item: a pair of woolen mittens, which I deemed practical, and Sophie, "retro."

By four P.M., I had resigned myself to a fruitless day. I shepherded Sophie toward the Underground, steering her away from a long-haired vagrant on the street corner. To my horror, she brushed me aside, ran up to the malingerer, and flung her arms around his scrawny, tan-colored neck. It transpired that the young man was Nicolas, the elder brother of her school friend Jessica and a distant cousin of Lady Zara Phillips.

When did the upper classes forget how to dress?

TUESDAY, JANUARY 8

There is a circus in the village. First I saw the gaudy pink and yellow posters, then I saw the line of caravans desecrating the village green. I have told Jeffrey to make sure that all our valuables are safely locked away. When I was a little girl, circuses meant candy floss, lions, and clowns. Now, they mean Lycra-clad Latvians and a dramatic spike in local crime rates.

"Gypsies," Miss Hughes said to me in a loud whisper at the newsagent. "You can't trust them."

I crossed my arms and shook my head. One cannot say such things, not in this day and age. It is acceptable to mistrust Latvian performance artists because they are not a racial group, but I am afraid Miss Hughes's views border on prejudice.

"You can't generalize like that," I told her firmly. "Not everyone conforms to a racial stereotype." I smiled broadly at Mr. Rasheed, the newsagent, but he must have been too busy counting the coppers, with which Miss Hughes always, pays to notice.

In any case, Sophie has gone to the circus, despite my admonitions that her time would be better spent practicing her French or removing her flaking nail polish.

WEDNESDAY, JANUARY 9

Last night was the first bell-ringing practice of the year. Fortunately neither the bells nor we ringers had rusted over during the Christmas break. Everyone was there—Reginald, the vicar; Daphne, the postmistress; the indomitable Miss Hughes; Gerald, the history teacher, and his wife, Rosemary—and everyone was just the same, with the notable exception of Rosemary. She was wearing lipstick. Bright red lipstick. Her hair, which is of the curly brown variety, had been swept up into a high ponytail, lending her the appearance of a muddied poodle. There was a strange gleam to her eye and flush to her cheek. High heels had replaced orthopedic sandals.

When she visited the ladies during our tea break, I speculated to Miss Hughes that Rosemary had perhaps undergone a "New Year, New You" makeover. Miss Hughes said she thought it was the menopause.

THURSDAY, JANUARY 10

Reginald, the vicar, came round for a cup of tea this morning. He wished to talk about his son, David, a pasty-faced nineteen-year-old who drives the van of the visiting library. Poor Reginald has brought up his son according to his liberal beliefs, preaching the importance of tolerance and open-mindedness. As a result, David has converted to Kabbalah, some sort of mystic sect favored by celebrity gym fanatics such as Madonna. Apparently, this explains why he has taken to wearing a red wristband. Last time I saw him, I thought he had simply visited the municipal pool.

Reginald stared pensively at his cup of peppermint tea and asked me for advice, with a little tremor of anxiety in his gentle voice. I suggested that he should either find David a girlfriend or enroll him in the Territorial Army. Both options would dramatically reduce his free time and thus his ability to indulge in unorthodox religious experiments. Reginald pointed out that he was a pacifist, and we both fell silent.

Then I had a sudden moment of inspiration. Sophie! Religious eccentricities aside, David is a very decent sort of young man, with a polite way of talking to his elders and clean fingernails. He could be a positive influence on her. Admittedly, she leaves for the Ardèche on Sunday, but they could always be pen pals. There is something ineffably romantic about penning letters to a dear and distant acquaintance, about yearning for someone far away across the seas; besides, it might improve her grammar.

FRIDAY, JANUARY 11

Reginald and David have just left, the latter with a slight limp. Sophie has shut herself in her room in disgust. Things did not proceed entirely as planned.

I did my best for poor Reginald. Once the vicar and his son were strategically positioned in the drawing room and had dried themselves off from the tea that Natalia had spilled over their laps, I went to fetch Sophie from her room. I told her that David, a charming, intelligent, and sensitive young man, was waiting downstairs. She asked if I meant "that retard with the gay hair." This was not a promising beginning.

Nevertheless, I coaxed her downstairs with the offer of a slice of my Madeira cake. I had already hidden most of the chairs in the kitchen, so the only seat available was next to David on the sofa. At the sight of my daughter—dressed, inexplicably, in a ballet tutu and leggings—David's pale features lit up and his protuberant ears almost waggled in delight. If only he would shave the peachlike fuzz off his upper lip he would be perfectly eligible.

Reginald and I chatted away, subtly alluding to David's achievements, including his certificate from the council for services to the visiting library. However, Sophie merely stared at a small mark on the wall—perhaps she too has noticed Natalia's sloppy cleaning standards.

Eventually, Sophie broke her silence and asked why David was wearing a bracelet. He replied with a long-winded and impassioned account of Kabbalah, which concluded with the offer of enjoining her into the faith. Sophie looked blank. David must have misread her confusion for tacit consent, because he suddenly took her small hand in his large, gangly one, and produced a spare red bracelet from the pocket of his chinos. Sophie leaped to her feet and kicked him in the shin like a mule. I was wholly ashamed of her. If she had to resort to violence, she could at least have slapped him in the face like a lady.

SATURDAY, JANUARY 12

Reginald telephoned to apologize today. I told him it was quite unnecessary: he is not responsible for his son's erratic behavior. If we were to be held to account for our children's every misdeed, then a certain shop assistant at Selfridges would still want my head on a platter after a six-year-old Sophie kicked over her pyramid of champagne flutes in a fit of pique.

If an apology is due, it is from Sophie. I tapped on her door in order to suggest as much, and was greeted with a very grudging "Yeah, come in." I did so, and found a scene of devastation. Given that she leaves for France tomorrow, I had been hoping to observe neat stacks of belongings ready to be packed. Instead there were clothes strewn across her unmade bed and unvacuumed carpet willy-nilly, bottles of nail polish tipped over magazines, half-burned candles nesting with chocolate bar wrappers and pots of unidentifiable unguents. Even though Sophie says she wants to save the planet, there were shopping bags of new but unworn clothes from Topshop and Primark, all presumably made in some sweatshop in India or Cambodia then shipped halfway across the world. Much to my chagrin, I even spotted one of my French silk nighties, which had been slashed down one side and pieced back together with a row of large safety pins. I gesticulated toward it and she calmly announced that it was her new dress, but she wasn't quite sure about the color. This adds insult to injury. Everybody knows that peach is very flattering on the complexion.

It was useless trying to remonstrate with her against such a backdrop. I will instruct Natalia to clean the room from top to bottom on Monday. She could do with the exercise, instead of stretching out on the leather sofa in Jeffrey's study at every opportunity. She may be slim for now but these Russian types are quick to develop a stout bottom.

SUNDAY, JANUARY 13

Sophie is gone. Jeffrey and I drove her to the airport this afternoon. We stood on the cold tarmac outside Gatwick's North Terminal, the wind whipping around her overfilled drag-along suitcase. I gave her a firm hug, Jeffrey patted her on the back. She felt very thin and fragile in my arms. For a moment I thought she was crying, but just as I went to comfort her she claimed that her hair had blown into her eyes and swore disgustingly.

When I got home, I tried to distract myself by talking to Darcy, but I fear that Natalia has been teaching him Lithuanian. Either that or he has bird flu. He made a strange, harsh noise when I tried to get him to say "She sells seashells on the seashore." I called Rupert, who told me that unless Darcy shows other symptoms beyond talking funny I shouldn't worry. Reassured, I asked him what he'd been up to today and he said he had been "downloading MP3s," or something even less intelligible than a parrot's Lithuanian.

MONDAY, JANUARY 14

Today, I finally decided to have words with Natalia. I have had enough of her attitude, her cold soups, her collapsed soufflés, her lackluster dusting, her scattered underwear. If she is to give Sophie's room the deep clean it requires, she will have to raise her standards. I positioned myself in the leather swivel chair in Jeffrey's study, then summoned her.

She did not present herself with the air of anxious deference I had been expecting. Instead she sauntered in and leaned against the wall, with one hand in her jeans pocket, the other twirling the strange tawny streaks that thread through her long, black hair. I informed her that her cleaning was below par and that she had better buck up, but she merely shrugged and looked baffled. I told her to get her act together, but she just stared. I told her to stop leaving her undergarments on the radiator. Again, she looked flummoxed. In desperation, I drew a diagram. She was wide-eyed, but when I stabbed at the drawing insistently with my pencil, she nodded slowly.

I believe that I have bent her will to mine.

TUESDAY, JANUARY 15

My attempt to discipline Natalia has backfired. Yesterday, Jeffrey came home from work and headed upstairs toward his study. I followed him so that I could tell him all about the latest Aga malfunction on the stairway. He opened the door to his study and we were both greeted by the unsettling sight of Natalia cleaning the room in her underwear, which was scant, black, and dotted with little shiny red hearts. It appears that as well as struggling with English, she is incapable of deciphering a simple diagram. Mother never had problems like this in her day. Jeffrey had to lie down to recover from the shock. Englishmen are not accustomed to such spectacles.

WEDNESDAY, JANUARY 16

I bear grim tidings from bell ringing. Last night I opened the door to the belfry at precisely 7:30 P.M. and was greeted with the usual waft of cold, stony air and the sight of Gerald standing in the shadows. His presence was nothing unusual in itself: the man is punctual to a fault, a habit instilled by twenty-five years of teaching to the bell at the local boys' school. And yet he failed to return my cheery "Good evening." When I said it again, he looked up at me with bloodshot eyes and a morose expression. It was then that I noticed the change to his appearance. Ginger stubble spread across his face like an exotic fungus. His usual crisp checked shirt and lustrous leather loafers were gone, replaced by a muddied sack-like pullover and a pair of slippers. His beige chinos lacked their usual immaculate crease down the front. There were purple shadows under his eyes. Tufts of hair protruded from his ears.

"Dear Gerald!" I said. "What on earth has happened to you?"

"It's Rosemary," he said, in a small, cracked voice. "She's gone."

"On the Women's Institute's away week to Tunbridge Wells? Don't worry, she'll soon be back. I'd have gone myself if I could trust Natalia to look after things."

But she had not gone to admire the architecture of Kent. Rosemary, Brown Owl for the village Brownie group, star fund-raiser of Surrey Conservatives, loyal wife to Gerald and mother of his two grown sons, had run away with a trapeze artist from the visiting circus.

I am summarizing this information so as not to try your patience: it took me, and subsequently the other bell ringers, half an hour to wheedle the truth out of Gerald. At one point, Reginald had to revive him with a shot of the alcohol we keep next to the biscuit tin to clean rust stains off the bells. The man was quite incapacitated with shock. I can't blame him. None of us saw it coming, although, come to think of it, Rosemary did perform a particularly emotive rendition of Queen's "I Want to Break Free" at the Rotary Club "dinner and divas' karaoke" fund-raiser last year. At one point she tore a clump of her hair out for emphasis. I informed Miss Hughes as such when poor

Gerald went to the lavatory, and she agreed that the rot had set in long ago.

THURSDAY, JANUARY 17

I wonder if there's any special technique for persuading an adult son to divulge a little more information about his life. The unsettling events at bell ringing have made me ponder how little we sometimes know about those who are close to us. Given the usual tenor of my conversations with Rupert, I am unlikely to be enlightened anytime soon. Last night's exchange was typical of its genre. It went something like this:

"Good evening, Rupert. How are you?"

"Hi, Mum. Fine, thanks."

"So, tell me what's new!"

"Oh, not a lot."

"How's work?"

"Fine."

"How's the flat?"

"Fine."

"Are you warm enough?"

"Yes."

"Are you wearing that nice scarf I bought you for Christmas?"

"Yes."

"Have you watered your houseplants?"

"Mum, I told you—they're cacti."

And so on and so forth, until eventually I'm compelled to fill the silence by gabbling on about Rosemary, the bell-ringing adulteress, and Natalia's sluttish underwear.

He is my own flesh and blood, and yet it alarms me sometimes that I know so little about the daily realities of his life. In all his twenty-five years, he has never once brought a girlfriend home, and for the amount of information he voluntarily imparts he could just as easily be a tap-dancing Martian as a software specialist in Milton Keynes.

FRIDAY, JANUARY 18

While lying awake last night pondering my son's reticence and romantic ineptitude, I was struck by a brilliant idea. I was tempted to jab Jeffrey in the ribs and share it with him immediately, but he was snoring so peacefully I was loath to disturb him. Instead I will share it with you. It runs as follows.

In two weeks' time, Rupert will celebrate his twenty-sixth birthday. To mark the occasion, I will organize a small party, and I will invite girls, as many girls as I can muster. Once they are assembled, I will present Rupert with gifts that underline his attractiveness to the modern female. These will include:

A rugby ball. For all the newspaper articles I read about the rise of the so-called "metrosexual," there is no doubt in my mind that most girls still hanker after a good old-fashioned muddied oaf.

A compass. To underscore the rugged, outdoorsy image, and also demonstrate his protective side. Should a young couple lose their way, it is always best for the man to be prepared.

A book by Jeremy Clarkson. Again, this will mark him out as bracingly free of namby-pamby metrosexuality. No woman goes weak at the knees for a liberal democrat.

A puppy. What woman can resist a young man in possession of a suitably doe-eyed hound? Clearly, I am thinking of something in the Labrador direction, not those vicious pit bull creatures that poor people keep, though I can't fathom why fake gold jewelry would require a guard dog.

MONDAY, JANUARY 21

I do not wish to sound remiss in my wifely devotion, but I was almost relieved when Jeffrey returned to work today. I have heard nothing this weekend but ski talk, and frankly it chills me to the marrow, as if I were already stuck on some wretched, blizzard-swept peak. The annual trip to St. Moritz organized by Jeffrey's law firm looms, and I am duty-bound to accompany him.

While Jeffrey derives an intense, childlike delight from the sport, I view it as nothing more than a likely means of breaking my bones and destroying my dignity.

It is impossible to maintain a tolerable level of decorum while clad in a waterproof duvet with two planks, two poles, hat, gloves, goggles, tissues, sunscreen, ChapStick, emergency snack, wet wipes, and lipstick all attached to one's person. What's more, one is always at risk of being crushed by an avalanche or a German snowboarder.

Jeffrey's brother, Edward, came for dinner on Saturday and the two men spent the entire evening regaling one another with competitive tales of black diamond runs and off-piste derring-do. Harriet, my long-suffering sister-in-law, rolled her eyes at me in sympathy but there was little we could do. I tried to change the subject to my plans for Rupert's birthday and the rising cost of hot chocolate in the Alps, but it was to no avail.

My one comfort is that Sophie will be joining us for the trip. She will not be able to wriggle out of a constructive tête-à-tête if we are sealed inside a ski lift thirty feet above the ground.

TUESDAY, JANUARY 22

Reginald came to see me today. I presumed that he wished to discuss how best to provide Gerald with suitable pastoral care and support ahead of this evening's bell-ringing practice, but it turned out that other matters, closer to home, pressed upon him.

As he dunked a biscuit in his tea (an unpleasant habit, but I let it pass), he informed me in his usual timorous voice that David had renounced Kabbalah. Before I could congratulate him, the troubled look in his moist gray eyes silenced me. David, it appears, has renounced his former faith in favor of Islam. He is attempting to cultivate the fluff on his chin into a fist-sized beard. He has renamed himself Abdul Mohammed Ahmed Aziz, and has taken to draping himself in a black-and-white checked neck cloth. He has thrown Reginald's organic sage and mustard seed sausages in the bin, and gone through today's *Guardian* scribbling over any exposed female flesh with a black felt-tip pen. (I felt he should have done the same thing for the words, but kept that to myself.)

By the time Reginald had finished mingling his concern for his son's intolerant zeal with a few paeans to the noble history of the Islamic faith, his biscuit had disintegrated and his tea had gone cold. I did not know what to say. His predicament is alien to me. My family has always attended church but none of us is religious.

Nevertheless, I sincerely wished to help poor Reginald. I told him to bring David along to Rupert's birthday party. A good party with a few pretty girls and a bowl of rum punch may just shake him out of his stringent beliefs. Or, if it does not, he can sulk in the corner and thus act as a foil to cast Rupert in a more favorable light.

WEDNESDAY, JANUARY 23

Bell ringing last night. Poor Gerald's condition has deteriorated. His nasal hair is rampant, his slippers encrusted with grime. We tried to carry on as usual, but the poor man just could not ring his bell with enough vigor. At one point he was so over-come with emotion that he asked me to hold it for him. I made sure I washed my hands afterward.

THURSDAY, JANUARY 24

Exciting news! The ladies from Church Flowers are on board for Rupert's birthday party. Pru has already vouched for her daughter Ruth, a primary school teacher and keen amateur dramatist, being free, and the other ladies are all making similar inquiries of their relations.

One of them has even put me in touch with a Labrador dealer. The more I think about it, the more I congratulate myself on this part of the plan. Rupert was a sensitive, responsible sort of child who, unlike Sophie, never went through a phase of pulling Dar-cy's tail feathers, so I'm sure that he will be very well suited to looking after a dog. His landlord won't have cause to complain—if anything, a watchful pet would be a bonus for the property. Rupert could train it to snap at any wood pigeons or tramps loitering outside.

FRIDAY, JANUARY 25

Today I informed Rupert of my plan for his birthday. I telephoned him at work so that he would be less likely to miss my call. It would be going too far to say that he greeted the news with unmitigated joy; and yet, after half an hour or so of gentle persuasion, he began to see the merits of the scheme and agreed to cancel his reservation at the Brasserie Blanc in Milton Keynes. I offered to send out invitations to the friends who were meant to eat with him, but he could not remember their addresses. It is so sad that the Internet has ruined the memories of the young.

SUNDAY, JANUARY 27

Jeffrey has dropped a bombshell on me. Although he is, in general, a most unobjectionable sort of husband, there are moments when he intersperses months of conjugal calm with the sudden announcement that, say, the senior partner at Alpha & Omega will be dining with us that very evening, or that he will be leaving in two hours for a golf weekend in Morocco.

Today's news was more shattering. In the brief interim between finishing his pudding and picking up *The Economist,* just as Natalia was clattering about with the dishes and I was listing the arrangements for Rupert's party, he calmly announced that we would have to cater for an extra guest next weekend: Ivan.

Dear readers, you cannot know the dread that these words provoke. Ivan the Terrible, as I think of him, is Jeffrey's most disreputable friend, a coarse, lumbering, foul-mouthed, foul-breathed, yellow-toothed reminder of a most unfortunate chapter of my husband's past.

Jeffrey met Ivan at Durham University when he was going through his Communist phase. This was before we were dating, I hasten to add. Deciding at the age of nineteen that progress was repellent, Jeffrey had a fleeting fixation with the Soviet Union, which led to his friendship with Ivan, the son of Russian émigrés, and the stenciling on his dormitory wall of a hammer and sickle. By the time I began dating Jeffrey, he had completed an internship at Alpha & Omega, joined the Young Conservatives, and whited out the offending symbol, so my conscience is clear. Ivan too has long abandoned any semblance of Communist sympathies in favor of the cut and thrust—and Armani suits—of the business world. The only legacy of his past is his reluctance to pay to get his teeth fixed.

And yet you will understand that the arrival of such a man is by no means a welcome development when one is carefully orchestrating the correct backdrop for one's son to fall in love with a primary school teacher.

MONDAY, JANUARY 28

Today I took Jeffrey's Land Rover out to pick up Poppy, a very fetching three-month-old black Labrador puppy with a damp nose, a perky tail, and boisterous brown eyes. I am not the sentimental sort—I do not, like Sophie, cry over episodes of *Animal Hospital*—and yet I must admit that I have something of a soft spot for dogs.

I grew up in a rambling old place in the Cotswolds surrounded by collies and horses; if it were not for Jeffrey's allergies I would have bought myself a chocolate-brown Labrador years ago. In the end Darcy has made a splendid—and allergen-free—substitute, though he is never going to bow down or fetch a stick. He once gnawed his way through a Christmas tree, but it was not the same.

Poppy must remain hidden until Friday. I do not stoop to keeping secrets from my husband as such, but there are some things it is simply better for him not to know. The mere mention of a puppy would doubtless start him off sniffing and sneezing.

I have enlisted Natalia's help. This is not always a straightforward procedure, but for once the girl has stepped up to the mark. As soon as she saw Poppy she threw her arms around her neck, stroking her ears and wittering away in her odd foreign tongue while I explained about Rupert's party, Jeffrey's allergies, and the need for canine concealment. I showed her how to measure out the dog food and top up her water bowl. Her eagerness to help with Poppy impressed me. I may reward her by popping in to Marks & Spencer to buy her some more comfortable underwear.

I am convinced that this would improve her mood, which might have a resulting effect on Jeffrey's too. Whenever she enters a room, he starts to look uncomfortable, and then leaves it, then once she has left, he comes back again. Her moodiness is obviously too much for him to bear, and I worry that all that coming and going must put a strain on the poor man.

TUESDAY, JANUARY 29

My neighbor Tanya stopped by for a coffee this morning. She's a youngish woman—around the thirty mark, although she dresses more like a girl Sophie's age—whom I've grown rather friendly with over the past year or so. This is despite the fact that she wears hoop earrings and insists on shortening my name to Connie, which sounds vulgar when pronounced by anyone other than Jeffrey, and only then is all right in an intimate setting.

Tanya doesn't have much to do with her time, and there aren't many other women her age around here who don't have little children to look after. She used to be a PA, or whatever they say now for a secretary, on her husband, Mark's, trading floor, but I suspect that that was only a means to an end. They moved into a new, rather flashy faux-Tudor house with a lawn like a billiard table and regimented little rows of waxy green shrubs, so she can't even get into renovating or gardening. Which leaves her plenty of time to pop by, sip a cup of black coffee, and lick the cream off one of my scones (she "doesn't do carbs" or some such nonsense).

I invited her to the party on Friday and she agreed immediately, offering to bring some "nibbles." She gave me a strange look when I told her all about my plans for Rupert, and seemed to be about to say something when the sound of vigorous barking came from the utility room. I decided to take her through to meet Poppy, although this was, in retrospect, a mistake. Tanya shrieked in horror as Poppy uncoiled herself like a tightly wound spring and inflicted a flurry of grubby paw prints all over her tight white jeans. I tried to clean them up with the dish cloth, but Natalia must have already used it to wipe Jeffrey's marmalade off the kitchen table, so I might have made matters worse. After that, Tanya left promptly to go into London for a "St. Tropez and a Brazilian." I told her she shouldn't drink too many cocktails if she was driving.

WEDNESDAY, JANUARY 30

Poor Gerald still hasn't rallied his spirits: he cut a thoroughly miserable and disheveled figure at bell ringing last night. What's more, he appears to have developed a full-fledged phobia of men in Lycra. He told us that trapeze artists swing through his nightmares, and that he was trapped in his own home for half an hour yesterday morning waiting for a string of cyclists to disappear from view.

I'm not without sympathy, but he does need to stiffen his upper lip, instead of looking at me with that beseeching expression that reminds me of Poppy whenever I walk past the box of dog biscuits. He's a grown man. It's time he took matters into his own hands.

I invited him to Rupert's party, which can't come around soon enough. Poppy is not easy to hide. Jeffrey started sneezing this morning, but luckily I managed to convince him that he was coming down with a cold, and sent him off to work with a flask of hot lemon and whiskey.

THURSDAY, JANUARY 31

Ivan the Terrible is here. I write this late at night, hunched over the computer in the study, the sound of raucous laughter and clinking glasses echoing up the stairway. I had actually attempted to go to bed, but Jeffrey was playing his accursed Led Zeppelin album so loudly it made my bedside table rattle.

It has been a trying evening, from the moment I saw Ivan amble through the door, trample mud into my oatmeal carpet, and clasp Jeffrey in a bear hug. He was dressed in blue jeans, a black suit jacket, and a white T-shirt, above which graying chest hair spooled grotesquely. The smile on his face reminded me of the velociraptors in the film *Jurassic Park,* which made Rupert wet the bed when he was nine. I only just managed not to recoil when he kissed me on the cheek. He is the sort of man who always makes as if he were going to kiss you on the lips, causing you to angle frantically to one side, before swerving at the last moment and laughing throatily.

Throughout dinner I tried to smile serenely, even while Ivan clacked his teeth against his cutlery and scattered bread crumbs willy-nilly across my new damask rose tablecloth. Natalia, however, was not so accommodating. Perhaps there is some lingering, deep-seated animosity between the Lithuanian and the Russian races; perhaps she resented having to work late and miss *Britain's Got Talent.* I do not condone rudeness toward guests, of course, but I had to dab my napkin to my mouth to stifle a small laugh when she spilled tomato and basil soup all over Ivan's white Ralph Lauren T-shirt.

Ivan, for his part, responded to her hostility by flirting outrageously. At least, I presume he was flirting: he kept muttering to her in a foreign language with a lascivious expression on his face. It all reached a climax at dessert, when he pinched her bottom just as she was leaning over to pour cream on Jeffrey's profiteroles.

Natalia let loose a barrage of what I presume was abuse in what I presume was Lithuanian, Ivan roared with laughter, Darcy started squawking, and Jeffrey went to the drinks cabinet for a whiskey and soda. Then Natalia fled to her room and put on *Britain's Got Talent* at full volume, while Jeffrey reciprocated with Led Zeppelin.

Every time Ivan visits, Jeffrey attempts to relive his lost youth. What he doesn't realize is that, much like communism, it is best consigned to the dustbin of history.

 FRIDAY, FEBRUARY 1

I wish the laws of hospitality had not compelled me to taste some of Ivan's foul vodka last night. I need a clear head today to focus on the challenges ahead. Before the party, I must take Poppy for a walk, teach Natalia how to make smoked salmon and cream cheese vol-au-vent, decorate the house with flowers (I thought white lilies would be best—attractive yet not too fussy, which is just the look Rupert should aim for), chill the champagne, wrap the gifts, impinge some basic human decency upon the character of Ivan the Terrible, and pick up my favorite dress—soft gray wool with a cowl neck—from the dry cleaner's.

SATURDAY, FEBRUARY 2

12:33 A.M.

Once again I find myself hunched over my keyboard late at night, pouring my heart out into the boundless ether of the Internet, gnawing my nails with angst, and ruining all my careful work with the buffing block.

Rupert's party was not the triumph that I had been anticipating. He is not smitten with Ruth—or any of the other girls in attendance, for that matter—and he is no longer speaking to me.

Jeffrey is sleeping in the spare room. He says this is because he does not wish to wake me with the cough caused by "that wretched mutt," but I fear this is only partly the truth. Ivan the Terrible enjoyed himself, but this in itself is a sad indictment of my attempts to provide a civilized party.

The evening began well enough. The guests arrived, Pru, Ruth, and Miss Hughes with homemade tarts and fairy cakes, Gerald with a light coating of dandruff, Tanya with a tray of cellophane-wrapped vegetables and hummus from Waitrose. Reginald arrived with David, who wore a black-and-white scarf enveloping half his head. I suppose it did at least disguise his weak chin. Ruth squealed with delight and asked if he was Lawrence of Arabia, adding that if she had known it was fancy dress she would have worn her unicorn outfit.

Once everyone was assembled, I made a brief speech that emphasized Rupert's many qualities—including his bravery when he recently removed a spider with visible leg hair from the bathtub—and then we moved on to the presents. I gave him the Jeremy Clarkson book, the compass, and the rugby ball, while he managed to contain his joy in his usual understated way. Ruth rushed in with a small package tied with silver ribbons, from which *The Little Book of Clouds* emerged. Rupert thanked her with a shy, restrained sort of half-smile.

Then it was time for what I thought of as my pièce de résistance: Poppy. I signaled to Natalia, and together we went to the utility room. While Natalia held her still, I attached a big blue bow to her neck. Natalia looked puzzled, though not as puzzled as Poppy, who wriggled onto her back, then snapped and pawed at the ribbon. We led her, skittering sideways, into the drawing room. A hush fell across the room. Then Jeffrey and Rupert broke out in unison, Jeffrey crying "What on earth?" and Rupert, something that sounded like "What luck."

Poppy, overwhelmed by the size of the audience, finally wrenched off her ribbon and galloped about the room in giddy delight, nipping Miss Hughes in the varicose veins and snapping at David's trailing head scarf. I lost a shoe trying to catch her, and knocked over two vases of lilies, but I thought that the loss of dignity was worth it as I prepared to hand her ceremonially to Rupert. Just as I had planned, Ruth clasped her hands together and sighed tenderly.

And that was the moment when things went sadly awry. Dear readers, it pains me to write this, but my own son refused to accept his gift, pushing Poppy gently but firmly away. What's more, as soon as Natalia grasped the situation (the girl never listens), she started wailing that she loved Poppy and would not let her go to the cold heart computer man and threw her arms around her neck. She shrieked as I tried to prize her steely fingers off Poppy's collar, Jeffrey launched into a sneezing fit, and the cacophony was interrupted only when Poppy vomited wetly on the Persian rug. It appeared that Natalia had fed the poor creature half the smoked salmon and cream cheese vol-au-vents. This was perhaps just as well given that she had made such a dreadful fist of them.

We were at an impasse. Ivan downed his vodka, and Rupert, who is normally a restrained drinker, followed suit. Emboldened, my son said that there was no question of the dog coming home with him. Jeffrey said that there was no question of "it" staying here, and sneezed. Eventually Gerald came forward, with tears shining in his eyes, and said that he would give the poor abandoned, neglected creature a home, and that Natalia could visit as often as she liked. This placated her enough to clean the vomit off the rug.

Afterward, the evening passed in something of a blur. Jeffrey turned up the music, Ivan the Terrible took hold of Ruth and whirled her around so fast that her glasses fell off, and he trod on them with his crocodile-skin loafers.

I felt like Rupert was doing the same thing to my heart. He drank vodka, ate fairy cakes with his mouth open, and threw his Jeremy Clarkson book on the fire.

 SATURDAY, FEBRUARY 2

11 A.M.

I woke late today, to the sound of my mobile bleeping. It was a text message from Rupert, which read: *Dear Mum, tks for party + presents. Sorry re dog. Poppy will be v happy with Gerald. Love, Rupert.*

This is more contrition than Ivan the Terrible is likely to muster, despite the fact that he trampled mud into my carpet, smashed a valuable porcelain vase, and manhandled the girl I had earmarked as my son's future bride.

When I went downstairs he had already commandeered the kitchen, strewing it with various jars of grotesque pickles, which reminded me of miniature amputated crocodile limbs, and drinking vodka from my Denby Imperial Blue teacup. He was whistling some kind of garish folksy tune which he interrupted to say "Good morning, Konnie" (I could tell it was a *K*) and slap me on the bottom.

Jeffrey emerged, looking well rested. He kissed me briefly on the cheek and said, "No hard feelings, eh?" which could have meant either that he did not resent me, after all, for triggering his allergy or that he wanted to check that *I* did not begrudge *him* for banishing an innocent puppy. My husband is a man of few words and many possible meanings.

In any case, both men left to play golf, leaving me to tidy the house and ponder the previous evening. I think I can draw the following conclusions from the unfortunate events:

I will need a more subtle and ingenious method to overcome Rupert's natural shyness and net him a wife.

Lithuanians are more sentimental than they look.

Never invite Ruth to a fancy dress party.

Never feed a dog canapés.

As Shakespeare would say, "Sweet are the uses of adversity."

SUNDAY, FEBRUARY 3

Just occasionally, it feels as though God answers my prayers. In church today, Reginald instructed us to take a few quiet moments to commune with the Holy Father, open our minds to Him, and lay bare our hopes and fears. I closed my eyes and asked Him to get rid of Ivan, who left two dirty towels on the landing floor this morning. When I got home, I found a note on the kitchen table from Jeffrey (who couldn't attend church because of a headache, poor man) saying that Ivan had business in London and that he had taken him to the station.

I suppose that, in the spirit of Christian compassion, I should spare a thought for Ivan's colleagues, whoever they may be, now forced to bear his company. His employment is a source of some mystery to me, allowing him, as it does, frequent and extensive free periods for hunting, shooting, golfing, and importuning the wives of his friends. Ivan claims that he is in the "dynamic human resources solutions" business and holds investments in commodities. I think this is the Russian way of saying that he has his fingers in a lot of pies. I hope that at least one of them burns him.

MONDAY, FEBRUARY 4

I decided to write a letter to Sophie today ahead of our ski trip. She prefers to correspond by e-mail, text message, or, more frequently, telepathy (this is the only possible explanation for her long bouts of silence), but I remain attached to the more traditional means of communication. Proper letters do not constrict one to a minuscule number of characters (my texts always spill onto two, three, or sometimes six messages) or carry computer-demolishing "viruses." Besides, I like the smell of envelopes.

This is what I wrote:

Dear Sophie,

I hope you're well and enjoying the eco lodge.

Est-ce que tu fais des progrès en français? I always found that conjugating the irregular verbs before bed, while brushing my hair one stroke per word, was the best method of getting on. A fine mind and a fine head of hair will both stand you in good stead later in life.

We're all well here. On Friday we had a party for Rupert's birthday which was good fun, if a little messy. I do worry about your brother sometimes, but we'll talk about that another time. Perhaps you have some nice young friends, preferably with an interest in information technology and good teeth, who might like to come and stay for the Easter holiday?

I hope you're looking forward to the ski trip—Jeffrey tells me he has e-mailed you the travel details. Don't forget your thermals! I've enclosed a 50 euro note so that you can get a nice haircut before you leave. Just because you're living in a French river for a year doesn't mean you need to turn into a savage.

With love,

Mum

TUESDAY, FEBRUARY 5

I decided to buy Natalia some new underwear today. The girl needs cheering up. This morning I saw her standing in the utility room with a half-empty box of dog biscuits in her hand

and a tear dripping down her plump cheek, causing a streak in her orange makeup.

She may still be upset about Poppy, her temperament may be naturally surly, but I'm sure that the constant chafing of her polyester underwear can do nothing to help. After combing through her drawers to find her size (34C, and 10, something I last aspired to in 1983), I went to Marks & Spencer and bought her a box set of T-shirt bras and briefs in beige, white, and pale pink. Mother would no doubt be shocked at the thought of giving a "servant" such a personal present, but times, and cotton/elastane mixes, move on.

When I got back, I interrupted Natalia as she was flicking a duster slowly back and forth across Jeffrey and my wedding photo with a faraway expression on her face. She has the attention span of a Ritalin-dependant gnat. I told her I had something for her, and she jumped, no doubt feeling guilty for her slapdash dusting. She looked confused as she pulled the boxes out from the shopping bag, but when I explained that it was a present to make up for Poppy she started crying yet again. The poor girl. She must have gotten really attached to that dog. I do hope I haven't misjudged things. It was so much easier in Mother's day, when all one had to do was give them a sixpence at Christmas.

WEDNESDAY, FEBRUARY 6

Last night we welcomed a new visitor to bell ringing: Poppy. Gerald, who is clearly the sentimental type, didn't want to leave her home alone. She may well possess a better innate sense of rhythm than Daphne, but her manners are markedly worse. She started howling as soon as the ringing got under way, pausing only to leap at the fluffy handholds on each rope. I had to feed her all the chocolate biscuits I had brought for our break to distract her. She was not grateful. After gobbling the lot, she trampled on the biscuit crumbs, barked twice, then urinated on Miss Hughes's handbag. Gerald had to throw himself in front of Poppy and act as a human shield to prevent Miss Hughes from beating her to a pulp with her walking stick. He will not be bringing her next week.

THURSDAY, FEBRUARY 7

A text message arrived from Sophie: *Yo big momma, got gr8t hair cut, its wikid!! Can u transfur more cash 4 ski jumpa? Luv soph xxx.*

I did not feel that it merited a response, far less a financial transaction.

FRIDAY, FEBRUARY 8

The suitcases are packed. Jeffrey's skis stand in the hallway like a totem pole to the pitiless gods of the piste. There is no escape. We leave for St. Moritz tomorrow at five A.M.

I have left Natalia with six pages of laminated instructions, including details for sewing the missing buttons back onto Jeffrey's shirts, polishing the silver, and switching the lights on and off at regular intervals to deter burglars. A week of solitude can't be an easy prospect, but she is putting such a brave face on things that I even caught her whistling as I was dragging my luggage toward the door. I knew the underwear would help.

I bid a long and solemn farewell to Darcy. He looked back at me with his glittering black eyes, ducking his head to run a claw rakishly through his emerald feathers. For once, he did not respond to me in Lithuanian. He simply cawed, "Oh, Jeffrey," in a breathless tone, which I found rather touching. He might have mixed up his owners, but at least he was expressing himself with a proper, and English, sense of loyalty. The memory will give me a warm feeling as I face the frigid slopes of the Alps.

SATURDAY, FEBRUARY 9

I have arrived. So has Sophie. Her hair has been cut so that it hangs just below her left ear, then gets gradually longer in a sort of hideous diagonal until it falls to shoulder length on the right side. The nape of her neck has been "undercut," which appears to be an alternative expression for "shaved to a piglike bristle." It has been bleached a peroxide blond, annihilating the subtle tones of her natural color and making her look like a barmaid.

I do not have time to describe my outrage, as the porter is carrying our belongings to our room as I type on the lobby computer and Jeffrey is giving me a puzzled look.

SUNDAY, FEBRUARY 10

Everything is worse than I thought, and I am not just referring to the aberration that is my daughter's hairstyle. Do not get me wrong: the hotel is charming, the mattress firm, the hot water piping, the alpine views from our balcony sweeping and majestic. It is the company and the skiing that have proved problematic.

On previous trips, Jeffrey and I would always team up with Andrew, a senior partner at Alpha & Omega, and his wife, Barbara. Barbara is a woman after my own heart, a retired schoolteacher with firm views about necklines and weak indifference to snow sports. Together we would ski a few leisurely blue runs then stop to drink hot chocolate, take in the fresh air, and discuss the character flaws of our respective children. I looked forward to catching up with her and finding out if her daughter ever did admit that she had cheated on her seventh-grade music theory paper.

Now I am perhaps never to know. Jeffrey did not feel fit to let me know in advance, but in the space of a year, Andrew has jettisoned Barbara and taken up with Amanda, a twenty-eight-year-old lawyer with a superabundance of glossy black hair and a waist that is offensively small, even in a ski suit. What's worse, she is an unnaturally zealous skier, zipping past the men with consummate ease. Jeffrey said that it was marvelous to see a woman so good at it, but this did not stop him from poling his way forward in a frenzied fashion every time she overtook him.

You can imagine that I was not comfortable on the slopes with such company. Sophie insisted on going off for a snowboarding lesson, so she was no help. I held them up on every run, but just as I was about to offer to go back to the hotel and leave them alone, the weather closed in. Amanda carried on unperturbed, her tight black ski suit bobbing and fading in the swirling white fog. Jeffrey and Andrew followed her. As the visibility diminished, so too did my fragile sense of balance. I turned left, and it was as if the slope veered away to the right. I turned right, the piste veered up to greet me. I stopped. An eerie silence descended. Snowflakes gathered in the folds of my ski jacket. I felt dizzy. There was only one thing for it. I did what any Englishwoman would have done in the face of such adversity: I had a cup of tea.

Luckily, I am always well prepared. I had a flask of Earl Grey and a packet of currant biscuits from the hotel room in my pocket, so I scooted off the side of the piste, patted the snow into the semblance of an armchair, and settled down to wait for the weather to lift. To pass the time, I counted snowflakes. Mother always said that patience is a virtue. Just as I got to 5,683, I heard a strange whirring overhead. No sooner had I realized that it was coming from a helicopter than I saw two skiers wearing orange snow patrol vests waving their arms and shouting. It was a horrible moment when I connected the two.

I do not wish to dwell on the mortifying details of my afternoon, but suffice it to say that Amanda insisted on alerting the mountain rescue team when I failed to appear at the bottom of the mountain. Luckily, Andrew has some business connection with the mayor of St. Moritz, who agreed to write off the expense.

MONDAY, FEBRUARY 11

After the trying events of yesterday, I have decided to spend today enjoying the hotel pool and sitting in front of the fire with a good book. Jeffrey did not spend much time trying to persuade me to do otherwise. He appears more embarrassed by the rescue debacle than I am. Every time he hears anything that sounds like a helicopter he flinches; the distant drone of the chambermaid's vacuum set him off this morning.

In any case, a day at the hotel gives me plenty of time to update you on the subject of Sophie. I had hoped that her time away from home would make her grow up a little and teach her how to behave in the company of others. Sadly there is little evidence to support this view.

Take last night, for example. I knocked on her door for a little chat just before dinner. I had thought that my brush with death (or at least a nasty cold) on the mountain would have stirred up her daughterly concern, but she hardly looked up as I went in, and continued to apply what looked like globules of bright blue ear wax to her hair. I asked her what on earth it was and she replied, "Mirage extra-hold sculpting crème." She was wearing a white vest top under which a fluorescent pink bra of the sort not stocked by M&S was clearly visible, with a pair of denim hot pants layered over sparkly tights. The one nod to the fact that we were twenty-one thousand feet up in the Swiss Alps in winter, and not in Barbados, or indeed a brothel, was a gigantic pair of faux-fur-lined suede boots. I asked her when she planned to dress for dinner and she merely glanced down at herself and shrugged. I had no luck either persuading her to change or getting her to tell me what she had learned from counting sticklebacks. The only subject that enthused her was her "awesome" snowboard instructor, Jake. Having once glimpsed said instructor on the mountain, holding her hands to keep her upright, dressed in ludicrously baggy trousers and an oversized bobble hat that reminded me of a baby's bonnet, I struggled to concur with her opinion.

I was worried about the impression she would create at dinner, particularly because she was seated next to a bright young lawyer named James, who was smartly dressed in a blue shirt and chinos. She regaled him with the story of my "mental" rescue, twirling the long side of her hair through her fingers for emphasis. James did not notice me rolling my eyes and buttering my roll with dismissive energy because he was too busy staring at her bra. I hope that this is because he too noticed that it clashed with her top and tights.

TUESDAY, FEBRUARY 12

Little to report today. Stayed at hotel. Finished *Heart and Soul,* Maeve Binchy's latest. Jeffrey, meanwhile, looks finished. After a couple of days of skiing he lumbers up the stairs like a grizzly bear that has been shot and stuffed.

WEDNESDAY, FEBRUARY 13

Sophie is still effusive about snowboarding and little else. I asked her if she wanted to spend the morning in the pool with me but she said she felt that she'd just reached an important point with Jake, her instructor. I suppose her determination is to be admired, though I wish she'd find a more appropriate activity: it is hardly very ladylike to spend so much time with her legs spread, even if snowboarding is in fashion.

THURSDAY, FEBRUARY 14

Valentine's Day today. Jeffrey appears to have taken a principled stand against the trite commercialism of the occasion—the last gift he gave me was a pair of silk stockings in 1985. They're still in the back of my drawer, in between a sewing kit and a lavender cushion. I'm not the mawkish sort—it's not as if I yearn for teddies clutching hearts or dozens of roses—and yet some small, tastefully wrapped token of affection would make a welcome change.

With this in mind, I decided to ease my feet back into the vicelike grip of my ski boots and scale the mountain to meet Jeffrey, Andrew, and Amanda for lunch. I managed the one blue piste leading to the rendezvous without mishap and found the two men sitting at a table near the fire, stretching their legs out in contentment, white goggle marks glaring against their scarlet faces. As soon as I had sat down Amanda came over with some drinks. She had drawn a little heart into the foam on top of both Andrew's and Jeffrey's beers. Before I could say anything about this she was air-kissing me on both cheeks and telling me loudly how brave I was to get back up here after the helicopter rescue.

After lunch, just as I was deciding whether a schnapps would help or hinder my descent, there was a noise of chairs scraping back out of the way and four men in dinner jackets appeared, carrying musical instruments. They positioned themselves pointing toward Amanda and began playing Handel's "Entrance of the Queen of Sheba." Andrew had hired a string quartet to serenade her at seven thousand feet. I thought this was more than a little outré, and glanced at Jeffrey to see if he would roll his eyes along with me, but he was distracted by the bleeping of his BlackBerry. I wondered who could have been texting him while he was on holiday but he muttered, "Work," and stuffed it back into his pocket.

After that I came back to the hotel for a long bath. Tonight there is a Valentine's gala dinner at the hotel, and because I will be enjoying Jeffrey's undivided attention, I want to look my best.

11:05 P.M.

What a to-do! I don't know whether to feel ashamed of my daughter or admire her. She certainly provided a little Valentine's Day drama.

I had dressed carefully for the occasion, putting on a mauve silk blouse, a black knee-length skirt, a wraparound merino wool cardigan, and black patent leather shoes. I went to Sophie's room to check that she too was wearing something smart. She opened the door and appeared before me in a pink T-shirt with the words "i look better naked" printed in gold, a pair of black leggings, and gold stilettos. I pulled the door shut and counted to ten. I knocked again and went in. After a small chat on the value of modesty and a threat to stop paying for her snowboarding lessons she gave in, and reluctantly changed into a minidress with spaghetti straps worn under a zip-up hooded pullover. It was not ideal, but it would have to do.

Her curious outfit didn't seem to trouble James, however. We were arranged at long tables decked out with tiny paper hearts, candles, and flowers, with couples sitting together and everyone else jumbled up. Sophie was looking well, the fresh air and candle-light making her pale complexion glow. Luckily she was sitting next to James, who was attentive to the point that I started to wonder whether he would agree to a church wedding and what sort of diamond a junior lawyer's salary would buy. I tried to ask Jeffrey—subtly, of course—but he was no use. He seemed distracted throughout dinner, and failed to give me any opinion whatsoever on whether a marquee would fit in the garden. Perhaps the altitude had gone to his head.

After dinner, we went through to the bar, and I observed James yawning, stretching, and placing his arm around the back of Sophie's chair. It was reassuring that however much some things change in the world—public school fees, the color of tights—certain manly stratagems remain the same.

My reflections were cut short by the entrance of a tanned young man with a hooded top a little like Sophie's and half an inch of elasticated underpant sticking out from his jeans. He walked up to Sophie, took a disgusted glance at James, pulled her up from her bar stool, and kissed her. Before I could elbow Jeffrey into action to protect our daughter from this brazen and spiky-haired interloper, Sophie kissed him back. I suddenly realized that I recognized him from our first day here—it was Jake, the snow-boarding teacher. James jumped up from his chair, spilling his gin and tonic, and shoved him in the chest. There ensued the sort of ungainly tussle that could not be more removed from the traditional idea of a romantic duel. Fists were swung; fists mostly missed their targets. Hair was pulled. At one point, so was Jake's underpant elastic. Sophie watched with her hands over her cheeks. It wasn't clear whom she was rooting for, but I hoped it was James. Eventually, the bar staff managed to separate them. Jake took one look at Sophie and stormed out, scattering chairs in his wake. James said he felt a little shaky and went to lie down. Sophie ordered another drink. She must have inherited her sang-froid from Jeffrey.

I shall have words with her. A well-brought-up girl should know better than to encourage two young men at the same time. And yet, I can't deny that it is gratifying to see my daughter admired, despite her disastrous dress sense. And at least, unlike those terrifying news reports one sees about feral girls running wild in the streets, she was only causing the fight, rather than participating in it.

SATURDAY, FEBRUARY 16

Back home, at last. It is a welcome refuge of peace, sanity, and temperate weather after such an eventful week in the Alps. The house is fairly clean, Darcy appears sleek and well, even Natalia seems pleased to have us back.

The farewells in St. Moritz were not straightforward. I managed to stay calm while Amanda air-kissed me once again on both cheeks and simpered that I simply must stay in touch if I knew how to use e-mail, but only just. Before parting from Sophie, I tried to convince her of the relative merits of solvent lawyers versus itinerant antipodean snow-sport instruct-ors. She conceded that James was "fit," which I hope means fit for the purpose of a serious relationship with the prospect of mar-riage.

8:32 P.M.

I just went to have a bath, but my bottle of sea minerals bath oil is empty. It was three-quarters full before I left. My fluffy white dressing gown is missing. So is my Estée Lauder moistur-izer. Natalia!

SUNDAY, FEBRUARY 17

Natalia was unrepentant when I questioned her about the missing bathroom items. She merely fixed me with her cold, inscrutable eyes and said, "Not knowing." I didn't have the energy to argue. I needed to keep all that for visiting Mother, who was in a testy mood because the new lady in the bedroom next to hers had snaffled the last slice of sponge cake at tea. I muttered something about the importance of sharing and loving one's neighbor, but from the look in Mother's eye, I fear that she was in more of an "eye for an eye, tooth for a tooth" sort of mood. She asked me to bring her a cake tin and a padlock next time I visit.

MONDAY, FEBRUARY 18

Last night I phoned Rupert, and a wonderful thought occurred to me. After I had told him all about St. Moritz and he had agreed that stopping to wait for the blizzard to pass was the best course of action, and that James was a better catch than Jake, conversation petered out. We seem to have reached a tacit agreement not to mention his birthday party. Finally, I resorted to filling the awkward pause by chatting about the day's headlines, including news of a roller-skating squirrel, which I had read on the BBC's Web site. It was then, while pondering the limitless variety of the Internet, that the idea occurred.

Why not put Rupert's profile on an Internet dating service? Only last week, I read an article about a choir mistress who found love at the age of fifty-nine with a retired greyhound breeder. If there is hope for them, there is hope for Rupert. And surely the advantages of such a discreet and convenient dating service would outweigh any minor invasions of his privacy. I kept this to myself while I was on the phone, of course, but in my head I was already composing an advertisement along the following lines:

"Handsome, professional 26-year-old with own flat and teeth

seeks respectable lady for companionship and potential marriage. Must have good sense of humor and love musicals. Virgin preferred. No feminists, socialists, sailors, or divorcées. No piercings below the ears, no tattoos or unnatural hair dye, please. Must be kind to animals, including parrots."

The choice of dating Web site is, of course, key. I typed "online Internet dating" into Google (Rupert once explained to me that Google is a little like direct inquiries, and I am rather proud of my prowess). The results that popped up almost immediately were staggering. There were dating Web sites for women seeking "sugar daddies," for men seeking policewomen, for those desiring "large and lovely connections," for wine lovers, for vegetarians, and for those seeking people to engage in acts of such specific physical athleticism that I snapped the lid of my LapTop down in horror before opening it again, slowly, transfixed in spite of myself.

This will take some thought. Things were so much simpler in my day, when Jeffrey and I simply locked eyes at a Durham Conservatives cheese and wine evening.

TUESDAY, FEBRUARY 19

Over dinner this evening—a shepherd's pie, which Natalia burned on top to a blackened crust—I decided to test out Jeffrey's opinion of my plan to advertise Rupert on the Internet, and to see if he would help me choose an appropriate Web site. I thought it would be sensible to get a second opinion after the debacle of Rupert's birthday party, and my unsuccessful attempt to set up Sophie with David. However, Jeffrey's opinion was not easy to obtain. It took him an inordinate amount of time to grasp what I was suggesting and why. As soon as understanding dawned, I put down my fork and stared expectantly at him, but he simply shook his head slowly, said, "Don't be ridiculous, woman," and took out his copy of today's *Financial*

Times, which he then erected like a giant peach windbreak between us.

Men. It is all very well for him to dismiss my concerns, but he is not faced with the same daily reminders of what we are missing out on. I am a fifty-three-year-old woman. Everywhere around me, my friends and contemporaries are booking ivy-clad idyllic rural churches, erecting marquees or welcoming their grandchildren into the world. Edward and Harriet already have both a three-year-old grandson and a bouncing baby granddaughter. The only thing my children have taken responsibility for is a cactus and a goldfish that died when one of Sophie's school friends poured a raspberry martini into its tank.

WEDNESDAY, FEBRUARY 20

I am sorry for wallowing in self-pity yesterday. It does not do to dwell on my problems. Bell ringing last night certainly put them into perspective. Gerald remains in a bad way. A dog may be a man's best friend, but unfortunately it does not appear to make an adequate replacement for a wife of thirty years who raised two sons and held a certificate in pastry cookery. Gerald's cheeks are pale, his demeanor hangdog, his clothes soiled. He mopes, moons, and misses his turn at the Reverse St. Sylvester. Something must be done, and I think I know what. Gerald is crying out for a woman's caring touch. Rupert is not the only man in need of my assistance in this area; my track record in this department may not be impeccable, but duty calls.

There is not what you might call an abundance of single women in the village with an interest in campanology and dogs, but once again a thought has occurred. Miss Hughes. She is the only unattached lady at bell ringing, and I am quite convinced that she grew up in the sort of place that was crawling with Labradors. She has never married—something to do with an orthodontist who ran off with her sister—but love can blossom late, like in those *Saga* advertisements of tanned sixty-year-olds holding hands on silver beaches. And despite the walking stick, she can't be more than a year or two Gerald's senior.

As if fate were on my side with matters of the heart, as soon as I got home the telephone rang, and it was Bridget, an old university friend who now works in publishing in London and is practically an expert on Internet dating. As she is a divorcée this is only to be expected, though I thought it best not to ask if she had signed up to "wine lovers" or "large and lovely." After I had told her that Rupert enthusiastically backed the plan—an exaggeration, I admit, but he did evangelize about the Internet's ability to connect one with like-minded people when he persuaded me to start this blog, so he can hardly object—she recommended that I look at the dating section of whichever newspaper he reads online. This turned out to be sterling advice: I have just had a look at the *Daily Telegraph*'s Web site, and it does indeed carry a dating service, called Kindred Spirits, that looks most promising. All I need to do now is finesse the wording. "Handsome, professional 26-year-old with own flat and teeth" or "Professional, handsome 26-year-old with own teeth and flat"? I must get this right. I would hate to annoy him.

THURSDAY, FEBRUARY 21

A disturbing incident at Church Flowers today. Usually the proceedings could not be more soothing: we meet, we select some seasonal blooms, we arrange, we place them for maximum effect in terms of both catching the light and concealing cobwebs, we stop for a cup of tea, and repeat the above. Today, however, Pru came over to me with a hard look in her eye. Her lips were pursed so that her fuchsia lipstick latticed out into her powdery cheeks. Perhaps she was troubled that I had taken the last stem of gladioli? Unfortunately not. It appears that the consequences of Rupert's birthday party continue to ripple beyond the bill for getting the rug dry-cleaned. Pru informed me that, as I had requested, her daughter had fallen "head over heels" for my son, as befitted her "sweet, trusting nature." I was rather taken aback. As far as I could tell, Rupert had done nothing to encourage Ruth. He had even left her gift—*The Little Book of Clouds*—wedged behind the U-bend of the downstairs lavatory, which is hardly consistent with a *coup de foudre*. Besides, the party was weeks ago.

However, Pru insisted that Ruth was still so smitten with Rupert that she cried herself to sleep at night because he never replied to the photo text message she had sent of herself with a heart painted on her cheek. Apparently, she "felt something click" when she first set eyes on him, and she just knew from the intense look in his eyes that he felt the same. I did not know what to say beyond wondering why it had taken her this long to say something and speculating that Rupert's contact lenses could have been irritating him, but I thought it best to keep all that to myself. Pru clearly expected a more substantial explanation; I also noticed that the other ladies had put down their blocks of flower arranger's foam to listen. It was a delicate situation.

On the one hand, I would like Rupert to settle, and Ruth is superficially a very reasonable candidate. She is attractive enough to look the part in a wedding photo, if only she would do something about her frizzy hair, but not so pretty that she would always be chased after by other men. She is a primary school teacher, which indicates an admirable fondness of children, as well as unlimited access to paper supplies. And yet, despite the prospect of numerous grandchildren and an inexhaustible supply of staplers, I can't help but worry that her evident emotional volatility would not equip her well for, say, a Christmas lunch with Ivan the Terrible and Mother. I decided that diplomacy was the only option. I also decided that now was not the moment to ask my fellow flower arrangers for help with the wording of Rupert's Internet dating profile. Instead, I told Pru that Rupert was the shy sort whose silence indicated that he was overwhelmed by emotion; and when she asked for his address to pass on to Ruth, I could hardly refuse.

I may leave Kindred Spirits alone, just for a few days.

 FRIDAY, FEBRUARY 22

3 A.M.

I have woken from a fearful dream. Ruth had chained herself to the railings of Rupert's flat in Milton Keynes and set herself on fire in the manner of a protesting Cambodian monk. Suddenly, the scene switched to a wedding, Rupert was quenching the flames with vintage champagne, and instead of a wedding dress, Ruth was swathed in white bandages. Poppy was eating the wedding cake and Ivan the Terrible swung from a chandelier by his toenails. I elbowed Jeffrey awake and told him all about it, but when I asked him what it meant he said, "Too much Roquefort," which I felt lacked either psychological depth or sensitivity of feeling.

SUNDAY, FEBRUARY 24

Perhaps I am psychic after all. Perhaps, despite my misgivings about the sort of people who wear tie-dyed clothing and smell of sandalwood, there is indeed something to the realm of the supernatural. My dream was almost a premonition. Do not be alarmed: there have been no acts of self-immolation on the steps of Conifer Court, the block of smart new flats where

Rupert lives. There has, however, been a disturbing visitation. Rupert called today, and I could tell by the way he called me "Mother" rather than "Mum" that something was up. He demanded to know how "she" had found out where he lived. I am ashamed to say I feigned ignorance, suggesting that if he meant Ruth, then she must have tracked him down on MyFace or one of those other Internet youth clubs I keep reading about in the newspaper.

Rupert was silent for a few moments, and then said in a softer, frightened-sounding voice: "Do you know what she did, Mum? When I got back from Sainsbury's yesterday there were Post-it notes, maybe a hundred of them, stuck on my front door in the shape of a heart. In the middle was a Polaroid picture of her with her phone number written on it in black felt-tip pen. She was wearing an angel outfit. It's creepy. What do you think I should do?"

My first thought was to shop at Waitrose rather than Sainsbury's, but I bit my tongue. Then I realized that this was, if anything, an opportunity, and asked him if he had any girlfriends that she might happen to see him hand in hand with. At that point he went quiet, and then muttered something about having to rush off to water the cactus. He must be covering up for his shyness. I am more convinced than ever that Internet dating is the only way ahead.

MONDAY, FEBRUARY 25

Dear readers, I have had a nasty shock. I feel like the very computer I'm typing on is contaminated. My fingers are sweating. The Internet is truly a wilderness, filled with strange creatures, littered with booby traps. All I wanted to do was visit the *Daily Telegraph*'s dating section on Rupert's behalf, and I ended up stumbling upon a horrible secret.

Jeffrey had left the computer on overnight, which is not like him. He often sits in his study late at night with a glass of scotch, studying the value of his investment portfolio, coming to bed with a twinkle in his eye. But I digress.

This morning, I noticed that he had left the computer on standby overnight, something he has tended to avoid since Sophie told him that by doing so he was responsible for submerging the Maldives. When I jiggled the mouse to get rid of the screensaver, a picture of a familiar-looking blond girl with a big grin and extravagant cleavage appeared on the screen. Upon closer inspection I realized that I was in fact on the Web site Facebook, registered somehow under Jeffrey's name, and on some sort of fan page. I realized that the girl in question was that *Blue Peter* presenter latterly more famous for getting caught snorting cocaine with a rolled-up fifty note off the chest of a disheveled rock musician. The fan page contained a display "wall" of comments from admirers, including "shez so hot I used to watch her on telly she could cover me in stiky bak plastic any day" and "nice t**s." With a small stab in my heart I noticed that Jeffrey had simply written "phwoooooaaar!" Well, when I say Jeffrey, I suppose I mean Jeffrey's Internet manifestation, which consists of his real name and an accompanying picture of Roger Moore dressed as 007. He is clearly living out his fantasy on the Internet. I just feel so hurt that this fantasy includes a perky postadolescent TV presenter who is my polar opposite in looks and dress sense. If he is going to salivate over another woman, the least he could have done is to choose a nice cultured type. What's wrong with Mariella Frostrup, for goodness sake? Or Nigella Lawson?

Natalia was cleaning in the study when I made my discovery. I gasped, so she came over to investigate. When she saw the page, she got quite upset too. The girl obviously feels for me: perhaps I shouldn't be so harsh on her.

Now that I've calmed down, I have a dilemma to contemplate. I'm not sure whether to simply shut the images of that smile and that cleavage out of my mind and pretend that nothing happened, or have it out with Jeffrey, or set myself up on Facebook and "cyberstalk" him. In any case, I shall not post Rupert's dating profile for the time being. I do not believe in omens, of course, but you will agree that the timing is not auspicious.

TUESDAY, FEBRUARY 26

Today I took a long hard look in the mirror, which is something I've tended to avoid doing since the age of thirty-six. I took a deep breath. I stared at my reflection; my reflection stared back. The eyes are still acceptable, green, wide-set, with the almond shape that Jeffrey used to admire. It is around, above, and below the eyes that matters deteriorate somewhat. There are crow's feet. There is a small crease between my eyebrows. There are lines connecting my nose to either side of my mouth that no rejuvenating night cream has been able to erase. Moving downward, my décolletage has the texture of an overripe peach. Why were there no warnings about sunscreen in the Provence villas of the 1970s? Farther south, my figure is rather good for my age, a size 12 that can be upholstered into something approaching svelteness with the appropriate underwear. All in all, the effect is much like my favorite armchair: an elegant silhouette, but frayed around the edges. I can't help but feel that this is how it should be for a woman of my age and experience. It is the spectacle of "mature" women like Madonna cavorting about in gym shorts that is abnormal, not a little natural decline. I do not wish to get my skin hoiked up so I resemble a startled cat, or Botox my forehead into bongo drum tautness, or wear a leotard. And yet, just every now and then, I would like to make Jeffrey say "phwoar."

I wonder what he sees when he looks at me. Does he see the young girl he married, slight, smooth-cheeked, or does he see the slack-jawed old woman waiting to get out? Does he even see me at all?

WEDNESDAY, FEBRUARY 27

Bell ringing provided a welcome distraction from my musings last night. I think many women would be happier if they turned to a rousing communal activity rather than magazine questionnaires to lift their self-esteem. As soon as I set foot in the belfry, Reginald bustled over to tell me that David had thrown his Arabic checked scarf in the composting bin and renounced Islam for good. Had elements of the Koran troubled him? I asked. Had he belatedly realized that Jesus Christ was the way, the truth, and the light? Reginald shook his head and said that David had been unable to locate a halal barbecue chicken pizza.

Gerald was there, sans Poppy, looking red-eyed and introspective. To break the silence, I mentioned something along the lines of here we are again and doesn't time fly, and he replied with a trembling voice that I looked more radiant with every week that passed. After yesterday, I could have kissed him, albeit after swabbing him with disinfectant first. He really is too good a man to waste. It's just a shame that Miss Hughes couldn't be there last night because she was laid up with her bunions.

THURSDAY, FEBRUARY 28

Church Flowers today, and I was a little anxious in case Pru wanted to stab me in the back with the pruning shears. As it happened, her behavior could not have been more different from our last encounter. She came up to me, placed a small, limp hand on my shoulder, and said, "Constance, Ruth has told me everything. You are so brave. Both you and poor, dear Rupert." She blinked at me, displaying puffy eyelids coated in lilac shadow, smiled, shook her head, and passed me five stems of hothouse peace lilies. What on earth was she referring to? Had she been drinking the flower-food sachets? However, never one to look a gift horse in the mouth, I decided to simply smile graciously and ignore the inquisitive glances of the other ladies. The Lord, and Pru, move in mysterious ways.

9:05 P.M.

I have telephoned Rupert's landline, left a message on the answerphone of his mobile, and sent him six text messages, all to no avail. What is he playing at? What has he said, or done, to Ruth to make Pru behave in such a strange way? Does he not realize that I am being gnawed at from within by suspense? Even Jeffrey noticed I was jumpy when I dropped the salt cellar into my soup and splattered him with winter vegetables. I hope Rupert makes contact soon. It is not as if he has any reason to avoid me.

FRIDAY, FEBRUARY 29

At five o'clock this morning I awoke from a dream in which Jeffrey was James Bond, I was Miss Moneypenny, and that *Blue Peter* hostess was emerging from a turquoise sea in a string bikini. I sat behind my desk, prim and powerless, as Jeffrey walked out the door and onto the beach without a backward glance. When I woke up I noticed that there were little red indents in the palms of my hands from where I had dug in my nails. There was only one thing to do. I had to find out what Jeffrey was thinking. I had to join Facebook.

As soon as Jeffrey had left for work and Natalia had gone to the supermarket, I shut myself in the study and typed "Facebook" into Google. I followed the instructions to register, pausing when it asked me to select an image. I was torn between wanting to use a holiday photo of myself ten years ago, an image of the queen, an elegant swan, an owl, apple blossom, a church spire, or Miss Moneypenny wearing a pencil skirt suit. However, the dilemma was resolved for me when I realized I didn't have the faintest idea how to add any sort of picture. I called Rupert, and Sophie, but as neither answered I was forced to accept the default image of a royal-blue question mark, which hardly cuts a dash. At least the rest of the process was easier. For my relationship status I put *married*; for religious views, *Church of England*; and for politics, *Conservative, but Kenneth Clarke, please, not David Cameron*.

Once I had finished registering, it helpfully asked me if I wished to look up any friends. I am not sure if "friend" is the correct term to describe a husband of thirty-three years, but I typed in Jeffrey's name, and, sure enough, among all the other unknown and inferior Jeffrey Hardings, there was his little 007 picture. My heart jumped to see it. Being rather new to all this, I was not quite sure exactly what would happen when I got to this stage, but I had presumed that I would be able to access all of Jeffrey's information, find out who his "friends" were, which fan clubs he had joined, how he described his religious beliefs, how many semi-naked television presenters he was adulating. To my intense disappointment, I could do none of this. The only options were to "add as friend" or "send a message." After hesitating for a few moments, I clicked on the former. It told me a "friend request" had been sent. Will he say, for a second time, "I do"? Will he be pleased to meet me in cyberspace? Will he be angry? Will he see my name pop up on his screen and feel a sudden stab of shame at his "phwoooooaaar's"?

While I pondered these questions, I decided to look for my

children too. There were a number of Rupert Hardings, none obviously my son, although one, which featured a picture of Oscar Wilde, did claim to be in Milton Keynes. This could be my Rupert: he always loved English at school.

It was, alas, easier to find Sophie. She was instantly recognizable, wearing a pink bikini and a sombrero, with a cocktail in one hand and a can of whipped cream in the other, sitting astride what appeared to be a rugby player's shoulders. I sent her a message saying *Never allow anyone to take a picture of you that you would not want your mother to see. Love, Mum.* I felt it best not to befriend either her or the potential Rupert. Children do have very firm ideas about privacy these days.

After that I managed to track down my friend Bridget—who had a very glamorous picture, a side-on shot of her with waved hair and crimson lipstick, smoking a cigarette through an old-fashioned holder—then I joined a group of "fans" of the National Trust and another for parrot owners, called Paratweets. When I heard the scrunch of tires on the gravel indicating that Natalia was back from Waitrose, I was amazed to see how much time had passed. Now I can understand how people can turn into Internet addicts and squander their whole lives wandering aimlessly across the Web. With that in mind, I turned the computer off and went down to help Natalia unpack. Then I went back upstairs, turned the computer back on, and updated my "status" to *is annoyed that the housekeeper has once again forgotten the Serrano ham.*

SATURDAY, MARCH 1

At last, a telephone call from Rupert. "Hi, Mum," he said, in a cheerful but brittle voice.

"What did you tell her?" I demanded.

There was a small silence, and then he said, "Mum, you've got to understand. She was freaking me out. She pushed a parcel of homemade cookies through the letter box. She waited outside my flat, hiding behind the recycling bins. She was wearing a mohair beret."

I had to concede that, notwithstanding her enthusiasm for home baking, this was not ideal behavior, or dress, for a prospective daughter-in-law. "Very troubling," I said. "So what did you say?"

He cleared his throat, then told me. I listened in awed silence.

Ruth, Pru, and, by extension, half the village are now laboring under the delusion that my son has leprosy. Not just any sort of leprosy: Rupert persuaded Ruth that he had a latent yet virulent form of the disease, which was activated by emotional excitement. He told her he picked it up when he was volunteering at an orphanage in Bangladesh. Apparently, a tear fell from her eye as she said that he was perfect, too perfect, and unreachable, like a perfect sad story. Then she left.

I hardly knew what to say. I was part appalled, part impressed by his powers of invention. Though of course I detest deceitfulness, I will have to keep it in mind for the next time the Jehovah's Witnesses call.

3:27 P.M.

I logged on to Facebook and changed my status to *is alarmed to hear that son has leprosy*. Jeffrey has still not added me as a friend. Do I say anything?

SUNDAY, MARCH 2

Once again, Jeffrey has shirked both church and visiting Mother for a game of golf. His absence at least gave me a chance to reflect. I studied the faces in the congregation, the white morning light falling equally on taut young foreheads and furrowed old ones, on squirming children and tired-looking mothers, on glasses and mustaches. I wondered how many of them endured the same troubles as I did, how many husbands were Facebook voyeurs, how many sons were wriggling out of relationships. I imagined few would go as far as to feign leprosy. Every now and then Reginald's sermon—something about the futility of material wealth—distracted me, but I mostly managed to blot him out.

After that it was onward to The Copse, where Mother was in a better mood because the *Antiques Roadshow* had featured a silver cow creamer rather like her own. She asked after Jeffrey, Rupert, and Sophie, and I replied noncommittally. Looking at her sitting there, a sturdy old woman crisscrossed with the green wool of her cardigan, chin hanging softly like a turkey's, wedding band cutting a wedge in her finger, I realized how much of her life was a mystery to me. When I was a little girl in Shipton-under-Wychwood it simply wasn't the done thing to consider my parents as human beings, much less human beings who had a "relationship" with each other. Father was the village vet, mother came from a wealthy family with aristocratic connections, and together they were an unassailable parental unit. As long as I tied my own shoelaces and washed my hands before tea I was largely left to my own devices. But perhaps it was not too late to find out more about my own mother, to learn from her lifetime's worth of wisdom and apply it to my own marriage.

"Mother," I said. "What was Daddy really like?"

She paused, put her glasses on, looked at me, and said, "Big feet. Liked mustard. Would snore if he slept on his left side, not his right."

This was not quite what I had been angling for. I tried again.

"You were married to him for fifty years. What's the secret of being happy for so long?"

She snorted. "Make sure he slept on his right side. Put his socks and underpants to warm on the Aga on a winter morning. But what do you mean, 'happy'? What are you asking me all this for?"

At that point I decided to drop the subject and made some bland remark about the number of daffodils in the nursing home gardens.

When I got home, Jeffrey still wasn't back, so I signed on to Facebook. He still had not made me his friend. Bridget had written me a nice note, though, including a startled inquiry into Rupert's health. I wrote back to reassure her. I had a friend request from a girl at school who used to smell of mothballs, and whom I've not seen since our twenty-year reunion. Judging from the hairstyle, her profile picture dated from that period. She certainly looked at least ten years off fifty-three, but I approved her anyway. Then I checked on Paratweets and left a comment advising others that linseed oil was the perfect remedy for dull plumage. After that I changed my status to *is pondering the gaping chasm between the generations* and logged off.

MONDAY, MARCH 3

Today I called on Tanya. It's been a whole week since I discovered Jeffrey's Facebook page, and I'm no closer to deciding what to do beyond waiting for him to reply to my friend request. I need advice from a woman of the world, which I believe Tanya is because she sometimes wears a pink velour Juicy Couture tracksuit. When she answered the door she was red-faced and out of breath, her highlighted hair scraped back in a pastel-pink headband. "Hiya, Connie, don't mind the state I'm in," she said, ushering me in. It transpired that she had been exercising to a Girls Aloud dance DVD. I suppose it must burn more calories than gardening, but I can't help but feel that it is less beneficial to the mind, and herbaceous borders.

While she went to make coffee, I was left to study her living room. It was vast, cream, and pristine, with a peculiar sort of remote-control fire, chocolate-brown leather sofas that made my hands feel clammy, ethnic vases filled with dead twigs, and a giant painting of oblongs doing battle with triangles, which I took to be modern art. When she got back, she handed me my coffee in a Starbucks mug and asked how I was doing. I decided not to beat about the bush.

"Tanya," I said. "I found out that Jeffrey has been eyeing up other women on Facebook. What does it mean? What should I do? Does it matter?"

She looked at me and laughed. According to her, Jeffrey's transgression is trivial. She explained that, as a stockbroker, Mark spends half his leisure time "with his face between a lap dancer's ***s," and that she wasn't troubled in the slightest. Such was her insouciance that the two of them would go through her fashion magazines together, giving the girls marks out of ten for their faces and figures.

"He can look where he likes, but at the end of the day, I'm the one with the wedding ring," she said, wiggling her elegant fingers. "And besides, he knows that if he does actually cheat, I get the house, I get the car, and I'll chop his bollocks off with a pair of nail scissors."

I didn't quite know what to say. I have never directly threatened Jeffrey's genitalia, but I rather hope that the sentiment was implicit.

In any case, I came away feeling much more cheerful, and at dinner I was emboldened enough to ask Jeffrey how he was enjoying Facebook. He started sawing his steak vigorously and said that he'd closed down his account because he kept getting friend requests from Nigerian spammers.

TUESDAY, MARCH 4

I have been grappling with a dilemma. After several days of pondering the wording, and one or two abortive efforts, I had filled in Rupert's profile for Kindred Spirits. I had persuaded myself that the ends (a wedding, grandchildren) justified the means (impersonation, deceit). And yet, hand hovering above the mouse, ready to click SUBMIT, some small inner voice—perhaps representing God, or my inner conscience, it can be hard to distinguish between the two—persuaded me to stop. I wondered if a different approach wasn't called for, one less likely to rub him the wrong way and result in him ignoring my text messages. And so, having thoroughly browsed the site, I decided to whittle down a short list of eligible girls to tempt him with before presenting him with a ready-written profile and asking for his permission to proceed. So far I like the sound of the following three:

Name: Flossie
Age: 24
Height: 5 feet 5 inches
Employment: PR/marketing
About her: I'm a positive, happy girl whose fun to be around, friends tell me I'm spontaneous and sociable, I like Strictly Come Dancing and take ballroom classes, sure you'd give my slinkey moves a 10!
Looking for: a nice smiley man to chillax with, maybe a serious relationship, maybe marriage and babies, who knows?!

(Notes: Nice but dim. Probably pliable. Unlikely to have a

career significant enough to impede producing grandchildren. Good height. Query: what does chillax mean?)

Name: Karen
Age: 32
Height: 5 feet 6 inches
Employment: Arts administrator
About her: I enjoy the simple things in life: a home-cooked meal, a walk in the park, a good book. I'm shy but if you take the time to get to know me, you won't be disappointed.
Looking for: I've had my heart broken before so I'm looking for a kind, honest man who won't dump me for a bimbo with a boob job.

(Notes: She is 32 and sounds desperate. Would marry quickly. Cheap to maintain.)

Name: Jackie
Age: 26
Height: 5 feet 2 inches
Employment: Stable hand
About her: Straightforward country gal. Love horses, dogs, country pubs, proper puddings.
Looking for: A rustic lad to share long walks and Sunday lunches.

(Notes: After Ruth, straightforward is good. Likes animals. And perhaps she will drag Rupert out of his flat and put a little color in his cheeks.)

Now all I have to do is give him a call. Wish me luck!

6:32 P.M.

I have called Rupert. It did not go as planned. Everything has been in vain: my research, the little talk I had rehearsed ten times in my head before picking up the phone, the profiles I had printed out. How can one boy be so stubborn, so resistant to either reason or romance?

The conversation went something like this:

"Hello, Rupert, how are you?"

"Fine."

"How's the job?"

"Fine."

"How's the flat?"

"Fine."

"Now, Rupert, I've been thinking. I don't want to be intrusive, but I keep reading about how hard it can be for young people to find their soul mates in today's highly pressured environment, and I wondered if you had ever considered online dat—"

"MUM!"

"Please don't interrupt, Rupert. I am sure you could meet a very good sort of girl on the *Daily Telegraph* Web site. In fact, I've already found three. Now, listen to this: 'Straightforward country gal. Love horses, dogs, country pubs—'"

"MOTHER!"

"Now, Rupert, please don't interrupt. What have you got to lose? You wouldn't even have to go to the bother of writing your own profile, because I've done it for you. Listen to this: 'Handsome, professional twenty-six-year-old with own flat and teeth seeks respectable lady for companionship and potential marriage—'"

There was a click. He had hung up. If I didn't have to hurry off to bell ringing, I would spend the evening wallowing in despondency, visualizing a towering hat aisle whose wares are always positioned just out of reach.

WEDNESDAY, MARCH 5

Once again, bell ringing drew me out of myself. I was forced to abandon all mournful thoughts of yawning empty marquees and apply myself to ringing. Bell ringing is a far more intricate and demanding activity than people realize. I feel certain that counting out the complex rhythms has helped Miss Hughes maintain her mental sharpness. She was back last night in her usual form, poking Daphne when she mistimed her entry and asking Reginald why he had failed to make sure the floor was swept. I looked at her, and I looked at Gerald, who was sniffing loudly in between rings, and I wondered.

Gerald is fifty-nine, shuffling his way toward retirement from the history department of the boys' school. He is currently an emotional car wreck, but prior to Rosemary's departure he was a steady, contented sort of man, who collected and pressed rare wildflowers and would take his children on holiday to Hadrian's Wall. Happiness to him was a rare orchid, or a well-preserved portcullis.

Miss Hughes, on the other hand, is slightly his senior, retired from a career as a doctor's receptionist. I believe she used to find happiness in informing patients that there were no available appointments until a week from Thursday. She has substituted this for waving her stick at the village youths for dropping litter. I doubt whether Kindred Spirits would award them a "five heart" compatibility rating, and yet I believe there are reasonable grounds for hope.

Gerald is now meandering hopelessly through life, threadbare, at a loss; his closest relationship is with a four-month-old black

Labrador. Miss Hughes could be just what he needs to whip him back into shape. And Gerald might be just the project she needs now that she has successfully stripped all the ivy from her privet hedge. With this in mind, during our tea break I decided to ask Miss Hughes some questions designed to cast her in a favorable light for Gerald.

"Tell me, Miss Hughes," I said. "Have you ever been tempted to get yourself a dog to keep you company in the cottage?"

"A dog?" she said, one thin eyebrow arched, before informing us all that the only purpose of dogs was to collect birds that had been shot, and that anything else was just piffle. I watched Gerald closely; rather than attending to Miss Hughes's words he was staring straight ahead with a distant, dreamy look in his eyes and a piece of lint hovering on his mustache. This may take more work than I had anticipated.

THURSDAY, MARCH 6

A horrific thought has occurred to me. I have been dwelling, once again, on Rupert's failure to bring home a girlfriend, and also on his reluctance to agree to my plan to put his profile on the *Telegraph*'s dating service.

I do not wish to countenance such an idea of my own flesh and blood, whom Jeffrey and I have done our best to raise on the straight and narrow, but I can no longer quell my doubts.

Could Rupert's preferences and predilections lie in another direction? Could I have been fundamentally mistaken about him all these years?

Could he, in short—I can scarcely bring myself to type it— could he be a closet *Guardian* reader?

I am not sure whether to confront him and demand to know the truth, or whether, in cases such as these, ignorance is bliss.

🍃 **FRIDAY, MARCH 7**

A text message from Rupert. It read: *Hi Mum, sorry I hung up. Love Rupert.*

Oh, Lord. You know what they say about liberal guilt. Perhaps it is true.

🍃 **SATURDAY, MARCH 8**

A strange conversation with Natalia. I suppose, due to her partial grasp of the English language, all conversations with her are strange, but this one was marked by its alarming subject matter as well as its style. I was just taking a stroll in the garden, enjoying the spring sunshine and checking that the new gardener had put enough bulbs down last year, when Natalia appeared. She had been taking sheets down off the line and was carrying them in a big bundle. "Mizziz Harding," she said. "I want talk to you." It was like being spoken to by a pillowcase with eyes. I took the laundry hamper from her, and put it on the ground. She looked suddenly exposed, and put one hand in her pocket and used the other to twirl her hair. She said that she had a big, big favor to ask. She said that she had a twin sister, Lydia, who was very sad because her boyfriend was a bad man and he had left her for a blond woman with a job in a bank and a big car. I nodded sympathetically, reflecting on the universal nature of the scoundrel, but wondered when she would get to the point. She said that her sister was studying but had a break for Easter, and that she had saved some money and maybe could buy her Lydia a ticket to come and stay and see some of England and get happy again.

Readers, do not think I have a heart of stone. I was not unmoved by this story of Lithuanian love and loss. In normal circumstances I would have welcomed this suffering twin, despite the many hazards that a double serving of Natalia could produce.

But she wanted her to visit at Easter, the very time that Sophie will be back from her eco lodge, ready perhaps at last for a few nice chats and a shopping trip for a new spring mackintosh. I regret to say that Sophie and Natalia do not get along, Natalia resenting Sophie's mess, Sophie resenting Natalia's habit of moving her things about, humming loudly, and allegedly once stealing her black-cherry nail polish. An extraneous Lithuanian would put her in a foul mood for the whole week and ruin my plans. It was not to be.

I told Natalia as kindly as I could that Easter week would not be possible, but that Lydia was welcome to visit another time. She stared at me in silence, her heavily made-up eyes narrowing to wavy black lines. Then she picked up the laundry, staggered once under the weight, and walked away.

SUNDAY, MARCH 9

Jeffrey surprised me at breakfast. I was calmly decapitating a boiled egg and reading a feature in the newspaper about "trophy wives" when he said that there was something he wanted to talk to me about. I put down my teaspoon. This was a rare event.

"It's about Natalia," he said, increasing my surprise. The affairs of our housekeeper are not usually his concern. However, she was apparently so upset by my refusal to allow her twin to visit that she had appealed to his higher authority. "I really think we should let her have her way, old girl," he said, the prospect of a distraught young girl putting a compassionate gleam in his eye. "What harm could it do?"

I was torn. I am usually happy to follow Jeffrey's guidance in all matters except for the color of table linen, but on this occasion I felt something within me rebel. I had plans for that weekend involving our daughter. I had already handled the situation with the housekeeper. If I am in charge of domestic affairs, then I am in charge of domestic affairs, come what may. I told him that I didn't think it would work and went steadfastly back to reading the newspaper. (I wonder if Tanya counts as a trophy wife? She is certainly much younger than Mark, and very pretty in a soap-opera-star sort of way, but I can't help but feel that her dark brown roots must rule her out.)

Jeffrey was clearly in a conciliatory mood because he followed me to church without complaining and then listened to Mother tell the same story about how the new foreign nurse had hidden her slippers twice. He must really pity Natalia. Beneath that cool, dignified, English exterior he has a heart that melts like our reduced-salt Lurpak butter.

MONDAY, MARCH 10

Where to start? It has taken me six vials of Bach Rescue Remedy, an hour of lying in a darkened room, and the help of a Facebook support network to calm my nerves enough to write this blog.

This morning, Darcy escaped. Darcy, my beloved parrot, my most loyal companion. I have always guarded so carefully against this happening. Every time I let him have a flutter about the conservatory to stretch his majestic wings, I always check and double-check that the windows are shut first. It was Natalia's doing. It must have been. She has the motive, and the malice.

Today at about 10:00, I let Darcy out of his cage and shut the conservatory door firmly behind me to go and pour myself a cup of coffee in the kitchen. At 10:05 I was gazing out at the lawn and thinking that I must get the new gardener to tackle the moss when I saw something out of the corner of my eye: a glint of emerald plumage rocketing off above the rhododendrons. It took me a moment to understand what I had seen. When I did, I have to admit that I abandoned my usual notions of feminine restraint and bellowed like a stricken ox.

The next few hours passed in a blur. I ran across the lawn and out onto the street in my bare feet. I ran up the pavement, grit sticking into my soles, and watched as his little silhouette faded away into a heartbreaking nothingness.

I went back to the house. I cried. I summoned Natalia and shouted at her. She shrugged. I phoned Jeffrey's office and pleaded with his PA to haul him out of a meeting.

And finally, I went back out again, and as I was pacing the streets, squinting at the horizon, Tanya drove past in her big black Toyota four-by-four. She was so kind that I will never again look askance at her hair extensions.

As soon as she understood the situation, she packed some Waitrose organic muesli to use as bait, and drove me around the village green, then Surrey Heath, Richmond Park, and eventually as far as Hampstead Heath. We came across a few clusters of parakeets, each of which made my heart surge, but none contained birds of Darcy's stature. After four long hours, we had to return empty-handed. My mouth was dry, my stomach cold and tight.

And then . . . well. We got home. Tanya hugged me, then I got out of the car and walked slowly up the drive. I went inside. Everything looked as it did before—Jeffrey's golfing umbrella leaning against the hat stand, a vase of lilies starting to drop pollen on the oak table—but the feel of the house was empty, desolate. I went through to the kitchen and looked out the window at the lawn, the last place I had seen my poor parrot. I looked, and looked again. Dear readers, there he was! Perched blithely in the apple tree in the middle of the grass, his branch bobbing in the breeze, staring right at me, I am sure, with a sharp and mischievous look. A few enticing words and Brazil nuts later, and he was back in his cage. My heart sang, even if the first word he uttered was Lithuanian.

I took a padlock from Jeffrey's shed, locked his cage, and threaded the key onto my white gold necklace next to Mother's locket. I lay down to calm myself, then went on Facebook and told Paratweets all about my ordeal. They were the only ones who could understand. *OMG pour you. Thats worse than the day my daughter hid in the laundry cupboard for 2hrs*, said one. After Googling *OMG,* I smiled sadly in agreement.

Although the knot in my stomach started to loosen and the thumping in my head started to fade, one problem remained: Natalia. She has shown me what she is capable of if I refuse to allow her sister to stay. I changed my status to: *Do I capitulate to domestic terrorism?*

 TUESDAY, MARCH 11

I am weak. I have given in. Lydia is coming.

Do not, however, think it is all my doing: I was tempted to pack Natalia off back home, clutching her Big Ben tea bag box and other pathetic memorabilia, after yesterday's act of treachery. But once again, Jeffrey has intervened. Last night over dinner I told him all about Darcy's disappearing act, almost choking on my salmon en croute as I explained that the whole dreadful affair was almost certainly Natalia's fault. I suggested it might be time for a new housekeeper, mentioning too her slovenly dusting and her habit of leaving her tarty underwear lying about. This did not have the effect I had expected. Jeffrey looked distant for a moment, before flicking into his lawyer mode (I can tell when he does this because his chest sticks out and the frown line deepens between his eyes) and intoning gravely on the principle of innocent until proven guilty. Apparently, there was no prima facie evidence to prove beyond all reasonable doubt to a fair-minded group of people that Natalia had indeed released a parrot named Darcy. There were no fingerprints, no DNA evidence, nothing beyond assumptions and suspicion. This young girl, who had an unblemished record and her whole life in front of her, could well have been framed.

Sometimes I think Jeffrey is wasted on tax. Once he had finished, he took a long swig of his wine, and said, in a normal, quieter, voice, "Besides, the economy's buggered, my pension's on thin ice, and she's cheap."

He's right, of course, although I find it hard not to feel rather distant from the swirling waters of financial Armageddon. The letters offering me platinum credit cards continue to arrive on the doormat, albeit a little less frequently, and only last Sunday, I learned from the *Sunday Telegraph* magazine that there is a six-month waiting list for a Mulberry handbag—named after some upstart fashion model barely Sophie's age—which costs twelve hundred pounds. As long as it is so easy to borrow money to buy unaffordable things, I'm sure the economy will perk up soon.

And yet Jeffrey would not budge. Natalia stays, and if I am not to walk around in a constant state of fear it means that Lydia will be coming to stay too. She will have to sleep in Rupert's old room, and I'll be damned if I'm moving his collection of old comics and computer manuals to make space for her cheap eastern European cosmetics.

WEDNESDAY, MARCH 12

Bell ringing provided a more sympathetic audience last night than Jeffrey did. I told them all about Darcy before we started ringing. Miss Hughes said it just shows that these eastern Europeans would sell their own grandmothers for a pair of gold earrings; Reginald said, "Let he who is without sin cast the first stone," and looked confused; Gerald touched my shoulder and said, "Poor you. I know what it feels like to be abandoned."

Even though I was preoccupied with the trauma of Darcy's escape, I did not forget my other business at bell ringing: Gerald. Trying to gauge Miss Hughes's tastes, I asked her whether she liked Reginald's new rust-colored pullover, and if she thought men should experiment with color. She wrinkled her nose. "That color reminds me of a septic tank," she said. "But I do like a man who can carry off a nice bit of purple." I repeated this loudly—that men looked nice in purple—so that Gerald could hear. Then I hurried home to check on Darcy.

THURSDAY, MARCH 13

Today I baked a walnut cake and took it to Tanya to thank her for her help. She didn't look her usual self when she answered the door. I told her she seemed pale and asked if she was feeling okay, but she laughed and said she was just trying to save money by skimping on the fake tan. Apparently Jeffrey is not the only one to notice that there is something amiss with the economy: Mark, her husband, is so worried that he has fired the cleaner and capped Tanya's allowance. As she opened the fridge door to get milk for our coffee, standing in front of the luminescent shelves of out-of-season strawberries and blueberries, Marks & Spencer ready meals and macrobiotic yogurts, she told me she didn't know what else she could cut back on. I said that at least they had the house, and she smiled thinly. I think she looks better without the tan anyway; more fragile, the first fine worry lines tracing out from her eyes, but prettier. I kept that to myself.

Then it was off to Church Flowers, where everyone kept staring at me in sympathetic silence, no doubt distracting themselves from the azaleas with thoughts of my son's leprous lesions, then home. I went on Facebook and found I had friend requests pending from two classmates, one of whom looked old, the other fat. I changed my status to *is suddenly feeling more cheerful.*

Although not as cheerful as Natalia, who, since the news of her sister, has been going about the house singing with a louder monotone drone than usual. She even made me a coffee with a squirt of whipped cream and half a crumbled chocolate biscuit on top, which I presume was meant to be a treat. Not wanting to dampen her all-too-rare good spirits, I waited until she wasn't looking to spoon the top off into the bin.

FRIDAY, MARCH 14

Sophie flies home in less than a week. I had offered to get Jeffrey's PA to organize a train trip back, given her environmental zeal, but she said that an eight-hour journey would make her "go mental." I sent her the following e-mail (which, after one eleven-minute phone conversation to Rupert for instructions, I have now successfully managed to "copy and paste"):

Dear Sophie,

I hope you're still enjoying yourself and the weather is nice. Do remember to wear sunscreen if it's getting warm—you will thank me for this advice when you reach my age, believe me. Pale is interesting. Just keep repeating that to yourself.

It's been an eventful week or so—I nearly lost Darcy, and tried to lose Natalia! I will tell you all about it when you're home. I'm looking forward to a good catch-up. I'll take you for a cream tea and a little shopping trip in Tunbridge Wells—my treat.

See you on Thursday. We'll be waiting for you at the airport at two.

Love,

Mum

For once, she replied promptly:

Yo mo, can I bring zac?
soph xxx

I struggled to recall her ever mentioning a Zac. I wrote back:

Dear Sophie,
Who is Zac?
Love,
Mum

She replied:

my best m8, ul love him. he's booked his tikit. seeya!!

So not only do I have a supernumerary Lithuanian to contend with, but also an unknown man who seems likely to impede both shopping trips and tête-à-têtes. What's worse is that I have no idea what his relationship with Sophie is. What are his intentions? Are they indeed just friends, or might he be a "soulm8"?

SATURDAY, MARCH 15

Today, I finally summoned the courage to call Rupert. If he is indeed a *Guardian* reader, the best hope of a cure will be to treat him kindly and expose him to a more sensible point of view, or simply wait ten years for him to grow out of it. I may send him the *Spectator* once Jeffrey has finished with it to hasten the process. In any case, I felt it was time to mend fences (locally sourced and sustainable ones, no doubt) and ask if he would come over and help me check out Zac. He was his usual polite self on the phone, if a little quieter than usual, but agreed that he would be there for a nice leg of lamb next Sunday. At least he hasn't turned vegetarian.

MONDAY, MARCH 17

A few sunny spring days and the garden has turned into a wilderness. Thank heavens that Randolph, the gardener I hired to replace Douglas after he retired last summer, was at work today. He is the American (hence the old-fashioned name and straight, white teeth) nephew of Daphne's husband, who is from New York. Randolph is in Europe for a gap year, which seems to be a necessity for this generation of young people in the same way that growing up and getting a job was for mine. Still, he is a polite young man who insists on addressing me as madam, even if he mitigates the effect by saying "I'm Randy!" every time he meets someone new. I declined to abbreviate his name. Once I'd gone back into the conservatory, he took off his T-shirt before starting work, even though it's still only March and I haven't yet moved my cashmere cardigans to the spare room wardrobe. Perhaps all those muscles have an insulating effect. I watched him over the top of my magazine as he took a spade to the flower beds, his long, lean frame bending to and fro. It's a shame he's just a gardener. Hose him down, give him an MBA and a light gray suit, and he would make a rather nice catch for someone like Sophie.

TUESDAY, MARCH 18

News, real news, of a wonderful sort! Enough to push Jeffrey's Internet antics to the back of my mind. At last I can start buying those matching Marks & Spencer baby cardigans and booties that I keep lingering in front of whenever I pop in for a pair of tights. Tanya is pregnant. She came around this morning and told me over coffee and a slice of my homemade lemon cake. I thought it wasn't like her to get through a whole piece rather than just picking at the drizzle icing. Her voice was uncharacteristically quiet as she put down her plate and told me her news. The slight weight gain that she'd attributed to her failure to follow Gwyneth Paltrow's macrobiotic diet, and attempted to exercise off with dance aerobics, was in fact a sign of her pregnancy.

She'd been so worried about Mark's job that she'd hardly thought about the possibility. "But he must be delighted," I said. She looked at me, blinked, and twisted her fingers together. "He is," she said after a pause. "But when I told him he went as white as my soy milk and had to sit down for five minutes. Then he said, 'F*** me,' then he cried."

I told her that everyone expressed their joy in different ways. Jeffrey, for example, drank three scotches when I told him I was expecting Rupert, and another six the day he was born. She smiled wanly. I know she is worried about finances, but Mark is a sharp, successful young man. I remember at Rupert's party he was telling Jeffrey all about some amazing opportunity in the credit default swat market or some such gobbledygook that only the truly intelligent could hope to understand. Left to my own devices I would stick all my money under the mattress, but luckily Jeffrey looks after the finances. Anyway, I'm sure the financial crisis will soon blow over so that Tanya can relax and start decorating the nursery. Will she be going for pink or blue, or yellow, as is the fashion these days? I may buy one of those lovely wooden train sets. That would cheer Mark up too.

WEDNESDAY, MARCH 19

Readers, I believe my plan is working! At bell ringing last night, Gerald was resplendent in an extra-large purple T-shirt with the silhouette of a stallion and the words "Wild Thing" written on it. He must have taken Miss Hughes's words in earnest, though I think she was imagining something more in the line of a nice jaunty tie. What's more, just as we were leaving the belfry, he turned to me, cheeks flushed with the vigor of ringing, and said, "Constance, I need to talk to you about something. Alone," with a meaningful look in his eye. At last. He must want my advice on how to proceed with Miss Hughes. Just think, by the time Tanya holds a christening for her baby they might be able to attend together, as a couple. The only problem is that I have so much to do with all the guests arriving for Easter that the earliest I could arrange to meet him in the village tea shop was next Wednesday. I suppose that true love can wait.

THURSDAY, MARCH 20

Little time once again. Sophie and Zac have arrived, the latter wearing those chunky rectangular glasses that signal that he too may be a *Guardian* reader.

Lydia is here too. She is, as I suppose is only to be expected, the exact image of her sister, even down to the shoulder-length dark hair streaked through with highlights. You would have thought that twins would have the good sense to at least opt for different hairstyles. Even Jeffrey looked bemused. "But how will we tell them apart?" he said, running a hand through his own thinning hair, as soon as Lydia had wheeled her pink plastic suitcase out of the hall. "How on earth will we tell them apart?"

FRIDAY, MARCH 21

At last, some time to myself. Sophie and Zac have gone to the cinema to watch some film involving Angelina Jolie and a flying monk. I'm writing this on my LapTop in the conservatory, from which I can see the twins relaxing in the garden. Lydia seems a sweet girl, though I'm not sure if this is because of her personality or because the only words she seems to know in English are "please," "thank you," "excuse me," and "Cadbury chocolate."

She must share her sister's physical hardiness though. It can't be more than fifteen degrees outside but the two of them are out there sprawled on the patio (I have resisted the trend for "decking," which belongs on a ship and nowhere else) wearing short ruffled skirts and listening to music on shared headphones. I worry they'll catch their deaths of cold, or distract Randolph from planting the petunias.

SATURDAY, MARCH 22

Everyone assembled for breakfast this morning. Natalia cooked a fry-up for herself, Lydia, and Zac, and Sophie nibbled on the chocolate cereal that she still hasn't grown out of. Jeffrey sat in a corner eating toast and marmalade, occasionally peering out from behind the side of the *Financial Times Weekend* at the hubbub. I hope our guests don't annoy him too much. Despite his sympathetic streak, he must be counting down the days until Lydia, at least, departs, taking her piercing "Girls Just Want to Have Fun" ring tone with her.

After a while, Sophie pushed her cereal bowl to one side, went over to the window, stared out, and asked, "Who's that?" I looked out. Randolph was there, mowing the lawn, his shirt tied around his waist, seemingly immune to the sharp spring chill. I explained that it was the new gardener, brought in to replace Douglas. "This one's an improvement," she said, pressing her nose against the glass.

A few minutes later, after Jeffrey had disappeared to his study, there was a gentle knock on the back door. I opened it and there stood Randolph, shirt back on but unbuttoned to expose a few dark curls of chest hair, standing with a delicate pink spring tulip in each hand. "Hi," he said. "I'm Randy." Sophie dropped her spoon into her cereal bowl with a little splash. But they were not for her. "For the ladies," he said, gesturing at Natalia and Lydia. Natalia looked a little cross; Lydia giggled. Or it might have been the other way around—I cannot for the life of me tell which is which.

In any case, I took the flowers from him, and said thank you very much in a firm voice so that he took the hint and walked off, turning his head for a last grin at the matching Lithuanians. He may well have a ravishing smile but he has taken unwarranted liberties with my spring flowers. Seeing as the damage was already done, I found two slim vases for the pilfered tulips, and handed them to the twins. Sophie walked out, almost knocking her chair over and leaving her breakfast things scattered behind her. Zac followed, with an apologetic look on his face. He seems a nice boy; it's just a shame he is too short and freckled to be considered a romantic prospect.

Natalia—it must have been Natalia because she knew where the dishwasher tablets were kept—tidied the breakfast things away, while Lydia stared out the window, twirling the tie of her pale-pink polyester bathrobe between her fingers. I hope she stays away from the stove, as it looks like it would go up in flames in a flash.

I should have liked to go after Sophie to comfort her, to tell her that one grubby American is not enough to waste half a bowl of chocolate hoops over, but the front door clicked. She had left with Zac. I suppose it is for the best: I have a Sunday dinner to shop for, and as Mother is coming around tomorrow, I have to find the most tender joint of lamb or her dentures will stick.

SUNDAY, MARCH 23

Sunday lunch was not the harmonious gathering of guests and family that I had hoped for. From the start, Mother seemed totally adrift. She could not understand how Natalia, the house-keeper, and Lydia, the sister of the housekeeper, could be sitting down with us at the dining room table, wineglasses shining in front of them, napkins on their laps, looking to all purposes like part of the family (had it not been for their matching "Eurovision Song Contest 2006" cropped T-shirts). In her day, there was a separate door for the servants, a separate table for them to eat on, separate dishes; their separate lives would intersect with the family only in carefully stipulated ways. I remember as a little girl her telling me off for playing hopscotch with the cleaning lady's daughter—as an only child I always craved company. Even then I suppose she was old-fashioned, clinging to her world as the fifties gave way to the alarming currents and hemlines of the sixties.

I confess I am a little like her in that respect; I believe there is a right way of doing things and a wrong way, that traditions should be respected, that you should put lemon in a gin and tonic, not lime. And yet I am also aware that we are in the twenty-first century now. Natalia is, despite occasional evidence suggesting the contrary, a human being in her own right, and as Sophie frequently says, I have to "get real." Not that I explained any of this to Mother, of course. It is simply too late in the day. She refused to understand any of Natalia's polite, if thickly accented, questions, and instead talked exclusively to Jeffrey. Zac was another source of bemusement to her. After meeting him she presumed he was Rupert's friend; I explained that, no, he was Sophie's friend, and she asked me if his intentions were honorable. We were in the kitchen at this point and Rupert patiently explained that they were "platonic friends," as was quite normal for lots of boys and girls now, but she merely harrumphed and said she would be watching what he did with his hands under the table.

As if dinner were not strained enough, no sooner had I started clearing up than I spotted Randolph through the kitchen window, shirtless and besmirched, scattering seed. Sunday was supposed to be his day off. Soon enough he sauntered over, knocked on the door, and, still bare-chested for Mother, Natalia, Lydia, Sophie, and me to see, asked if he could come in to "take a slash." I asked him what he was doing here on his day off and he said he couldn't keep away, winking at the twins before wandering through to the downstairs bathroom, leaving muddy footprints behind him. Mother nearly choked on her port.

MONDAY, MARCH 24

I woke to the sound of screaming. Had the house caught fire? Was Randolph stalking the landing with a gun, revealing himself to be another tormented American teenager with a chip on his shoulder and revenge in his eyes?

No. Natalia had a frog in her bed. This unfortunate state of affairs only became clear when I had dashed out of my bedroom brandishing the pepper spray I keep in my handbag for emergencies, followed by Jeffrey, sleepy-eyed, holding a baseball bat at a limp angle. The latter, at least, was superfluous.

When we reached the source of the screaming, we found Natalia, shuddering, dressed in a short shiny black nightie, pointing at her bedclothes. She was quickly joined by Lydia, dressed in an identical slip, and the two girls confided quickly in Lithuanian, clasped each other, and shrieked. I wanted Jeffrey to do something but he was still so drowsy that he simply stood there staring at them, transfixed. After a few long moments, Natalia (or Lydia?) grabbed a coat hanger, and gingerly used it to pull back her duvet.

It was then that we saw it, a small squat amphibian, which took a grotesque leap forward and landed squarely on Natalia's lilac-colored pillow. Having grown up in the countryside, I am not squeamish about such creatures; and yet I would rather not touch them when there are other perfectly good means of remedying the situation. I gave it a quick blast with the pepper spray. Natalia and Lydia left the room choking; the frog sat quite still, stunned. I made Jeffrey seize the moment by taking off one of his bed socks and scooping the green interloper up into it. He quickly knotted the end and stood holding his wriggling bundle when Sophie and Zac finally emerged to check out the noise.

Zac, rubbing his eyes, hair standing on end, looked truly baffled, then alarmed. Sophie, I noticed, seemed bright-eyed, with a trace of mud on each kneecap. Would she have? Could she have? I suppose her time studying the ecosystem of the Ardèche will have made her quite capable of catching the odd frog; and yet I don't like to imagine my own daughter capable of stooping to such spite.

Once Jeffrey had taken the sock and deposited its contents under the bushes at the edge of the garden, I made everyone a cup of tea. We were a silent group, Natalia and Lydia sitting close together, wrapping their fingers around their mugs, each of them no doubt wondering how such a thing had come to pass. Sophie was the first to speak. "Someone must have put it there," she said. Natalia and Lydia looked up as one. "Someone who knows the outdoors, who knows where to find gross things like that. Someone who knows us, and the house too." She paused. Everyone looked down, perplexed. "And why was Randy lurking about here yesterday? It was his day off."

Oh, dear. Was she right, or was Randolph (I do wish she would use his full name) being framed? Either way, Natalia whispered a translation to Lydia, who promptly burst into tears. Who could blame the girl? She fled one country in despair at the sort of man who would cruelly dump her for a rich girl, only, one assumes, to find solace in a man who now appears to be the sort to smuggle amphibians into her sister's bed. I felt I had to intervene. "But Sophie," I said pointedly. "Why on earth would Randolph do such a thing?"

She was unfazed, and took a long sip of tea before replying: "Oh, you know what men are like. He probably thought it would be funny."

Natalia again translated for Lydia, who listened with fresh tears running down her puffy cheeks. Then she stuck her chin out and declared something that Natalia translated back into English (of a sort) as "She says she hate men. All men are whole asses. She from now will be girl who like girls." Jeffrey looked a little woozy, perhaps from his exertions with the bed sock, and said he needed to lie down.

TUESDAY, MARCH 25

Before taking Sophie and Zac to the airport today I finally got a chance to talk to my daughter alone. Zac had gone out for a run—like many short men, he seems to take a perverse pride in his physique—leaving Sophie in the conservatory trying to teach Darcy to say something that sounded like "Comin' atchaaaa." Fortunately she failed. I settled down in a wicker chair and waited for her to stop pretending she didn't know I was there. Eventually she looked away from Darcy, who was shifting uncomfortably from one foot to the other saying "Atchoo," turned to me, and said, "All right, Mum?"

I decided to bite the bullet. "Yes, I'm fine, thanks, but I'm a bit worried about *you*, Sophie," I said. "Jealousy is a terrible thing." I stared at her in the hope that she would cave in, or at least show some sign of embarrassment or remorse, but instead she stuck her hands firmly in the pockets of her slouchy jeans and stared right back at me through narrowed eyes rimmed with thick green kohl.

"Yeah, I know," she said. "I saw the look on your face when Aunty Harriet told you that Laura had got engaged." I could tell that this line of conversation was going nowhere. I will never find out if my daughter is guilty of a frog-related crime passionnel; she will never confess.

Instead I turned the conversation to safer territory. I asked if she was enjoying herself in the Ardèche, and she said it was "all right"; I asked if she'd made lots of nice friends, and she said "'spose"; I asked if her French was getting better, and she said "'spose." She then perked up a little and said she knew how to give a boy a brush-off by telling him to do something unspeakable with a pinecone—I paraphrase so as to spare your blushes, dear readers. I know I should have told her off but I couldn't suppress a small giggle. I gave her a hug, and actually felt her hug me back. I felt less bleak than usual when I drove her, and Zac, to Heathrow. It will be Lydia's turn at the end of the week, and then I hope things will return to normal.

There was no bell ringing this evening because of the Easter break, but after such a hectic few days I was quite happy to sit back on the sofa and watch *Location, Location, Location*. It featured a couple who had spent £100,000 on a two-bedroom flat in Clapham in 1996 and, having added a "feature wall" of glass bricks and painted everything white, were selling it for £375,000.

Jeffrey and I bought our house in 1988; even without any novelty see-through bricks, Lord only knows what has happened to its value since then.

And now I must get an early night: tomorrow I am finally meeting Gerald, and I will need all my wits about me to steer him safely into the arms of Miss Hughes.

WEDNESDAY, MARCH 26

I have just returned from my rendezvous with Gerald. We met in Café Milano, or what used to be the village tea shop before it underwent some spurious Continental makeover. Gerald was there already, perched uncomfortably on a chrome bar stool and clutching a paperback copy of *Anna Karenina* with clammy-looking hands.

He was wearing a lavender-colored corduroy suit, with a crumpled white T-shirt underneath. Either he is taking Miss Hughes's preferences to heart, or he has managed to lose all his blue shirts and sensible trousers at the launderette. When I went up to him and said a cheerful "Hello," he appeared ill at ease, perhaps because he was nervous about the conversation that would ensue, or perhaps because he was bamboozled by the café's terminology of lattes and Americanos. I took matters into my own hands. I was an Englishwoman in an English tea shop; there was no need for me to ask for anything ending in *o*. I asked for one cup of tea, one white coffee, and a couple of biscuits, fixing the waitress (I will not say barista) with an unflinching smile. She gestured vaguely at the blackboard, which had all sorts of strange words chalked up in a curly hand, but I repeated myself, and eventually she simply nodded her head beneath her preposterous baseball cap and went to get the drinks. Gerald was looking at me with respect, no doubt admiring my powers of persuasion and hoping they would be as much use on Miss Hughes as they were on the waitress.

Once we were settled opposite each other at a small metallic table, Gerald finally looked me in the eye and asked, in a quiet voice, if I had any idea why he'd asked me here. I replied with a knowing smile that I thought I had an inkling. Heartened, he carried on, saying "It's just that, since Rosie left me, I've been so lonely. It's been the most wretched time of my life. I didn't think I'd get through it. If it hadn't been for Poppy and—and—" Here his confidence failed him.

"Bell ringing?" I suggested, with another encouraging smile.

"Well, yes, ringing has certainly been a refuge of sorts. It's taken me out of myself every week, and everyone has been so kind, especially, uh . . . You see, that might be why I've started to—started to develop certain feelings. . . . I've lost faith in marriage, Constance. Rosie just upped and left, after thirty-six years. She left her rings in the soap dish. What does it mean, *marriage*? That's why I'm telling you this, telling you about my—my feelings."

He stuttered to a halt, crumbling a biscuit (I will not say biscotto) to a fine powder with his right hand. I decided to leap in and fill the void. "It's Miss Hughes, isn't it?" I said. She was unmarried. Gerald jumped, slopping tea over the side of his cup and onto his saucer. "Don't worry, I guessed a little while ago. Your secret's safe with me," I reassured him, while he sat there staring, his facial muscles working as if to open his mouth, but failing. "She's a fine woman—knows her own mind, but nothing wrong with that. I'll do my best to soften her up for you." I patted him on the arm. Finally, Gerald snapped back to life like an elastic band that has been stretched for too long.

"Uh, yes, yes, of course, Miss Hughes. Uh, yes. So kind. Knew I could count on you. Uh. Fine woman. Bunions. Uh. Do you know, I've just realized that the launderette is coming around to fix a leaking pipe in ten minutes. Shall I get the bill?"

The poor man. He was obviously overcome with emotion at the mere mention of Miss Hughes's name. I can't wait for bell ringing next week!

THURSDAY, MARCH 27

Church Flowers today. Appearing in a cloud of perfume that smelled like air freshener (a little touch of Anaïs Anaïs is all I wear), Pru informed me in a hushed voice that Ruth was doing much better thanks to therapy.

"What for?" I asked.

"You know," she whispered, loudly enough for everyone to hear. "To help her get over the shock of what happened with Rupert. Her therapist suggested he might come along to one of the sessions. She can arrange a screen because of his—condition."

I said that it would still be too risky, and Pru nodded sadly. It is out of the question that Rupert should attend; he is terrified of Ruth, and besides, therapy is the worst American import since Britney Spears, whom Sophie once said she wanted to grow up to be. Rupert is not so far gone down the path of *Guardian* reading that he would need to pay a stranger to listen to him witter on about himself. That's what friends—and parrots—are for.

I got back to find the house filled with flowers. For a moment, I thought Jeffrey had made his first grand romantic gesture since 1989; but it turned out that it was all Randolph's doing. I caught Natalia and Lydia wandering among the milk bottles stuffed with irises and daffodils giggling. Natalia explained that she had told Randolph what happened with the frog and he said it wasn't him—and he'd then arranged the flowers to cheer the twins up. Which is all very well, except it has ravaged my borders. Jeffrey came in, eyed the floral superabundance, and said it was a sacking offense. He seems to have taken against Randolph from the beginning. I may not have agreed with him, but there was a certain compelling fury to his speech. Even Natalia looked chastened.

SATURDAY, MARCH 29

Lydia is gone; silence rules. Jeffrey obligingly took her to the airport. As soon as he came back he retreated to his study, no doubt savoring the newfound calm and quiet in the house. I saw Randolph in the garden, immobile, leaning balefully on his hoe until it sank three inches into the ground.

MONDAY, MARCH 31

Back to normal. Having instructed Natalia to give all the bedrooms a good clean and check thoroughly for concealed frogs, I settled down with a cup of coffee to check my e-mail. As usual, there were a few circulars from Waitrose and the National Trust, and nothing from Sophie—even though she promised before she left that she would e-mail me a photo of herself every Monday so I could check that she wasn't losing weight or getting her hair cut in any more unusual shapes.

And then, like a scab that one cannot resist picking, even though one knows the results are likely to make one queasy, I felt compelled to sign on to Facebook and find out whether Jeffrey had indeed abandoned his online persona. A search for his name revealed that his original identity had disappeared into the ether; but scanning farther down the page I saw something that made my stomach lurch: J Hardon, whose profile picture was Daniel Craig wearing a 007 tuxedo. I hope this is merely coincidence. I like to think of Jeffrey as a Roger Moore man to the core.

TUESDAY, APRIL 1

I called on Tanya today to ask her whether she thought that J Hardon was Jeffrey, and if so, what I should do. She seemed distracted, taking a bottle of pomegranate juice instead of milk out of the fridge and pouring some into my coffee, but eventually she said I should stop worrying, and gave me a thin smile. I think she's finding her first pregnancy tough. This is hardly surprising. I remember my brain went to mush when I was expecting Rupert: how Jeffrey laughed when he came home from work one day to find me upset because I had run out of matching wool while knitting the third bootie in a "pair." He put his briefcase down, took me in his arms, then laughed into my hair as he patted my stomach. I asked Tanya whether Mark was excited about the baby, and she shrugged and said he was never there, before opening the fridge, staring into it for five seconds, then closing it again, shaking her head.

WEDNESDAY, APRIL 2

What a disappointment! Gerald didn't come to bell ringing last night. I fear something drastic must have happened, because he knew full well that I was primed to butter up Miss Hughes for him. Perhaps his leak has deteriorated.

In any case, I decided not to waste the opportunity to have a quiet word in her ear—well, not so quiet, given her partial deafness and the resonance of our ringing. She is a woman with a no-nonsense attitude and a tendency to bellow "And your point is?" whenever she feels herself to be adrift in a conversation, so I decided to be forthright.

"Miss Hughes, I want to talk to you about Gerald," I said.

"Gerald?" she replied. "I thought as much. Dreadful sense of timing, that man. Do you want me to tell him to pay attention when he creeps back here next week? Or perhaps to smarten himself up a bit, trim that mustache?"

I considered this offer. It would certainly improve both the standard and the salubriousness of our ringing group. And yet I decided that, once started, I should not let myself be drawn off on a tangent.

"Well, that's not quite what I meant," I said, and paused to gather my thoughts. She frowned and began tapping her suede Footglove shoe against the flagstones, making a series of muffled thuds. Dithering was not going to help my case. I cleared my throat.

"I'm going to be open with you," I began. "There's no other way of saying this. Gerald doesn't need nasal clippers, he needs the love of a good woman."

"Really?"

"Really."

"What's that got to do with me?" she said, wrapping her arms firmly across her cream blouse.

"Well, to put it bluntly, I have reason to believe that the good woman in question is you. He has always thought very highly of you. You have stood here, shoulder-to-shoulder, pulling together, for the best part of fifteen years. Since Rosemary left he has begun to see you in a new light."

There was a strange expression on Miss Hughes's face—her eyes narrowing and curling up at the corners—which brought to mind for some reason a fox standing in front of a chicken coop.

"And how do you know all this?" she asked, smoothing back an immaculate curtain of iron-gray hair and securing it with a quick stab of her hairpin.

"He told me."

"Really?"

"Really."

And that was that. I hope Gerald resolves his plumbing problems before next week.

 THURSDAY, APRIL 3

I got back from Church Flowers to find Natalia reading a magazine—or rather, looking at pictures of girls with orange tans falling out of taxis—when she should have been at the supermarket. I chivvied her along. Edward, Jeffrey's brother, and his wife, Harriet, are coming around for dinner tomorrow night and the usual slapdash fare will not do. Last time I ate at their house, Harriet had her housekeeper make a perfect cheese soufflé, an act of incalculable malice.

FRIDAY, APRIL 4

11:59 P.M.

Readers, I think I've done something silly, or maybe two or three silly things. It's all Edward's fault, why did he have to top up my wineglass every two minutes? Why did he have to bring port? It went down too quickly just like wine but stronger especially the third glass. It's all Hattys' fault anyway, I never liked her that much funny nose with a bump on the bridge like a man always pursing her lips and how can she be a size 10 and ask for seconds? and why did she have to show me those pictures? The wedding album, laura in a cream strapless dress, fur wrap, hair curling around her face, smiling, there's harriet in the next one in her mother of the bride suit size 10 from jaeger and her hat and her glass of champagne. There's me and sophie sophie's wearing ugly ugg boots and scowling I tried to make her wear pretty cream shoes with a kitten heel I tried. And then the baby photos their son John's new baby girl, their second grandchild, pink face, pudgy, perfect, there's her big brother built like a little rugby player standing next to her and smiling. Why?

So I just called Rupert and sophie I went on facebook and I dont want to think about it anymore now I need two big glasses of water and some leftover chicken and bacon casserole with a fried egg on top and bed. Why didn't jeffrey stop me? I can here him snoring from here thats why

SATURDAY, APRIL 5

It is nearly lunchtime. I have slept late. Jeffrey has left for a game of tennis with Edward. The house is silent except for the dull clatter of Natalia unloading the dishwasher. I have taken two aspirin with a glass of sparkling water and eaten three chocolate Hobnobs. Physically, my condition is stabilizing. If only I could say the same about my state of mind.

I am embarrassed to see from my blog page that I started to inform you about last night's events at a time when I should not have attempted any form of irreversible electronic communication. Please ignore my observations on my sister-in-law, Harriet. Her nose, in fact, gives her a noble profile.

As you will have gathered, it all got a little much over dinner. Edward was generous with the wine, and Harriet was glowing with excitement because she had finally finished writing the calligraphy captions on the photo album of her daughter, Laura's, wedding, which took place last December. She also had the first photos of her son's baby daughter, whose christening we will shortly be attending in the North. Readers, it was an intoxicating combination. The more pictures I saw, the more I felt myself almost mechanically compelled to lift my glass to my lips. Harriet was too absorbed in the pictures to notice; Jeffrey and Edward were having some sort of heated argument on the state of the world economy, which they interrupted only to slosh out large quantities of wine. I heard incomprehensible snatches of their conversation as the photos started to merge into one multicolor smiling blur in front of my eyes.

After several hours of such activity, I remember hearing the heavy clunk of the front door shutting, then suddenly finding myself sitting in the conservatory with my legs tucked up under my skirt and my mobile in my hand. I called Rupert. I wish I hadn't; but the call history on my phone confirms that it was so. I first remembered the full details when I woke at six A.M. with a tongue that felt like the bit of carpet underneath the sofa. As far as I recall, the conversation went something like this:

"Hello, Rupert, it's me."

"Mum! Is everything okay? It's almost midnight."

"Yes, I mean no. The casserole was a bit dry around the edges. I told Natalia to use more stock but the stupid girl wouldn't listen. But, yes, don't worry, everything's fine. Except it isn't."

"Mum, are you okay? Have you been drinking?"

"Yes, I mean no! Stop changing the subject. I've been thinking and looking at lots of pictures and booties. What I mean is, I've been thinking about why you don't want to go on *Telegraph* dating."

"Mum, I really don't want to talk about that just now."

"Don't interrupt your mother while she's talking! What I mean is, I've been thinking and worrying and worrying and thinking and what I think is this. You're hiding something. You're not the person I thought you were."

"Jesus, Mum, are you sure you want to be having this conversation?"

"Never take the Lord's name in vain! But you wouldn't care, would you? You're probably an atheist. That would fit the picture. You probably donated money to that campaign to put "There is no God" on the side of a bus and laughed about it afterward with all your friends with their rectangular glasses and Converse trainers. Even David Cameron has Converse trainers now. You can't trust anyone."

"Mum, what are you going on about?"

"Rupert, you're a *Guardian* reader, aren't you? Just admit it. You want your father to be taxed to death and you wish that you'd been brought up on a wind farm run by asylum seekers. You've turned against us. You hate everything we stand for. You're a *Guardian* reader, aren't you?"

Then I recall that there was a pause before he said:

"Yes, Mum, yes, I am. I do read the *Guardian,* mostly online. Sometimes the BBC Web site too. But every Sunday I buy the *Sunday Times* because I like the supplements. I don't hate you and Dad. I think wind power should only ever make up part of a mixed-energy portfolio and, while I believe we have a moral duty to provide asylum to political refugees, I wouldn't swap you and Dad for the world, as hard as that is to believe right now. Now will you go to bed?"

"Good night, sleep tight, hope the bed bugs don't bite."

And that, I believe, was the end of the conversation. I must comfort myself where I may. He reads a newspaper that encourages him to think like a decent human being once a week. I can only hope that he doesn't skip Jeremy Clarkson's column.

After talking to Rupert, I remember trying to call Sophie. She didn't answer, but I vaguely recall leaving her a long message on the aesthetic horrors of Ugg boots. After that I went on Facebook and sent a beseeching message to my friend Bridget, asking if I could come and stay. She's childless and divorced, and so the only person in the world who can make me feel better about myself at the moment. The only problem is that it appears I phrased my message along those lines. I also sent a cocktail to all my friends and "poked" J Hardon. I have just changed my status to *is hungover and remorseful*, so hopefully Bridget will forgive me.

My phone has just bleeped. A text message from Sophie, reading: *momma k, was u pissd last night? largin it?? lol!!! xxx*.

I am going to lie down again.

SUNDAY, APRIL 6

Today I have been a model mother, daughter, and wife. I went to church, I brought Mother a bunch of flowers (the pollen made her sneeze, but the thought was there), I called both my children and left normal, sober messages on their answerphones, I cooked Jeffrey steak with homemade Diane sauce. I drank water with dinner. I shall make amends, I shall.

10 P.M.

Good Lord, my domesticity has been shaken by a message from J Hardon on Facebook. The good news is that it cannot possibly be Jeffrey. The bad news is that I have this scrawled on my "wall" like public graffiti for everybody to see: *u hot horny lookin for sexy time's?*

Jeffrey would never misuse an apostrophe.

MONDAY, APRIL 7

Thank heavens for that: Bridget has written back to me on Facebook, undeterred by J Hardon or my rudeness. Luckily, she is the tough, plucky type who is not easily offended. She wrote: *Dear me Constance, if life in the suburbs is getting you down there's only one solution: London! Come stay this weekend. Fun, frivolity, and fine food await. Bridge x.*

I'm slightly worried about what "fun and frivolity" might entail, but it can't be worse than reading 276 handwritten wedding photo captions. I replied that I would love to and booked my train ticket.

I thought Jeffrey would be bemused by my rash display of independence, but when he got home I took his briefcase out of his hand, hung up his coat, and told him about my plans, and he simply smiled broadly and said, "You have a ball." He really is most supportive at times. I will tell Natalia to make sure she looks after him properly this weekend.

TUESDAY, APRIL 8

Dear readers, dreadful news. Poor Tanya. I popped around to her house this morning to bring her a coffee and walnut cake and a copy of *You and Your Baby* magazine, which had a special feature on nursery decor, including the most gorgeous hand-carved white crib. As I approached the house, I noticed a few weeds poking up through the yellow paving stones of the drive—they must have laid off the gardener as well as the cleaner. I really should lend her Randolph, I thought to myself. When I got to the front door, it was ajar. I knocked but there was no answer. I pushed it open another few inches and shouted her name; it would be a shame to let the cake go completely cold. It was then that I heard a muffled sob emanating from the direction of the kitchen. I forgot all my scruples about intruding and went straight in, nearly dropping the cake as I kicked off my shoes. I found her sitting at her stripped-pine table, her hands knitted into her hair just at the point where the lengthening brown roots turned honey-blond, weeping. I ran over and put my arm around her. Whatever was the matter? Was it the hormones, or was something wrong?

"Something's wrong," she said, looking up at me with muddy

trails of mascara dripping down across her white cheeks. "It's Mark. He's lost his job."

Horrible as this news was, I have to say that my first feeling was relief: Mark had not been beaten about the head by a blood-thirsty asylum seeker or a resentful taxpayer and left to perish in a gutter; both Tanya and her baby were well. I put the kettle on, took two of Tanya's funny square plates out of the cupboard, and served the cake. By the time the tea was ready she was only sniffing intermittently, stroking her hands up and down over her bump. After half a piece of cake, she felt up to telling me what had happened.

Mark had been made redundant that morning. As soon as he got to work, his manager called him into his office and told him, as kindly as possible, that he would have to clear his desk. It was a conversation he had been dreading for months. Mark was a senior derivatives trader (whatever that means—Tanya tried to explain, but she ended up staring blankly into the middle distance, as did I). In any case, she impressed upon me the fact that, given the financial climate, his profession was akin to being a turkey in December. After the inevitable occurred, he blasted home in his Porsche, told Tanya the news, kissed her on the cheek as she stood there stunned, then left again to "clear his head." That was an hour ago. "He was still wearing his lucky cuff links," she said, another sob breaking out. She gestured to a small crate in the kitchen that contained all his possessions from seven years of work at the bank: a Reuters desk calendar, a small gift hamper from Fortnum & Mason, some folders, a dog-eared copy of the book *Investing for Dummies,* a pocket calculator, and a novelty Margaret Thatcher nutcracker.

"That's it," she said. "That's all he's got left." The sorry pile stood beneath one of many framed wedding photographs, which both our eyes drifted up toward. It showed the happy couple in

Barbados, Tanya wearing a sheath of designer silk with a stem of acid-pink hibiscus tucked behind one ear, her skin shining and nut-brown, her hair immaculately flaxen-colored. Mark was in a cream suit, open at the neck, a huge smile on his face. They had flown 120 people over, she said, for a ceremony on the beach, at sunset, flanked by candles, where they said "for better and for worse" with silver sand between their toes before cracking into Bollinger and lobster.

"And now I don't even know if we can afford a Bugaboo pram. What will happen to us if Mark can't find another job?"

I reassured her as best as I could and then, sensing that she wanted to be alone, I left, the pristine copy of *You and Your Baby* tucked discreetly under one arm.

WEDNESDAY, APRIL 9

What has become of the modern man? Jeffrey excepted, the male of the species seems lacking not just in employment opportunities and proper footwear but also in get-up-and-go. Take Gerald. Last night he scuttled into the belfry late, to take up his usual position by my side. Miss Hughes—who was resplendent in an olive-colored tweed skirt two inches shorter than usual—asked to swap places with me so that she would be next to him. Instead of seizing the opportunity to sidle up to her, as any red-blooded man would have done, he was quite put off his stroke.

THURSDAY, APRIL 10

Ruth appeared at Church Flowers like some mournful specter, dressed in layers of baggy white. As she approached me, blinking behind her purple plastic glasses with a self-pitying smile on her face and a book called *The Secret* clutched in her hand, I decided I had no truck with her nonsense. Just as she began to assert that the way to overcome sorrow was within, I cut her off.

"Now, look here, young lady," I began. "Have you found out that you're pregnant and that your husband has just lost his job? Have you been abandoned after thirty-six years of marriage for a trapeze artist?"

She was silent, her fey smile drooping.

"No? Well, then. I suggest you buck up."

Pru clucked indignantly, but I could tell from the look in her eyes that, secretly, she was on my side.

After arranging was over, I gathered up the leftover flowers and took them around to Tanya, who was struggling to peel a carrot and weeping. Mark had suggested she try cooking a meal from "scratch," and she said she had been shocked to discover that scratch wasn't in fact an Asian vegetable or a form of small, bristly wild boar. I introduced her to the stock cube and helped her make a shepherd's pie before leaving. I wonder where her friends are in such difficult times. She must have lost touch with her old colleagues after leaving work, and I suppose she moves in different circles from her school friends'.

When I got home I signed on to Facebook and changed my status to *Does anyone know anyone with a job for a banker?* No one replied.

FRIDAY, APRIL 11

I have packed a capsule wardrobe for my trip to London this weekend: black low-heeled shoes, smart black trousers, a stone-colored knee-length skirt, a black sleeveless fitted top, a primrose-colored cashmere cardigan, my cream Burberry raincoat, and a can of mace spray. I am all set. If you don't hear from me again, please write to the mayor and ask him to mount a search party in the Notting Hill area. I am so glad that that dreadful Ken Livingstone is no longer in charge. Never trust a grown man in a duffle coat, as I have told Sophie many times.

SATURDAY, APRIL 12

I must be quick. Bridget is in the shower and we will be scooting off to the Victoria and Albert Museum as soon as she's ready, and it's already taken me ten minutes to figure out how to use her funny white Mac computer. She told me something last night that I just had to share with you. My old university friend, with her first-class degree and her high-flying publishing career, has launched herself in a new direction. She is now a writer of erotic fiction under the pen name Bluebell Lahore. After a few glasses of wine, she explained that times "were looking pretty iffy" in publishing and that it made sense to have a lucrative sideline. "Even in a recession, women will always buy chocolate, makeup, frilly underwear, and dirty paperbacks," she said, grinning through blackberry-colored lips stained with red wine. I thought of Tanya with her carrot peeler and her roots, and I wondered.

"And besides, writing them's a breeze. There are only three plots you need to know. One: poor, downtrodden young heroine battles adversity; man A, who is also poor and downtrodden, falls in love with her, but she falls in love with man B, who is a rich, vicious love-rat; she has a steamy affair with man B then he breaks her heart then man A fights him then inherits lots of money then girl and man A live happily ever after. Two: feisty, successful young heroine bored in marriage to man A, who is dependable but dull, starts illicit affair with man B, who is a rich, vicious love-rat who breaks her heart, sending her back into the arms of man A, who in the meantime has started to work out and now has a six-pack and some handcuffs. Three: sweet, naïve young heroine saving herself for marriage with man A, her childhood sweetheart, when love-rat man B arrives on the scene and leads her astray; man A fights him wins back heroine but then she runs off with man B anyway for a life of passion."

I stood gaping at her, wineglass halfway up to my mouth.

"You see? Easy," she continued, unabashed. "All you need to do is make up a few names and places and you're laughing all the way to the bank. Maybe you should try it. You always had a way with words."

I was tempted to reply that this blog provided me with as much of an outlet for my writing as I needed, but I bit my tongue. Dear readers, I think it best that you're not joined by anyone who knows me. Instead, I muttered something noncommittal about being far too busy with bell ringing, then went to bed. I woke at three A.M., however, from a dream in which Gerald was in the belfry with a "Man B" name tag pinned to his corduroy jacket and Miss Hughes was swinging about on a bell rope wearing a frilly Victorian-style nightie with her hair streaming out behind her and her bunions showing. I looked down and realized that I was wearing one of Sophie's Topshop minidresses with the name tag "Girl A" attached to it. What does this mean?

I have no time to ponder an answer. I can hear Bridget's hair dryer.

MONDAY, APRIL 14

I am back home. My London adventure is over. For two days and two nights, I shared the life of a cosmopolitan single woman. I sat in Bridget's flat eating chocolate éclairs from the nearby French patisserie (making cakes is one thing the French can be trusted with), admiring the large bow windows, the antique book shelves, the pretty Oriental rugs, and doing my best to resist running my fingers across every surface to show up the dust. Bridget herself does not have the crushed look that I expected in a single, childless woman of fifty-three. In fact, she has fewer wrinkles than I do: I know, because I counted them as she was leaning forward over the breakfast table to concentrate on a crossword. She was wearing a brightly colored silk kimono at the time, and whistling cheerfully. Nothing about her expresses the idea that she has crashed through life's great hurdles. Over dinner at a smart restaurant, after I had spent half an hour bringing her up to date on the various shortcomings of Sophie and Rupert, she told me she was perfectly happy as she was, alone, and smiled serenely over her wilted green leaves and speck of sea bass. Perhaps she is simply putting on a brave face, or perhaps the Clarins beauty flash balm I spotted in her bathroom cupboard really works. After dinner she took me to some sort of forties-style club where everyone was wearing tea dresses and dancing. I'm afraid the martinis Bridget bought me went straight to my head and I had to take a taxi home. Bridget must have crept in like a mouse later because she didn't wake me at all. She must have gotten enough sleep, though, because when she appeared for breakfast she certainly had a spring in her step.

I think the weekend has achieved its aim. I am better equipped to cope with little Erica's—the granddaughter of Harriet and Edward—christening next weekend. If Bridget can be happy with no children, two bonsai trees, and a career, I too can be happy with my lot.

As if to reinforce the point, Jeffrey greeted me at the station with a lovely bouquet. I don't know what's gotten into him. He doesn't normally buy me flowers except when he's trying to make up for something, like the time he spilled his Bloody Mary on my Burberry trench coat. As far as I'm aware, none of my clothes has been inadvertently soiled recently. But spring is in the air,

I suppose. And underneath that slightly stern exterior, he does have a kind, even a passionate, heart.

TUESDAY, APRIL 15

Once again, a visit from a troubled-looking Reginald. I could tell something was amiss from the way he kept hooking and unhooking his thumbs through the belt loops on his chinos even as he stood on the doorstep. When he came in and sat down, the wisps of hair he pulls back across his flaking scalp flopped down over his eyes. He peered out through the graying strands like one of the rare breeds of long-haired sheep they have at the county fair. "Reginald, dear, whatever is the matter?" I asked.

"Two things," he said, patting his hair mournfully back into position.

"David has decided he's a Scientologist. And St. Mary's is being investigated by the Health and Safety Executive."

I didn't know what to say, or which piece of news was worse. I once watched a *Panorama* documentary on Scientology, which seemed to show that it was a mad cult filled with mad Americans wearing sunglasses who went even madder if anyone called it a mad cult. My only uncertainty is whether health and safety inspectors are as deranged as Scientologists. Reports in the newspaper would suggest that they are.

I comforted Reginald that it was doubtlessly just a phase that David would grow out of, and that I would help him complete the necessary "risk assessment" form for bell ringing.

WEDNESDAY, APRIL 16

Bell ringing last night. Miss Hughes's skirt has shrunk another three inches, revealing knees as thick and fleshy as a joint of ham. It was too much for Gerald, who bolted out of the belfry before the last note had sounded. I stayed late, however, to help Reginald with the form. Under the section "What are the hazards?" we wrote:

Ringers may hold on to rope for too long, be hoisted off the ground, fall, and die.

Ringers may be deafened by cacophony.

Ringers may be trampled by Gerald.

Ringers may choke on biscuits at break time.

Ringers may be thumped by Miss Hughes's handbag for failing to keep time.

I thought we should whittle it down a little, but Reginald was adamant that honesty was the best policy. Underneath the section "What are you doing to minimize risk?" we wrote:

Praying.

Underneath the section "What more could be done to manage risk?" we wrote:

Ringers to use common sense and, perhaps, ear muffs.

I hope that will do.

 THURSDAY, APRIL 17

Dear readers, I have done something rash.

Tanya came around for lunch today, but she hardly touched my homemade onion quiche with green salad, merely pushing forkfuls of food back and forth across the plate and sighing. I thought that perhaps I had oversalted the pastry, but it turned out there was an even worse explanation. She and Mark are going to lose the house. Pushing her lengthening mousy hair behind her ears, she explained that they were mortgaged to the hilt; Mark's bonuses had gone to pay for the wedding, the Porsche, the all-inclusive holidays to Sandals in Jamaica and luxury chalet trips in Méribel, the tailored suits and Jimmy Choo shoes. He had blown his redundancy payout on online gambling. Given the recent fall in house prices, they were in serious negative equity; repossession loomed. I stifled a small gasp of horror. Tanya's parents live in a flat in Billericay, Mark's in a flat in Spain. Neither is a suitable abode for a mother-to-be. I hadn't realized their situation was so dire.

I wanted to rail against Mark for his selfish irresponsibility, but something about the flat, resigned look in Tanya's eyes told me not to. She said that Mark had lost a stone from worry, while she could not stop comfort eating and had gained one, which she claimed was far too much weight at this stage of her pregnancy. She was distraught. Tears fell from her eyes, but this time there was no mascara to wash away. Readers, there was only one thing I could do. I invited her and Mark to stay for as long as it takes them to find their feet.

I hope Jeffrey doesn't mind.

FRIDAY, APRIL 18

I am still waiting for the right moment to tell Jeffrey about Tanya. He was in a bad mood when he got in last night— something to do with the share price of an Icelandic bank—so I didn't feel it was wise to raise the subject. Perhaps the christening of our little grandniece will cheer him up. I bought her a silver piggy bank; growing up in the North, I'm sure she'll learn to hoard her pennies. We leave for York as soon as he's back from work tonight, with Rupert in tow. Harriet just called to check that we were all set, with a gleeful flutter in her voice.

I will not be jealous.
I will not be jealous.
I will not be jealous.
I will not be jealous.
I will not be jealous.
I will not.

SATURDAY, APRIL 19

I am jealous. There is no point in lying to you. I am horribly jealous, from the top of my head, where this morning's blow-dry has now gone askew, down to my cream heels, dip-dyed in mud. This is a terrible thing to say, but at one point I wanted to slap Harriet's pink, glowing face. It was a perfect day, warm spring sunshine, branches of cherry blossom waving in front of the pretty church where the ceremony took place. Afterward there were glasses of champagne in a marquee nearby, Harriet flitting to and fro with a camera, little Erica a perfect plump-cheeked bundle in a little lacy white dress, kicking her feet in her little white booties. Harriet picked her up and carried her about like a trophy. By the end of the afternoon my cheeks were starting to hurt from the enforced smiling, so I made my excuses and came back to the hotel, leaving Jeffrey discussing golf swings with Edward.

As I sit here, squinting at the computer in the dim-lit hotel lobby, my only comfort is this. I watched Rupert closely as he chatted to the guests, who included a large group of young women in pretty dresses. He was quite at ease in their company, laughing and chatting. I couldn't tell from my vantage point if he was flirting, but he clearly wasn't intimidated by female company. Perhaps he is overcoming his shyness. Perhaps it will not be so long until I too have a wedding, then a christening, to organize.

SUNDAY, APRIL 20

What a to-do. I knew I should have told Jeffrey about Mark and Tanya sooner, but I was waiting for the right moment. Family get-togethers always seem to put him in a bad mood, so the weekend was not opportune. And how was I to know it would happen like that?

But I'm getting ahead of myself. We finally got home last night after a five-hour drive from the North via Milton Keynes, during which Jeffrey showed off his manly, indomitable spirit by driving consistently at three miles per hour over the speed limit. Once home, no sooner had Natalia helped us with our bags and put the kettle on than the doorbell rang. We were both puzzled. Could it be Reginald, with another health and safety form to fill out? It was not.

When I opened the door I was confronted by the sight of Tanya and Mark—still wearing his stockbroker braces—surrounded by boxes, with a hunted look in their eyes. There was a screech of tires as their taxi rushed away down the road. I thought better of asking what had happened to their Porsche. Trying not to panic, I welcomed them in and asked Natalia to help with their things while I rushed over to Jeffrey, who was striding down the hall to see what the fuss was about. I quickly whispered to him the gist of the situation, and he turned port-colored. Luckily, however, he is well bred to the point that it is usually impossible to tell what he's thinking.

Once they were settled in the guest room, I whipped up a few omelets for dinner, which we ate in silence. I would have asked Natalia to cook, but she kept staring mutinously at the new arrivals and saying "I not understanding." Neither did Jeffrey. Neither, really, did I.

MONDAY, APRIL 21

I cannot write for long. I must buy some casserole steak and give it a good going over with the tenderizing mallet. In doing so, I hope to make amends with Jeffrey. He was manifestly unhappy about the Mark/Tanya situation when I got to bed last night. I could tell by the way he clutched his book so hard that the tips of his fingers went white. It was the most upset I had seen him since I accidentally decluttered the spare room of his favorite golf clubs.

TUESDAY, APRIL 22

The atmosphere in the house is tense. Jeffrey didn't get home until after eleven last night, by which point my tender steak casserole was a congealed mess. Mark and Tanya must have noticed. He said he had been working on an important case, but when I was carrying his briefcase upstairs it fell open and four back copies of *Golf Monthly* along with an Andy McNab novel spilled out.

WEDNESDAY, APRIL 23

Bell ringing last night. Although I was anxious about leaving everyone at home to their own devices, I didn't want to miss practice, especially with the national ringers' contest coming up in a few months. Such divided loyalties are a woman's lot. Reginald certainly needs someone to help him focus: he looked quite pale and apprehensive last night. He told me that David showed no signs of relinquishing Scientology, and kept trying to convince him that Jesus—if he existed—came out of a volcano. What's more, we will have a health and safety inspector poking his nose into our practice next week. Apparently, our form did not reassure him that everything was under control. As if to prove his point, Gerald put his back out. Miss Hughes had asked him to help her pull her rope, feigning a weakness at odds with her oxlike strength. Gerald shuddered with what must have been excitement as he took hold of the rope and Miss Hughes briefly clasped her hands over his. It was too much for him. He yelped and rolled onto the flagstones, like a footballer after a flamboyant tackle. Miss Hughes knelt beside him and stroked his hair, which quickly revived him. He jumped to his feet and left, muttering his excuses. I do hope he won't be out of action for long.

When I got home, Jeffrey wasn't back and Mark and Tanya had gone to bed. There were Chinese take-out cartons and leftover prawn crackers in the bin. Tanya is still clearly not on good terms with "scratch."

THURSDAY, APRIL 24

Once again, I sneaked out of my fractious household to attend one of my regular activities—Church Flowers. It's just as well that I did. A wonderful thought occurred to me. Pru had not brought Ruth along this week because her daughter was going to a "chakra" class or something at the community center straight after school. I asked Pru what this meant and she said, in a monotonous, downtrodden sort of voice, "Chakra is the study of wheel-like vortices of energy." I raised one eyebrow, and stared at her in silence for several seconds. She relented. In something like her usual tone, she whispered vituperatively, "It's mumbo jumbo." I nodded sympathetically. And then, in my old adversary, I suddenly recognized a kindred spirit to poor dear Reginald, and an opportunity. Was Reginald not going through exactly the same ordeal with his son David? Might two young people forget their odd spiritual hobbies if they got together and focused on normal things, like two-for-one cinema vouchers and dinner at Pizza Express? I can only hope so. As I watched Pru at work with the gladioli, her pink and white polka-dot neck scarf drooping into the flower heads and her worried frown cutting creases into her forehead, I felt a strong urge to tell her my idea, but I held back. I need time to formulate a plan; especially after last time.

FRIDAY, APRIL 25

Mark and Tanya have been in the house for five days now. I feel it is time to take stock of this arrangement.

The advantages:

I have done the right thing. I look at Tanya sitting on my sofa, cradling her expanding bump, and I feel the same warm glow inside that I got when I donated Jeffrey's old LP collection to the annual Cats in Need jumble sale.

In Tanya, it is nice to have someone to talk to who talks back, which is more than can reliably be said of either Darcy or Jeffrey.

The disadvantages:

Jeffrey is peevish and resentful. He hasn't stooped to saying as much, of course, but he comes home later, drinks more, and in bed sometimes turns the light out when he can see that I'm still reading Joanna Trollope's *Second Honeymoon*.

Natalia is peevish and resentful. I found a copy of the newspaper *Socialist Worker* in her room. She has expanded her vocabulary to include the words *workload, exploitation, proletariat,* and *strike*.

Tanya leaves magazines like *Heat* and *Now* lying on top of my pile of *Ideal Home* and *Country Life*. I can't help giving them a quick glance, which then makes me feel bad because they are trashy, vapid nonsense and everyone in them is so much younger and thinner than me.

Mark shows no signs of finding another job and thus putting an end to their stay. While Tanya posts his CV on recruitment Web sites (which reminds me of my own fruitless efforts with Rupert and Internet dating), Mark is devoting his entire time to teaching Darcy to say "buy," "hold," and "sell." He must be missing the trading floor.

Today I found a half-eaten packet of cheese and onion crisps in the back of the sofa.

You will see that the cons outweigh the pros, and yet I don't think I would have done things differently given the chance.

SUNDAY, APRIL 27

Tanya came with me to church today. CityJobs.com hadn't turned up anything for Mark, so she decided to try prayer. The service ended with "All Things Bright and Beautiful," one of my favorite hymns. Tanya stood up with the rest of the congregation, but while everyone else sang she simply opened and closed her mouth like a goldfish. I asked her afterward if she had ever learned the words at school, and she shook her head. I asked her what songs she could remember from school, and she thought for a long time before replying "Puff, the Magic Dragon" and "Don't Cry for Me Argentina." I don't think either is quite as effective as moral ballast.

MONDAY, APRIL 28

A positive sign: this morning I found a half-empty bottle of Johnson's Holiday Skin self-tanning moisturizer in the main bathroom, along with a few telltale yellowish streaks on the hand towel. Tanya must be getting back to her old self. When I went downstairs, I found that she had neatly spread a cloth over the dining room table and laid out a variety of sequins, vials of brightly colored nail polish, tiny brushes, and what looked like flaked almonds, which she explained were fake nail extensions. Apparently she has always made decorative nails as a sort of hobby, but now she has started making them for friends of friends on Facebook for a small fee. I managed not to smirk at the lines of gaudy end products; at least she is being productive, which is more than can be said for Mark.

I found him in the conservatory, hands in his pockets, staring intently at Darcy, who hunched up his wings, swiveled his head, and stared back. I watched him for a few minutes from just behind the door. Every now and then, Mark would say something like "BP" or "BATS" or "RBS" and Darcy would quietly caw something back, at which point Mark would smile weakly and scribble in a notebook that I had last seen in Jeffrey's study. I sighed and walked away. Then I went on Facebook and asked the other Paratweets members if they knew whether birds were likely to be distressed by repeated exposure to an unemployed banker.

TUESDAY, APRIL 29

Another visit from Reginald. First he had a very kind chat with Tanya, during which he praised her nail enterprise with the words "Best keep busy—the devil makes work for idle hands," then he sat down for a cup of tea and a chat about the procedure for our health and safety inspection this evening. After we had arranged who would check the storeroom for dead mice and who would lock Miss Hughes's handbag away, he got up to leave and I noticed that he had three green sequins stuck to the seat of his cassock. I thought it best not to brush them off. After he had gone, Tanya came bursting into the living room with a smile on her face and said she had decided to call her new business Idle Hands.

9:45 P.M.

Dear readers, I am in a panic. Things did not go at all well at bell ringing. There was a spider in the biscuit tin. Miss Hughes was so busy staring at Gerald that she lost hold of her rope and it whipped up and then back down and smacked her in the face. Reginald tripped over his cassock in the rush to check that she was okay. The dust he stirred up gave Gerald a coughing fit. The inspector was scribbling so quickly he snapped the lead in his pencil. To top it all, I have just come home to find Tanya worried because Mark stepped out for some fresh air two hours ago and still hasn't gotten back, Darcy pacing side to side on his perch shrieking "Sell! Sell! Sell!," and Jeffrey shut in his study with *Golf Monthly* and a whole bottle of port.

WEDNESDAY, APRIL 30

Mark didn't come back last night. I have a horrible cold feeling in the pit of my stomach. I can't write for long because I must get back to checking with the police and the hospitals, and force-feeding Tanya Bach Rescue Remedy.

THURSDAY, MAY 1

Still no sign of Mark. Tanya is distraught. I'm so worried about her, in her condition. Even Jeffrey didn't retreat behind *The Economist* last night, but phoned all his contacts in the City in case anyone had spotted him. Natalia stopped threatening to strike, although I can't say for sure whether this is out of sympathy or because her workload has been reduced by a quarter. Mark's parents are flying home tomorrow. I did offer them a bed but they insisted on booking themselves into a Travelodge. How could Mark do this to them? The mattresses aren't even clean in such places.

FRIDAY, MAY 2

Dear readers, mixed news. Mark has been sighted, if this is the appropriate word for the discovery on Facebook of a photo of him at Spearmint Rhinos last night, swigging champagne straight from the bottle with a nipple tassel on his nose. Tanya had alerted her entire network of online friends, including several of his old colleagues, that he was missing, and one of them noticed the picture today and got in touch. Poor, poor Tanya. The good news is that her husband is alive; the bad is that he is an abominable, selfish pig. She has alternated between laughing with relief and crying with anger. He still has not made contact; his Black-Berry is switched off.

Darcy continues to screech "Sell!" I worry that he is suffering from executive burnout. Paratweets were unable to advise; apparently none of them has experienced anything similar.

SATURDAY, MAY 3

Mark is back. I was dusting the wooden blinds in Jeffrey's study (Natalia never gets into every nook and cranny) when I spotted a lone figure walking up the drive with an odd lopsided stride. I looked closer. It was him, wearing only one shoe.

After two hours locked in the bedroom talking to him, Tanya emerged and told me everything over a cup of tea. Mark was wretchedly sorry. Needless to say, he hadn't been able to cope with losing his job. His life had revolved around work to an extent even Tanya hadn't guessed at: it was where he spent the majority of his waking hours, where he had gotten used to the constant pressure, the buzz, the adrenaline highs and lows, the camaraderie, and the rubber chicken affixed to his monitor. Without it, he told Tanya, he felt like he was lying in a bath of ice getting more and more numb. These are obviously not the words that a wife and expectant mother wishes to hear, but Tanya had at least welcomed his honesty.

He went on to explain that he had kept a sense of purpose by gambling on his credit cards, but when the funds had dried up and they had to move here he didn't know how to face the future. He started noting down how he would trade a hypothetical portfolio of stocks that he followed on the London Stock Exchange Web site, but the final straw came when he made Darcy play too and my parrot's share tips outperformed his own. I managed to suppress a smile of pride at this point. He had dressed for work, got on a train to the City, and, in his own words, "gone a bit nuts." Tanya did not elaborate and I didn't press her.

Last night, he was lying on the pavement looking up at the streetlamps and the clouds, and realized that the pain he felt all over wasn't caused by the drink or the drugs or the bits of broken paving stone he was lying on, but by how much he missed her. Tanya's eyes misted over. I wondered what he meant by drugs and whether he had brought anything illegal into the house and whether, if he had, Jeffrey or I would get arrested and thrown into jail to rot, but once again I bit my lip and patted Tanya on the shoulder. She finished her tea and ate two oatmeal cookies, which I took as a good sign. Poor Tanya. Poor Mark.

SUNDAY, MAY 4

Mark is a changed man. Last night he apologized sincerely to me and Jeffrey for being "such a t***," and vowed that he would do everything he could to earn his keep while he was staying with us. He demonstrated this by loading our best wineglasses into the dishwasher.

MONDAY, MAY 5

No sooner had I waved Jeffrey off to work this morning and poured myself a second cup of coffee than I heard Mark on the phone, his voice back to its usual persuasive, bouncy tones, mentioning things like Idle Hands, microfinancing, growth opportunities, and recession-proof niches. This is another good sign. Tanya had left a tube of half-used Great Lash mascara in the bathroom. This is yet another good sign, although it suddenly made me miss Sophie, who uses the same brand. I decided to call her, on a whim.

I didn't really expect her to answer, as I presumed she would be in her wellies, knee-deep in the waters of the Ardèche, studiously counting stickleback, but she picked up after just two of those flat Continental bleeps. I could hear laughter and the repetitive thud of electronic "music" in the background. She quickly explained that they were celebrating after recording "s***loads of fish"—I told her off for her language—but that everything was fine, except that her allowance had run out because she had had to buy a special silk fishing net. Having agreed to transfer some more money, and checked that she was wearing sunscreen, wasn't drinking too much, and was eating enough, I ran out of things to say, so I decided to ask after her best friend, Zac. There was a confused silence before she said, "Zac? Oh, yeah, Zac. He's all right. Daisy's my best mate, she's wicked." This Daisy, it transpired, was an aspiring "DJ" who "rocked" on her iPod. Sophie declared that she too wanted to be a DJ. I reminded her that she had a deferred place to study sociology at the University of Bristol, which may not be the most relevant qualification, but she said, "Whatever, gotta go, smell ya later," and hung up.

WEDNESDAY, MAY 7

I suspected that we had not passed the health and safety inspection at bell ringing with flying colors when I opened the door to the belfry and found it strewn with crash helmets and what looked like sky-diving harnesses. Reginald was there, wandering about, kicking at them with the toe of his scuffed tan loafer, scratching his head so that his hair flopped over his eyes. This was not a good sign. "Reginald, whatever happened?" I asked.

"That man, that dreadful man," he replied, picking up a harness and despondently letting it fall to the floor. After some comforting and cajoling, I managed to extract the truth from him: the health and safety inspector had issued a harsh warning. St. Mary's bell ringers have one more strike and we're out. If we do not wear the requisite safety gear and comply thoroughly with all aspects of the 2003 Health and Safety Act, we will be disbanded, dispersed, muffled. I breathed in sharply in horror. Then I picked up a helmet, gave it a tentative sniff, and breathed out in horror. It had been requisitioned from the Boy Scouts.

By this point, the other ringers had assembled and were also eyeing the new equipment with distrust. I looked at them, I looked at the knots of stupidly colored canvas on the ancient gray flagstones, and I saw two worlds colliding. We had to adapt or die. I felt an almost Churchillian impulse rising in my chest. I cleared my throat and called out to my "friends and ringers," telling them not to fuss, to put on their gear and carry on, declaring that the noble spirit of bell ringing would not be snuffed out, even if we did look like adventure tourists from New Zealand. There were a few murmurs of assent; Reginald thanked me, Gerald had a tear of emotion in his eye, and everyone began donning their equipment. Everyone, that is, except Miss Hughes. She was wearing a dress—a light gray cotton dress with purple embroidery—for the first time in living memory—and her hair was coiffed into two immaculate shining wings of steely gray. She refused to ruin her hairstyle with "that stinking thing," patting the side of her head coquettishly. I tried to persuade her otherwise, as did Reginald, but to no avail. Thinking on my feet, I elbowed Gerald and whispered to him to have a go. "I'd do anything you ask, Constance," he whispered back, still clearly awed by my oratory. Then he told Miss Hughes to put the hat on and stop being a silly old bat. She complied, and we began.

What with the unwieldy harnesses and the strange sensation

of being hooked up to one of the overhead beams, our ringing was not quite of its usual high standard, but we did manage to muddle our way through a quick Bob. I felt quite triumphant. At the end of the evening, Miss Hughes took off her helmet, ran a comb with a mother-of-pearl handle through her hair, and asked Gerald if he would be so kind as to pay her a visit at her cottage to help her with some Cats in Need paperwork. As he hesitated, I elbowed him in the ribs and told him what a lovely opportunity it would be to do some good work. The man is incapable of running his own affairs. In any case, it did the trick, and he will be seeing Miss Hughes on Friday afternoon. Inspired by their example, I decided to push forward my plans to bring Ruth and David together, and asked Reginald if he would call in on Church Flowers this week to give the ladies a morale boost. He happily agreed. All is set.

THURSDAY, MAY 8

All the ladies were aflutter when I told them that Reginald would be visiting us today. Our dear vicar, with his portly physique, babylike cheeks, and thinning hair, can hardly be described as a pinup, and yet his entrance always causes something of a stir. Flower displays were turned to show off their best angles, two ladies simultaneously rushed to make him a cup of tea, and plump Doris, who keeps eating even though she has had two knee replacements and walks with a stick, offered him all the best shortbread biscuits. Reginald looked slightly ill at ease at this flurry of attention—I could tell by the way he kept running his finger around the inside of his dog collar—so it was easy to draw him off to one side with a query about one of the stained-glass windows. I beckoned Pru over too, and once they were both together, I wasted no time.

"Reginald, Pru, it seems that you both have something in common," I began.

"A shared interest in the history of stained glass?" hazarded Pru, while Reginald nodded thoughtfully.

"Not quite," I replied. "Pru, you have a daughter. She's a lovely girl, but her religious—or shall we say spiritual—tastes are a little, well, eccentric."

Pru glared at me defensively for a moment, and then, seeing Reginald's sympathetic smile, conceded that Ruth had thrown out her collection of porcelain owls because they were "bad feng shui."

I turned to Reginald. "And you have a wonderful son whose only vice is a weakness for Scientology."

He nodded. "I have to do something before he starts jumping on sofas," he said. "I heard about what happened on *Oprah Winfrey*. And I had them reupholstered only last year."

"Well, for the sake of your sanity and your soft furnishings, may I make a suggestion," I continued. "We get Ruth and David together. What they need is a little distraction, which they may well find in each other. And then there's a decent chance that their odd views will cancel each other's out."

It took a little more work to persuade them—Pru was cautious after the *affaire Rupert,* Reginald after the *affaire Sophie*—but eventually they both saw that the potential rewards outweighed the risks. Now all we had to do was engineer an occasion to bring them together. In the end, we decided that a showing of *Top Gun* on Jeffrey's new high-definition television combined with entertainment from the Psychic of Surrey, whom I found in the church's Yellow Pages, would do the trick. I will make the arrangements for a week from Friday. Pru and Reginald both left with a spring in their step, and I with a smile on my face.

FRIDAY, MAY 9

Today I tried on my bathing costume. In just over a week, Jeffrey and I leave for our annual two-week break in the Bahamas. Personally, I am not convinced that idyllic silver beaches, azure seas, and swaying palms can compensate for the ordeal of shoehorning my wobbly bits into a sculpted John Lewis swimsuit. What's wrong with visiting the ruins of Tuscany, or the relics of the Knights of Malta, or anywhere where a lightweight cotton shirtdress is appropriate attire? Unfortunately for me, Jeffrey insists that if he is going to sleep in a hammock with a Panama hat over his head, nothing but the most perfect tropical views will do.

As I was turning myself cautiously in front of the long mirror in the bathroom, rather like a turkey on a revolving spit, Tanya burst in. She was totally unperturbed by my seminude appearance, and merely complimented me (rather too kindly) on my figure, suggesting that I try "one of them bathers with the bits missing" along with her Johnson's Holiday Skin self-tanning moisturizer. I looked at my white, mottled flesh. I looked at Tanya's new honeylike glow. For a moment I was tempted, but then I thought of orange palms, streaky calves, footballers' wives, and the indignation of Mother, and I declined.

SATURDAY, MAY 10

As if to put us in the mood for a holiday, the weather was glorious today, so we decided to have a barbecue. Jeffrey isn't exactly the ruddy, outdoorsy type, nor is he interested in cooking, but as soon as the temperature nudges above 19 degrees, something primal rises in his blood and he strides off to find last year's charcoal briquettes. I invited Harriet and Edward, while Rupert agreed to drive down from Milton Keynes.

Conversation was a little strained at first—I could tell that Harriet was looking askance at Tanya, whose substantial bump protruded between a vest top and low-slung pink jogging bottoms, while Jeffrey and Edward took pains not to mention the City in front of poor Mark, who kept fetching plates and glasses and napkins. However, once the G&Ts were flowing and the steaks sizzling, everyone relaxed. Rupert arrived late with a nice bottle of Italian red, and spent a long time chatting with Tanya. Will I ever see him talking to a pregnant woman of his own?

Natalia, meanwhile, sulked inside. She is under no obligation to mingle, but she would nonetheless have been welcome to join us. Her behavior is so odd whenever Jeffrey is at home that it borders on the insolent. Perhaps she just dislikes men. If it were not for the tarty underwear, I would take her for a feminist.

MONDAY, MAY 12

Why is it that I can hardly turn on the television or venture forth on the Internet without being bombarded with news of the wedding of a footballer whose name I cannot even be bothered to type, which is taking place in some grandiose Italian villa today? From the level of coverage it is receiving, one would have thought he's third in line to the throne, and not some pasty-faced game player with perpendicular ears and the air of a convict about him. I resent being bombarded with news bulletins about his nuptials, especially when the prospect of a wedding within my own family remains as faint and far away as ever. His new wife, at least, I have some respect for. She could almost be upper class in the way that, though unexceptional-looking, she has managed to make herself look really very attractive through the power of grooming. I wish Sophie would take note. She has much better raw materials to work with: in fact, she would be quite beautiful if only she would apply a dab of pink blush and blow-dry her hair with a round brush.

When I went on Facebook, I saw that Bridget had joined a group called "I don't give a s*** about footballers' wedding." Though I disapprove of the language, the underlying sentiment was sound, so I joined anyway.

TUESDAY, MAY 13

The Surrey Psychic just called to check the details for Friday, when Ruth and David will finally be brought together. I felt like telling her that if she were really psychic she wouldn't need to ask for my address, but once again I bit my tongue.

WEDNESDAY, MAY 14

Everyone seemed to be getting used to the new safety gear at bell ringing last night; even Miss Hughes jammed on the helmet without complaining. Incongruously, Gerald already had a large yellow bruise around his left eye. Perhaps he was set upon by hoodlums on his way home from the tea shop. Nothing would surprise me these days. Miss Hughes was strangely silent, however, and failed to exude any sympathy whatsoever toward the poor man. This does not bode well for their fledgling romance. I decided to invite Gerald for a glass of sherry this afternoon to find out what was going on. He will be here any moment, so I had better dash.

THURSDAY, MAY 15

Well, I had a rather dramatic evening last night. Gerald arrived promptly at 5:30 P.M. with a bunch of wilted carnations and a box of Cadbury Milk Tray, which struck me as a simultaneously paltry yet excessive offering. At least Darcy will enjoy the chocolate Brazils.

His bruise had faded slightly, but he still winced as he lowered himself into an armchair. I asked him if had been beaten up by hoodlums, but he replied that his attacker had been much, much worse. Good God. Did he mean rabid Alsatians or unemployed eastern Europeans? Again he said no, and sighed deeply. "Constance, I don't know where to begin." He exhaled, looking at me across the rim of his teacup.

"Well, you could start by telling me what's going on with Miss Hughes. I did my best to put in the groundwork for you, and I thought it was going swimmingly until last night. Do you have any idea why she was so frosty? Have you had a lovers' tiff?"

He put down his teacup with an abrupt clatter and appeared to be choking. I went over to pat him on the back, but this only exacerbated the situation. Once I had sat back down and he was calm enough to speak, he looked at me with reddened eyes and said, "What you have to understand is that it was, it was—*that woman*—who did my eye in."

It was my turn to put down my teacup in consternation.

"Whatever do you mean? Why? How? What happened?"

In a quavering voice, he said that when he went to her cottage at the appointed hour to help with the paperwork, it soon became apparent that distressed cats were not uppermost on her mind.

"She sat me down, looked me in the eye, and said: 'You are a man. . . . I am a woman. Neither of us is getting any younger. It's about time we dusted off the cobwebs before we both seize up. I want you to come upstairs and—and—' Dear God, I can't repeat it, I can't!"

I wasn't sure what to say. She was clearly a bit more forward than I had anticipated, but wasn't this, ultimately, what Gerald had been wishing for, albeit perhaps with a few more nice dinners and a night out at the Rotary Club dance first?

Gerald shivered, shook his head, and told me that I'd completely misunderstood him. I was shocked. I like to think that I am a perceptive judge of character. Still, caught up in the drama of his story, I asked him what had happened next.

"I panicked," he said. "She had her gnarled fingers on my thigh and was leaning into me. Her breath smelled of Fisherman's Friends. My mind went blank."

"And then?"

"And then I told her the truth. I said that I could not go upstairs with her because . . . because I was in love with someone else."

"Gerald!"

"And then she struck me in the shin with her walking stick, belted me in the eye, and left."

"But who else do you mean? Who are you in love with?"

At that moment, the door opened and Jeffrey arrived. He is not the suspicious type—such things are beneath him—but he did look a little disgruntled to see Gerald in a prone and emotional state in his favorite armchair.

Poor Gerald's nerves must be shot, because he leaped from his chair like an electrocuted ferret and hurtled to the door, jabbering something about a plumber.

I cannot bear the suspense. Who has won his heart?

FRIDAY, MAY 16

I have to admit that after Gerald's shocking news yesterday I'm starting to feel a little less confident about my matchmaking skills. David and Sophie ended in disaster. Rupert and Ruth ended in disaster. Gerald and Miss Hughes ended in a livid bruise and a mystery. Yet what can I do? Every time I think I should end my meddling, I think of Reginald's earnest face as he tells me how he despairs of David, and I feel that it cannot be beyond me to put some things right in the universe. Besides, I've already invited Ruth and David to arrive at six o'clock today, and sent Natalia out to pick up *Top Gun* from Blockbuster. Tanya has been briefed to help, although she did raise her newly tweezered eyebrow when I told her about the plan. I've made sure that Jeffrey will be going out for a glass of wine straight after work and Mark is closeted in the study drawing up spreadsheets for Idle Hands. Everything is set. In fact, I can hear something now. It appears that the Psychic of Surrey has arrived, early, in a purple Ford Ka.

IO P.M.

Dear readers, triumph! Ruth and David have swapped numbers. Rupert, Ruth, Gerald, Miss Hughes—these are all temporary aberrations in my matchmaking career. I suppose I should also give Tanya some credit, given that she slipped the psychic a ten-pound note to tell Ruth that the man of her dreams would be a pale stranger born under the sign of the cross, currently wearing a green Marks & Spencer polo shirt. But it was, after all, my idea to bring them together. I sent a text message to Reginald and Pru saying *Mission accomplished!* As soon as I have aired out the house and got rid of the smell of incense my joy will be complete.

SATURDAY, MAY 17

Just a quick post to say farewell for two weeks. The Bahamas beckon. I am uneasy at the prospect of leaving home at a time when warfare threatens to erupt between Natalia and Tanya, Gerald is shrouded in romantic mystery, and Ruth and David may need my guidance to progress to their first date, but such is my lot. Rupert has promised to pop around and check on Darcy. Jeffrey has tested out his new snorkel in the bath. I have packed capacious swimwear, SPF 50 sunscreen (Mother always told me I looked like a peasant when my freckles came out), a broad-brimmed hat, beach towels, insect repellent, two Maeve Binchy novels, and a family-sized pack of wet wipes. I cannot bear it when my sunglasses get smeared. We leave first thing in the morning.

I went on Facebook and updated my status to *is off to the Bahamas*, but then realized that this might give legions of Internet thieves an open invite to ransack my house, so I went back and changed it to *is sitting just behind the front door with a gun*.

WEDNESDAY, MAY 21

I did not expect to be addressing you again for another week and a half, and yet I couldn't stop myself. My first reaction to the dreadful events of this holiday was to find somewhere to pour my heart out to you. My surroundings are not salubrious. I am writing from a clammy Internet café in Crab Hill, flanked on one side by a youth playing a computer game that appears to involve driving a car and shooting people and on the other by an elderly man studying the Web sites of Japanese secondary schools. The keys are sticky. You will understand that I am in desperate straits.

The holiday got off to an aggravating, though not a catastrophic, beginning. I had hoped to have a good tête-à-tête with Jeffrey, telling him all about Gerald, Ruth, David, and the preparations for the regional bell-ringing championship. However, he was so busy twiddling on his BlackBerry that even when I stopped midway through a sentence about the Surrey Psychic he did not notice. It took all my wifely duty and restraint not to hurl the accursed gadget into the Caribbean. However, these trials are as nothing compared to what happened next.

I can scarcely believe this is happening, but the wretched and despicable Ivan the Terrible has intruded upon our holiday. Jeffrey casually mentioned over dinner last night that by a "happy coincidence" (his words, not mine) Ivan and his fourth wife would be arriving at our hotel the following morning. I hid my rage by cracking open my lobster with unusual efficacy.

And so it came to pass that I spent today on the beach watching Jeffrey and Ivan tear about on noisy, smoke-belching jet skis in the company of Ivanka, who sported a gold thong bikini and truly impertinent breast augmentations. When the two men returned from the sea she giggled and flicked Jeffrey's bottom with her Versace-logo beach towel.

How is this to be borne?

I retired with a headache this afternoon, but this is merely a short-term strategy.

MONDAY, MAY 26

I have a dreadful confession to make. Once again, I am back in the Internet café, hitting the yellowing keys as if in purgatory. My conscience will not be silenced.

As you know, I have been suffering from severe provocation. The headache technique did not work for long; claustrophobia and resentment began to weigh. Why should I be driven from my husband's side by a would-be oligarch and his surgically enhanced strumpet?

Lying in my room listening to the drone of the fan going round and round, I formulated a plan. I think the combined effects of the heat and a rum punch may have made me reckless.

I returned to the beach with a large bottle of coconut oil that I had bought from the hotel boutique. Ivanka has skin the color of baked tangerines, but Ivan's complexion is the pale, sallow tone of someone whose ancestors have toiled in Ural salt mines, whether he drives an Alfa Romeo sports car or not.

Ivanka makes sure that he is protected from the sun by spraying him liberally with high SPF sunscreen from a large plastic bottle. I waited until Jeffrey and Ivan had gone to take a dip, and then mentioned to Ivanka that her lip liner looked peculiar. (This was hardly a lie—there is a substantial discrepancy between where her real lips end and where her coral-colored liner does.)

Once she had fled to the hotel bathroom mirror, I emptied the contents of the sprayer and refilled it with coconut oil. By the end of the day Ivan was scarlet and irate with pain. He and Ivanka left for Moscow the following morning.

Last night I lay awake, listening to Jeffrey snore and the fan whine, agonizing over a moral and philosophical quagmire. Did the ends justify the means?

SUNDAY, JUNE 1

Home, sweet home. Never has that sentiment seemed truer. Here, there are no oligarchs to fry, no sand to get stuck in my sandals. I can savor the gentle beauty of an English summer's day without being assailed by stinging insects, spicy food, sunstroke, or pangs of guilt. Randolph has done a sterling job on the garden; the borders are bursting with flowers, the lawn is an immaculate, uniform green. Once I have put the breakfast dishes away I think I will make some lemonade and take the newspaper outside to catch up with what's been going on in the world.

Here, at least, it appears that no major disasters have occurred over the past fortnight. When we rolled up the familiar curve of our drive late last night, I was anxious about what lay behind the sage-colored front door and closed curtains: had Natalia and Tanya ripped each other's hair out? Had Natalia gone on strike, leaving piles of stinking rubbish piling up like in that repulsively addictive program *How Clean Is Your House?*

I needn't have worried. The house was no dustier than usual, and the only major difference was that neat cardboard boxes labeled Idle Hands, with a swirly sketch of feminine fingers, stood stacked in the hall. Our mail had also been piled up tidily, and amid all the bills, which I left Jeffrey to deal with, were two postcards.

One was from Gerald. It had a faded Beatrix Potter illustration of two rabbits walking arm in arm and a tea stain on one edge, and read:

Dear Constance,
When will you return?
Gerald (bereft in the belfry)

The poor man clearly needs more help with his mystery romance. The second postcard was from Sophie. It had a lovely photograph of the Pont du Gard aqueduct, suggesting that my hopes that she would develop more mature, sophisticated tastes during her year abroad were not unfounded. Strangely, the postal stamp on it was in Spanish—some inept Continental postal worker must have confused Surrey for Spain and sent it on a circular course. Sophie's handwriting is admittedly dire.

I was just pinning the cards up on our noticeboard this morning when Natalia emerged, wearing a short pink summery dressing gown. When I saw her nails, I shrieked: they were scarlet at the base, as if she were bleeding, and gangrenous-looking. On closer inspection, however, it emerged that she was wearing a full set of Idle Hands nail extensions, painted in green, yellow, and red—the colors, she told me, of the "Lithuan flag."

I could hardly complain, as the odd appendages did not stop her from cooking a full English breakfast for Jeffrey, even though it was her day off. I opted for bran flakes instead, the memories of swimsuits and a whole roasted Caribbean pig sitting squat and pink on a bed of banana leaves still fresh in my mind.

MONDAY, JUNE 2

As soon as I had seen Jeffrey off to work this morning, I was distracted by laughter coming from the conservatory. When I went to investigate, I found that Tanya and Natalia had painted Darcy's claws pink and silver. It appears that Natalia is now a full-fledged friend of Tanya and supporter of Idle Hands.

Needless to say, I do not approve of this tampering with my parrot's natural state, and yet it is difficult to remonstrate with a pregnant economic refugee and a capricious Lithuanian—whose recent, and unexpected, alliance has restored a fragile sense of harmony to the household.

TUESDAY, JUNE 3

Jeffrey just called from work. This is such a rare occurrence that when I heard his voice on the phone I feared the worst. Had he gotten his hand caught in the photocopier? Had he dropped his onyx paperweight on his foot and crushed a toenail? Alas, the news was almost as bad. He was calling to let me know that he had invited Andrew, the senior partner at Alpha & Omega, and Amanda, the irritatingly enthusiastic skier, for dinner tonight. From the brisk tone of his voice, it was clear that he had no inkling that:

(a) Four hours is not sufficient time to make an obstinate Lithuanian remove all traces of nail extensions from the dining room, then shop, cook, and serve a meal of a suitable caliber for a senior legal executive and his hoity-toity "girlfriend."

(b) With six weeks to go until the bell-ringing championships, I can ill afford to miss practice for the third week in a row.

Such is a woman's lot. I suppose duck à l'orange will do.

11:32 P.M.

They have gone. Thank heavens, they have gone. I do not wish to dwell on the evening. It was not a resounding success. Suffice it to say that when we sat down around the table, Amanda leaped back up again with a recently painted nail extension dangling from the seat of her cream Nicole Farhi cigarette pants, and this set the tone. She made as if to laugh it off with a tinkling giggle, but I could see that there was ice in her eyes. After watercress soup, I served up the duck, and she said, "Quail, how lovely. It's my favorite starter—the portions are just the perfect size not to fill you up too much." Later, she asked me how many grandchildren I had and turned her nose up at my coffee because it wasn't fair trade.

How I yearned for the cool, musty calm of the belfry.

WEDNESDAY, JUNE 4

Another postcard from Gerald arrived today. It read simply: *Constance, I am lovesick. Cure me.*

There was no postal stamp; he must have pushed it through the letterbox. At least he is not too lovesick to walk.

I am itching to know who he is pining for, so I drafted the following on a plain cream card and sent Natalia off to put it under his door:

Dear Gerald,
Please feel free to come round and fill me in,
Constance

THURSDAY, JUNE 5

Dear readers, I have had a terrible shock. Despite the warm weather, I have goose bumps jostling underneath my peach sleeveless top. Perhaps you can guess what I am referring to. Perhaps you share Tanya's suspiciousness. In case you are of a more naïve and trusting disposition, I had better explain.

I was tidying the kitchen this morning, wiping the smears of jam from the place mats and sorting through the odds and ends of paperwork that Natalia never manages to keep off the table. Tanya came in just as I held Gerald's latest postcard in my hand. She caught sight of it over my shoulder and I heard her catch her breath. Presuming that she too was curious about his romantic plight, I began filling her in on the whole story— Rosemary running off with a trapeze artist, my heart-to-heart with Gerald in the tea shop, Miss Hughes and her shrinking skirt, and so forth up until the present state of affairs. Tanya kept saying "But Connie . . ." and trying to interrupt, but I insisted that she hear me out. Once I had finished, she folded her arms over her bump, shook her head, and said, "Don't you see?"

Then she explained that, to an outsider, it was glaringly obvious that Gerald didn't have a thing for Miss Hughes. She explained her interpretation of the events. At first, I could hardly give credence to what she was suggesting. I am a respectable woman. I had thought that Gerald, for all his crumpled trousers and emotional volatility, was a respectable man. Tanya waved the card in my face, determined to prove that he was not. I looked at it again. The illustration was of Winnie the Pooh unscrewing a jar of honey. Surely that was innocent of anything other than a little misplaced mawkishness. Then I looked at the words. I picked up his earlier postcard. I looked at the words. A clammy, prickly feeling spread down my spine. In one horrible, wrenching moment, I knew that she was right. How could he? How could I not have realized?

Tanya asked if I had replied to the postcard, and I mechanically repeated my innocuous note. She went white, despite her Johnson's Holiday Skin. Before I could agonize any longer, however, I had to leave for Church Flowers. Pru descended on me in a cloud of Lily of the Valley perfume, fluttering her hands, telling me how delighted she was—David and Ruth had been to the cinema once and to dinner twice, and Ruth had already given away her caftan to Cats in Need. But I was too distracted to revel in this success. All I could visualize was Gerald, standing in the belfry, clutching his rope and staring at me with longing in his eyes. No matter how much I tried to concentrate on wrapping my twine tightly around the rose stems, the image remained.

How could he? What to do if he comes around?

I shall hide. That is what I shall do. I shall hide.

4 P.M.

He is outside! Dear readers, this is terrible. I can see him through the crack in the blinds in the study, pacing back and forth on the gravel, a bunch of red roses in his hand. I have told Natalia, Mark, and Tanya not to open the door on any account. I have put the chain on. I am a prisoner in my own home.

I sincerely wish that Jeffrey wasn't allergic to dogs so that we would have a slavering Alsatian at the ready to set loose on him. Perhaps I should buy one of those large gloves and train Darcy to attack.

I have just taken another peek out the window. Thank heavens. He is walking away, holding the bouquet at a sorry angle.

FRIDAY, JUNE 6

I cannot hide forever. I must resolve this situation. As far as I see it, I have the following options:

Tell Jeffrey all and allow him to defend my honor as he sees fit.

Tell Gerald that I am joining a convent.

Convince Jeffrey that we should emigrate.

Shave my head and start dressing like Jacqui Smith in order to dampen his ardor.

I talked these through with Tanya, but she seemed to think a note would do the trick. I thought for a long time, and then drafted the following:

Dear Gerald,
I am a married woman. Kindly desist.
Constance

SATURDAY, JUNE 7

I hope the old adage that "No news is good news" holds true. The welcome mat was blessedly free of postcards from Gerald this morning, though I'm not sure if this is because he has been shamed into silence or because he knows better than to push his luck while Jeffrey is at home. My husband has a sturdy, rugged physique, even if the last thing he punched was the wall when England lost to Wales at rugby.

SUNDAY, JUNE 8

Still no word from Gerald. I went to see Mother alone, because Jeffrey said he wanted to mow the lawn while the weather was nice, and she once again raised her eyebrow as if to suggest that I must have done something terrible to have driven him away. I didn't dare allude to Gerald, or so much as mention bell ringing. There is something about that look she gets that takes me right back to the day I got caught stealing a piece of the Christmas cake she had been maturing for four months in the larder, whether or not I have anything to feel guilty about. Instead I told her the latest from Rupert, who has just been given a small promotion, and Sophie, who promises that she is practicing her French verbs "in her sleep." Mother sniffed at the latter piece of news and asked what was wrong with speaking English slowly and clearly.

When I got back, Jeffrey was lying on our garden recliner, asleep, with a gin and tonic beside him and luxuriant, unmowed grass surrounding it to the rim. I felt too cowed to reprimand him.

MONDAY, JUNE 9

Still no word from Gerald, and mixed news from Tanya. This morning, as we were having our usual eleven o'clock coffee together, she announced that she had something to tell me.

"It's good news, Connie," she said, with a confident smile on her face. She has finally taken to wearing maternity tops—pretty, colorful, crossover things—which are a marked improvement from the old gym wear. "Idle Hands has taken off," she said. "It was all Mark's doing. He drew up a business plan with graphs and everything and now he's found us an angel investor, just like on *Dragons' Den*!" I had to admit that I found this talk of angels and dragons a little hard to follow—it reminded me of the computer games Rupert used to play—but I didn't want to dampen Tanya's enthusiasm, so I smiled encouragingly.

"The best thing is that the business plan included costing for new premises—well, when I say premises I mean a two-bedroom flat with an open-plan kitchen/dining room, but you get my drift. With this investment we can afford to rent our own place. We'll be out of your hair!"

I bit down on my tea cake a little too hard, and felt my teeth crunch together. I will miss her. Of course I am delighted that her business is a success, and that her baby will be born into a proper home of its own rather than having to be stowed away next to Jeffrey's golf clubs, but I will still miss her company, her conversation. I gathered myself together quickly enough to congratulate her, then tried to concentrate fixedly on the time she switched off *Woman's Hour* to put on a dreadful pop song by some woman called Katie Perry.

TUESDAY, JUNE 10

What, I wonder, does one wear to a bell-ringing practice in order to discourage the advances of a certain man while also having to fit comfortably into a safety harness? Burlap sacks are out of the question. I stood in front of my wardrobe for so long pondering the question that Natalia was driven to vacuuming around my feet. In the end I selected a pair of black boot-cut trousers and a gray cotton T-shirt that had begun to stretch with age, hoping to convey an impression of austerity, but without quite looking like a hag. I left off the sweep of dusky peach blush and mascara that I usually wear, put on my stone-colored raincoat, and left. I'm not sure the effect was entirely successful—or perhaps, more to the point, it was too successful. When I got to the belfry, Reginald asked me if I had caught the summer vomiting bug.

Then Gerald arrived, and I busied myself with strapping on my harness and arranging my helmet over my hair so that a few strands poked out to soften the impression of being as bald as a coot. It wasn't until we had started ringing that I dared to look at him. Something had changed. He was staring straight ahead with a solemn expression on his face; he was wearing one of his old blue shirts, perfectly ironed; his nasal hair had been clipped. He didn't speak a word to me all evening.

WEDNESDAY, JUNE 11

Still no postcard from Gerald. I suppose he has paid attention to my request, which is more than can usually be said for Jeffrey.

While giving the utility room a bit of a spring cleaning I found a pair of Sophie's purple leggings, coiled up like an exotic snakeskin, in the corner. I thought of her wearing them with her funny little dresses over the top and felt that sudden, achy sensation of missing her, which can occur at the oddest of moments. I decided to call, and by withholding my number managed to get her on the first attempt. The line was bad. Sophie sounded muffled and there was a rustling like the lapping of waves on a beach in the background. I asked her if she was okay and she said that she was "thfine" and talking funny only because she had been practicing her French so hard. Just as I was asking if she wanted me to send over some Buttercup syrup from Boots she said that she had to rush off to hold Daisy's bucket and hung up. I hope she will get better soon. French is indeed a language to mangle any Englishwoman's vocal cords.

THURSDAY, JUNE 12

Reginald popped around in a positively effervescent mood today. "Constance, you are a genius," he said over a cold Pimm's in the garden, with a grin as broad as his sun hat. "It's all going swimmingly." By this I presumed that he meant the situation between David and Ruth, and I was right. It would appear that David has not attempted to persuade his father that he needs a psychological "audit" for more than a week, that he has started to wear Lynx deodorant, and that yesterday he took Ruth on a date to play mini golf. In short, he was showing all the hallmarks of becoming "normal." Pru confirmed that this happy transformation was a two-way affair at Church Flowers when she told me that Ruth had had a haircut for the first time in eighteen months. I tried to savor my triumph and not to reflect on the fact that had things been different, my own son would have been benefiting from Ruth's sudden swing toward neatly coiffed conformism. I comforted myself with the thought that I wouldn't in any case want Pru to be mother of the bride at Rupert's wedding, as she would no doubt want to have a say in all the organization. Judging by what she did with the freesias today, she is much too slapdash to be trusted with the table arrangements. It's a good thing that Reginald is the rumpled, forgiving sort.

FRIDAY, JUNE 13

Friday 13: unlucky for some, including one of Sophie's dim-witted "friends." I have just received the following e-mail:

yo momma k how ru and dad? could u ask ur friend whoz a nurse what to do bout an infected tongue? my m8 got it peerced last wk an she still cant eat. really sore. and has this wierd kinda puss coming out. anyhoo, gotta go . . . love ya lots
soph xxx

I thought for a long time, and then I replied:

Dear Sophie,
When you left primary school seven years ago you appeared to have a firmer grasp of the English language than you do now. I'm giving you the benefit of the doubt and presuming that the French sun has addled your brain (are you wearing sunscreen and a hat?), but just in case I'm going to pop a copy of Eats, Shoots & Leaves *in the mail for you along with that Buttercup syrup.*
Now, as to this friend of yours, the first thing I want to know is why you're spending time with someone who would do such

a disgusting and tasteless thing to herself. A pierced tongue? I thought that was the preserve of deranged, bat-eating heavy-metal fans.

But I digress. Unfortunately I'm no longer in touch with the nurse Natasha (who hasn't returned my Christmas cards since the time I asked her to take a look at Grandma's varicose veins), but I do remember that Grandma's cat once had an infected tongue abscess, and I think the treatment would be similar. She needs to bathe it in a strong salt solution. It will sting, but the pain may make your friend think twice about being such an idiot in the future.

I hope you're well and having a nice time. Not long now until you'll be home for the holidays!

Lots of love,

Mum

SATURDAY, JUNE 14

Mark and Tanya have gone. They were here for only two months, but it feels like the end of an era. At ten o'clock this morning I heard the diminutive crunch of Smart car tires on gravel as Mark pulled up in their brand-new lilac-colored company car, emblazoned with Idle Hands in a black curlicue font on the side; three hours and nineteen carloads later, they and their meager possessions had vanished. The house had that same big, immaculate, empty feeling it gets when Sophie has just left. I called Natalia to make some lunch, longing for a little bustle of any sort, but she was nowhere to be seen. I called Jeffrey, but in a strained voice emanating from his study he said that he was just in the middle of something and had his hands full. I went to talk to Darcy instead. He cocked his head and looked at me with his black, depthless, wise eyes, and said, "You're fired!"

SUNDAY, JUNE 15

Jeffrey came to church, and to see Mother, without complaining once. I can't keep up with him, I really can't.

MONDAY, JUNE 16

Dreadful news. My fingers are shaking so much I can hardly type. The director of the eco lodge just called. Sophie has not returned from a field trip to study the newt population of the Loire. He tried to reassure me. The lodge staff has checked her room and it seems that her passport and most of her clothes are missing. Perhaps she is homesick and on her way back? I told him that she would never have done such a thing without telling me. How else would she pay for the ticket?

He said there was one other thing I should know. Her friend Daisy has disappeared too. Perhaps they had gone off on a little trip together? I swallowed hard. It was possible, but so were many other scenarios. What if she has been abducted by drug smugglers to be used as a human mule? Or worse—by Parisian pimps? If only she had let me persuade her to keep a can of mace spray in her handbag at all times.

I feel ill. Jeffrey is on his way home. I hope he gets here soon.

TUESDAY, JUNE 17

Relief, of a kind. Sophie is safe, if a little woozy due to the effects of a piercing-related infection. I am too angry to say much more. Besides, I must book my flight to Ibiza.

WEDNESDAY, JUNE 18

I will have to keep this brief. Tanya is coming around to drive me to the airport in fifteen minutes for my flight to Ibiza Town. Jeffrey left for work as usual this morning, as if for all the world his only daughter were not holed up in some latter-day, sun-baked version of Gin Lane with a bolt of metal through her tongue. Just writing these words makes me shudder. I feel numb with shame and trepidation.

Sophie finally answered her mobile at three P.M. yesterday afternoon, after I had made the eco lodge director alert the French police, contacted Interpol, taken out an advertisement in the classified section of the *Daily Telegraph,* and wrenched approximately thirty-two hairs out of my head in desperation.

When she said hello she sounded as if she had a damp sock in her mouth. Her tone was dazed, then sheepish, then emotional. My relief was quickly subsumed by anger. She was not in the Ardèche valley. She was not even in the Loire, or the Tarn. She was in a flat in San Antonia, on a small, and by all accounts rampantly hedonistic, Spanish island that is not renowned for the rigor of its stickleback monitoring.

She was so befuddled by fever that she couldn't keep up the charade. I still find it hard to believe her capable of such dissimulation in the first place. This wretched new DJ friend of hers must have led her astray.

In any case, I have no further time for speculation. I have packed water-purifying tablets, lightweight clothing, disinfectant, insect repellent, cotton wool, and an emergency flare, and I am ready to depart. Heaven only knows what awaits. Wish me courage.

SATURDAY, JUNE 21

I am still alive. That is about the most positive thing I can say about my current situation. Even this state of affairs may not endure: an obstreperous airport security official confiscated my water-purification tablets.

Once, in happier times, I visited the Rodin museum in Paris. There I observed the famous sculpture *The Gates of Hell,* which featured writhing, contorted, debased, and demented human forms. That is what Ibiza reminds me of.

THURSDAY, JUNE 26

Sophie and I have returned safely from Ibiza. There were moments during the trip, such as when I was subjected to the reckless ineptitude of Hispanic taxi drivers, when I feared that I would never type those words.

When I got to the address Sophie had given me, a nondescript sixties-style apartment building, I climbed a set of concrete steps and knocked tentatively on the moldering door. This was hardly the bougainvillea-clad villa of expatriate fantasy. After two further raps, just as I was cleaning my fist on a wet wipe and wondering if the imbecilic taxi driver had taken me to the wrong place, the door swung open.

A skinny girl with an orange tan and headphones around her neck, who transpired to be Daisy, let me in, cheerfully saying "You're Soph's mum, right?" and showing no sense of shame. Passing through a tiny, hot, and messy flat, I found Sophie sprawled in bed, wearing a bikini, her feet tangled up in dirty sheets, with piles of Milky Way wrappers, bronzing lotion, flip-flops, *Hot* magazines, and makeup scattered around her. There were photographs stuck to the mirror of her posing with friends in clothes that would be too small to fashion a silk vest for a Siberian hamster.

"Hiya, Mum," she said woozily, smiling and grimacing with pain. I felt torn between the desire to take tender care of her, as any mother of a sick child will understand, and to put my hands on my hips and give her a good talking to. In the end, I oscillated between the two. Sophie spent most of the time burying her head under a pillow, perhaps through a belated sense of shame at her loathsome piercing, perhaps because whenever she emerged I made her gargle with saltwater.

The combined effects of the heat and the emotional stress gave me such a terrible headache that I had to raid the bathroom cabinet for some pills. They perked me up so much that I soon felt like taking a brisk stroll to get some fresh air, and I ended up walking the length of the bay and back fourteen times. Exercise can be terribly therapeutic. Blotting out the near-naked revelers and the ghastly, thundering, monotonous music, the natural beauty of the scene made me feel strangely euphoric.

The rest of my time there was much quieter. I nursed Sophie back to health, attempting to cook wholesome food in her tiny, dark kitchen, which was stocked with nothing more than a box of stale Frosties and a bottle of ketchup. I tried to ignore Daisy, which was easy as she was always either out or asleep.

As soon as Sophie was better, I booked our flights and here we are. Fortunately, she had to remove her tongue stud to pass through the metal detectors in the airport.

FRIDAY, JUNE 27

Sophie kept to her room today. I do hope she will perk up in time for her nineteenth birthday, which is next Friday. I'm going to organize a last-minute party: it will do her good to have something to look forward to. I'm thinking a marquee, ice cream, trifle, fairy cakes—all her old favorites. I might even book a magician. His first trick could be to make the tongue piercing vanish.

SATURDAY, JUNE 28

You'll be pleased to hear that the planning is well under way for Sophie's party. As it's such short notice (I had presumed she would still be in France), I decided—for once—to stint on formal etiquette and phone the guests rather than sending out invitations. The family will all be there, as will Reginald, David, and Ruth, and several of Sophie's old primary school friends with whom she has lost touch, and their mothers, with whom I have not. Rupert asked me several times what Sophie thought of the plan before agreeing to come. I don't know why he's being so stubborn. What's not to like about a party?

After some deliberation, I decided to invite Gerald along with all the other bell ringers. While not wanting to give him any inappropriate encouragement, I'm also anxious to get things back to a normal footing as quickly as possible, to avoid rumors of any description. Miss Hughes has almost a supernatural insight into other people's affairs, especially when her hearing aid is turned to maximum.

After making my phone calls, I dipped into Facebook for the first time in some weeks. I found that, once the initial excitement had worn off, it is a little like using e-mail, except with more advertisements and baffling invitations to turn all my friends into zombies. This time, however, I noticed the section for "events." After two hours of studious concentration, I was able to set up a page for Sophie's birthday party, complete with a lovely picture of a smiling clown. My Internet skills have certainly progressed since I first joined—Rupert would be proud. I invited Sophie, of course, and managed to remember a few of the names of her sixth form friends and invited them too.

I filled in the "event description" as *An afternoon of fun, fairy cakes, and magic to celebrate my daughter turning 19. Dress code: Ladies' Day at Ascot before it went downhill.*

8:30 P.M.

I am just testing my LapTop to make sure it still works. After dinner, Sophie swept out of the room and knocked a glass of wine all over it. I hope she grows out of her clumsiness soon.

SUNDAY, JUNE 29

A rather strained Sunday lunch today with Mother, who I picked up from The Copse, and Rupert, who drove down from Milton Keynes. Since Sophie had to hide her swollen tongue from her grandmother, and the only line of conversation that this same grandmother would take with Rupert was to ask him if he was playing cricket this summer, which he wasn't, and whether he was seeing a young lady yet, which he also, alas, wasn't, there was little in the way of lively conversation. At one point Mother said to Sophie, "Cat got your tongue?" and I found myself replying "If only" before I could stop myself. All in all I was relieved, for once, when Jeffrey opened up the paper before the pudding was finished, giving me an excuse to start clearing away.

MONDAY, JUNE 30

Today I attempted to have a heart-to-heart with my daughter. She has been at home now for nearly five days but has done little more than mope, watch television, and eat Ben & Jerry's ice cream directly from the carton. The summer stretches out ahead of her. She doesn't feel up to going back to the eco lodge for the final week of the project, and there are more than three months to fill before her first term at Bristol starts. At her current rate of activity, that would equate to twenty-four tubs of ice cream and ninety-six episodes of *Ricki Lake*. I fear for the effect on her mind, and her figure. Something had to be done.

I knocked on her door at eleven A.M. and was greeted with an apathetic "Yeah?" She was sitting up in bed, wearing a Little Miss Naughty vest top and painting her nails bluish black. I started off on a sympathetic note, examining her tongue and asking if it still hurt. From there I shifted to the soothing qualities of ice cream, the quantities of which she could look forward to at her party on Saturday, and beyond that to how many days lay ahead of her before the term began. Just as I was persuasively setting out how these days might constructively be filled by helping Miss Hughes with Cats in Need or signing up to be a Tawny Owl at the local Brownies group, she interrupted me. "Don't be such a mentalist," she said, yawning. "I've got plans, yeah?"

This I was not expecting. "What sort of plans?" I asked cautiously.

"Oh, I'm doing this TV thing in London." I stared at her, my jaw ajar. "Will be great practice for sociology," she added, sticking her tongue out between her teeth and narrowing her eyes as she applied a thick stroke of varnish to her last remaining nail.

"You mean a documentary? You'll be working on a documentary?"

"Yeah, yeah, that's it. A documentary."

"What's it about?"

"Oh, lots of people and how they get along, like."

"And this is an official work placement scheme that you've applied for?"

"Yup, gazillions of people applied. Didn't want to tell you earlier because I didn't know if I'd get in."

I felt rather pleased. This was more initiative than I had expected. Clearly Sophie had not squandered all her time absconding to sun-drenched Spanish islands. She was also thinking of her future.

"Well, that's wonderful news, well done, though you could have told me sooner. I was that close to calling Miss Hughes for you! But where will you be staying? Shall I give Bridget a call and see if you can stay in her spare room? She's got a lovely place, but mind that she doesn't make you eat French éclairs for breakfast. Or we could go and see if we could rent you a nice little flat for a few months?"

"Nah, it's all taken care of. The TV thing is . . . residential."

"You mean you'll have your own flat?"

"More like a sort of bunk bed."

"That sounds like fun! It'll be just like Guides."

"Yeah."

Only a well-structured internship would provide accommodations. After getting her to write down the name of the organizer and her telephone number, I left Sophie's room with a smile on my face, and didn't even nag her to pull her curtains and make the bed.

THURSDAY, JULY 3

Today I went out to buy the drinks for Sophie's birthday—after all, she will have been legally entitled to enjoy a peach Bellini or two for exactly a year. Also, Mad Marvin the Magician, whom I've booked as the entertainment, insists that he can't work without a two-liter bottle of Strongbow cider. Perhaps by some strange alchemy he turns it into something drinkable.

FRIDAY, JULY 4

I tried to coax Sophie out on a shopping trip with the offer of a pretty dress for tomorrow's party, but to no avail. Perhaps she is worried about the effect the recession is having on our finances and wishes to save us the expense. In any case, she spent the day lying on the lawn plugged into her iPod, smearing her pale skin with tanning oil. Worried that she would burn, I decided to execute what I think of as a "Reverse Ivan," and subtly swapped her oil sprayer for SPF 50 while she was dozing.

After an hour of gentle weeding (Randolph does a good job, but it pays to keep one's hand in), I could almost feel my freckles coming out, so I retreated indoors to check Facebook, which gave me something of a shock. There were thirty-six "comments" on the wall for Sophie's party, all from people I didn't know, all lacking in the basic rudiments of grammar and courtesy. The profile pictures did not inspire confidence either, ranging from Pamela Anderson to a hoodlum and a picture of a man's Calvin Klein underpants. The last comment was "comin atchaaa." I wonder if Jeffrey could reinforce the privet hedge with razor wire.

SATURDAY, JULY 5

The day has not begun well. Sophie is threatening to hide indoors because she has woken to find she has several big white hand prints against the dusky pink skin of her décolletage. She grabbed her bottle of tanning lotion from the kitchen table, stared at it in confusion, then threw it to the floor and stamped on it, leaving a greasy streak across the slate tiles, which I had only recently persuaded Natalia to scrub. Jeffrey gave me a funny look when I inquired about barricading the garden perimeter. The trifle has not yet set. I had better go.

10 P.M.

Where to begin?

As you will have gathered from my last posting, the start of the day was not promising. Things did not subsequently improve. Five minutes before the guests were due to arrive, Sophie was sitting at the kitchen table with her shoulders slumped, wearing a hooded top, minuscule frayed denim shorts, and flip-flops. I asked her when she planned to change, wondering if she had spotted the pretty, plum-colored sundress—just the thing to offset her pale complexion—that I had sneaked out to buy from John Lewis yesterday and laid out on her bed along with a matching glittery hair clip. She had. She said she wouldn't be seen dead in it and maybe I should give it to someone with no fashion sense, like Natalia. Natalia's English may not be perfect, but she was still able to catch the gist of Sophie's meaning, and as she was pouring a glass of juice at the time, she stumbled heavily to one side so that it poured, splashing, into Sophie's lap. Sophie screeched and threw her own glass of juice over Natalia in retaliation, and the fracas was stopped only when Jeffrey put down his paper and thundered "Girls!" in a rare intervention. At last, Sophie went upstairs to change, but the results were not as I had hoped. As the doorbell rang for the first guest, she emerged wearing an "Ibiza Rocks" T-shirt and what appeared to be latex leggings.

Still, I tried to put her unfortunate outfit to the back of my mind, and the first hour or so was rather pleasant. Ruth and David arrived holding hands, Reginald and Miss Hughes sat in the marquee eating trifle together, Harriet helped me carry out jugs of Pimm's and lemonade, and the pastel-colored balloons I had arranged earlier waved in the gentle breeze. Mad Marvin began his act by pulling a dove out of his hat (I was glad Darcy was safely shut indoors. I should not have liked to see him disappear again, if even for an instant), punctuating his performance with swigs of Strongbow. Though Sophie was pretending to fiddle with her nails, I heard her gasp and saw a smile spread across her face when the dove fluttered over to land on her shoulder.

And thus we may have continued, cheerful and relaxed, had I not spotted a familiar figure weaving haphazardly across the lawn toward us, followed by a bouncing black Labrador. Gerald, with Poppy. My heart flopped like a goldfish. He had come. Why had he come? I took Jeffrey's hand. He jumped, and asked what was wrong with me.

At this precise moment, a silence had fallen over the lawn while Marvin asked for volunteers to be sawed in half. Understandably, perhaps, given the empty cider bottle, none were forthcoming.

Gerald approached. His breath reeked of sherry, his complexion was flushed, but his short-sleeved shirt was immaculately ironed. He looked at Marvin, still fruitlessly beckoning, then looked at the assembled guests, then looked at me. "Constance, I would do anything for you," he bellowed, before pushing forward onto the makeshift stage, where the saw awaited.

Luckily, Jeffrey was preoccupied with chasing the lemon slice out of the bottom of his gin and tonic so that he could drink the last drop, but Sophie and Miss Hughes both gave me a quizzical look. "Bell-ringers' loyalty," I said, with what I hoped was a convincingly casual laugh, as Marvin packed a swaying Gerald into a purple sequined box. With a great flourish, he split Gerald in two, and I decided that this was a far safer state of affairs than having Gerald on the loose and intact. I had to prolong the moment. "A speech!" I declared, leading the magician off the stage by his elbow to the trestle table, where the glasses of champagne and peach Bellinis were laid out. Thinking on my feet, I waxed lyrical about my daughter and the joys of family life with her wonderful father, giving Gerald a meaningful look as he sweated in his bifurcated limbo.

When Gerald was subsequently reformed and released, he scuttled away across the lawn, leaving a little trail of sawdust behind him. Poppy stayed behind eating some fairy cakes that had fallen onto the floor, which was just as well. No sooner had conversation started up again than I heard the *thud thud thud* of modern "music" and saw a crowd of youths tramping up the gravel. The Facebook interlopers. I felt a cold clamminess on the back of my neck. "Go, Poppy! See them off!" I shouted desperately. She looked up, a smear of cream on her damp nose, and must have suddenly realized that her owner had left, because she bolted down the drive barking. To anyone who knows her, Poppy is as menacing as a baby seal. However, she succeeded in alarming the youths and saving us all from further disaster, thus proving herself far more useful than her owner.

After that, the mood was rather flat, and it wasn't long before everyone made their excuses and departed, leaving me to pick up the stray balloons that had blown into the flower beds and eat the last blob of trifle, which had already begun to congeal. When I asked Sophie if she had had a nice time, she said that it was "all right" and then asked me what I would do if I had to choose between, as she put it, "shagging Gerald, marrying him, or pushing him off a cliff." What a thing to say. I told her not to be so cheeky. The Bellinis must have gone to her head.

I didn't say anything to Sophie of course, but after long reflection, it would have to be either option one or option three.

MONDAY, JULY 7

Sophie has left. No matter how many times this happens—however many Christmas holidays or Easter holidays end with her wheeling her suitcase across the hall and swearing as it catches on the rug—it still ends with me sitting alone, blinking hard, in a house that feels heavy with silence. It was the same with Rupert. I think of Jeffrey busy at work in his open-plan office, poring over

his documents, staring at his computer screen, with phones ringing, colleagues bustling, perhaps a secretary bringing him a cup
of tea, if they still stoop to such things these days. Is he oblivious,
or does he feel it too?

I gave him a call to find out, but he said that he was on a con-
ference call with the Netherlands and the CFO of Allianz Banque.
I told him I was busy too and went to rearrange Sophie's sock
drawer. I hope she took enough pairs with her. I suppose it's a
normal sign of growing up, but she seems increasingly unwilling
to accept my advice or help. I would happily have driven her into
central London to her accommodations today, but she insisted
that I drop her off at the station so she could get the train in.
When I dropped her off and said, "See you soon," she said, "You
will, Mum, you will," with a strange look in her eye. Perhaps she
has already realized that she will miss me and is planning a trip
home.

TUESDAY, JULY 8

It is exactly one month until my fifty-fourth birthday. I
wonder whether I should start dropping mild hints as to what
sorts of presents would be appropriate, or whether such things are
beneath me.

The problem is that, left to his own devices, Jeffrey once
lurched from forgetting one year to giving me a necklace made
from pink diamonds and jet the next. I can only hope it was his
secretary's choice. I stored it away in my underwear drawer, where
it keeps snagging my 30 Derniers. After that it was an oven glove;
then a miniature foot spa. Sophie can be equally misguided. Last
year she bought me a disgusting book called *Belle du Jour: Diary
of an Unlikely Call Girl*. Rupert, at least, can be relied upon to
buy my favorite perfume or a smart neck scarf. He always seems

to find just the thing to compliment my complexion. If only the rest of the family would follow his lead.

WEDNESDAY, JULY 9

No sign of Gerald at bell ringing last night. I hope the combined forces of Jeffrey and Mad Marvin have not frightened him off indefinitely. There are only six weeks left before the championships and we can't afford to lose any of our ringers, no matter how rhythmically challenged. Miss Hughes seemed to blame me, and trod on my toe twice while executing a Plain Bob Major. She must weigh at least 14 stone. I have a livid bruise showing through my cream espadrilles. I suppose one must suffer for one's art.

10:30 P.M.

I am shaking. What have I done to deserve this? What? I taught Sophie right from wrong, I read her Ladybird Classics from the age of three, I gave her an apple a day, I taught her that she could achieve whatever she wanted if she worked hard. How can this have happened?

At nine P.M. this evening, just as I was watching David Attenborough's *The Life of Mammals* and Jeffrey was snoozing in his armchair, the telephone rang. It was Tanya. "Turn on your TV," she said in an odd voice.

"I have," I replied. "I'm watching a baby bat learn to fly."

"Wrong channel," she said urgently. "Put it on channel four."

By this point Jeffrey had woken up and was looking at me with a bemused expression. I needed his help to locate channel 4. Then we found it. We both stared. I thought for a moment that it was some kind of practical joke. We looked again. "Connie? Are you there?" echoed Tanya's voice, small and remote, from where the receiver lay. Jeffrey hung it up. We stared at the screen again.

The last piece of a monstrous jigsaw clicked into place. Sophie was not working on a documentary. Sophie was in an experimental new reality television program—mentioned only yesterday in a disapproving editorial in the newspaper—called *Dungeon*. Thanks to this said editorial, I am aware that the program involves twelve people being held in a ghoulish medieval-style dungeon who will be given challenges to win the right to daylight or food other than gruel. The "dunce of the day" will be put in replica plastic stocks. I am aware that it is only the latest in a long line of such programs, which are essentially cruel cynical freak shows allowing nonentities to build careers out of playing strip poker and weeping copiously at the mistreatment that they enthusiastically signed up for.

And there was my daughter, sitting on her prison bunk in her strapless purple Topshop minidress, giving a dwarf a foot massage.

THURSDAY, JULY 10

For a few soft, swirly moments when I woke up this morning, I forgot that anything was amiss. I wondered if it would be warm enough to go to Church Flowers without a cardigan and whether Jeffrey would have made himself coffee yet or waited for me to do it, as usual. Then I remembered.

A good night's sleep is meant to make most things better, but not, alas, all. Sophie was on *Dungeon*. As I lay there underneath my white cotton summer duvet set, Sophie was lying in a strange, crepuscular cell filled with stranger people, under the blinkless gaze of the television cameras. I got up and ran downstairs. Jeffrey had already left. He took things more calmly than I did last night, sitting ramrod straight on the sofa with a double whiskey while I paced and pulled out my hair; but he must be ruffled to have skimped on breakfast.

Natalia was emptying the dishwasher as I walked into the

kitchen. I am sure she was humming the theme song of the accursed program, as if to mock me. I left the house without talking to her, and hurried straight to the newsagent in the village, counting my paces and breathing in through my nose then out through my mouth in an effort to calm myself down. Rupert had called before the dreaded program had even finished last night, and had told me that I had to brace myself for a lot of publicity in the newspapers, but that it would all blow over in the end. And so, for the first time since the death of Princess Diana, I bought a tabloid. Not just one, but three: the new series had made the front page of the *Sun,* the *Mirror,* and the *Mail.* I couldn't look Niral, the soft-spoken newsagent whose son is the same age as Sophie, in the eye as I handed over my change.

Once home, I shut myself in the conservatory, put on my pink rubber gloves, and turned the pages. You can imagine my feelings when I saw that Sophie's official picture showed her angling her head with a coy look in her eye and sticking her pierced tongue out. With a hammering heart, I learned that her fellow contestants included the dwarf, a transvestite yoga teacher, a lap dancer from Brazil, an eighteen-year-old public school boy with a *Brideshead* obsession and a teddy bear named Aloysius (or "posh weirdo with Latin cuddly," as the *Sun* put it), a lesbian council worker whose job was to fill potholes, a Peter Andre impersonator named Phil, and a physics teacher with a Mussolini mustache.

It was all too much. The knowledge that my daughter's picture was being ogled by millions, that she was right now being broadcast via the Internet to perverts from Japan to Gibraltar. It was bad enough that time she wore a miniskirt past the Epsom Common Working Man's Club. The names and faces swam in front of my eyes. I called Jeffrey. His mobile was turned off. I called his office line; his secretary told me he was in a meeting with Andrew and the CEO of Hubris Consulting. I ordered her to interrupt the meeting and tell him to read the *Sun*. In desperation, I called the number that Sophie had left me. It rang twice, and a harried voice said, "Golden Noodle Restaurant. How can I help?" I hung up, tears of frustration building in my eyes. I ran up to Jeffrey's study, logged on to the Internet, and searched for a channel 4 contact number. After an hour of listening to recorded messages and grating music and being passed from pillar to post, I finally got hold of a producer. She sounded about twelve, and told me—in a voice that skipped between Received Pronunciation and Estuary English—that as Sophie was over eighteen there was nothing I could do, and that I should be proud that she'd made the final cut.

I hung up and spent ten dark minutes with my head in my hands, crying. And then I did what I always do when adversity overwhelms me: I recited Wordsworth's "Daffodils" ten times, then formed a mental list of people less fortunate than me, beginning with the workers who have to remove roadkill from the side of the motorway, and ending with Miss Hughes.

10 P.M.

Jeffrey and I have just watched the latest episode of *Dungeon*. How could we not? The imagination is a terrible thing; it is worse to guess at what images of one's daughter are being beamed around the world than it is to confront the mortifying reality head-on. Not that this was an easy task.

The "cell mates," as I am apparently meant to think of them, were set a challenge. They were given an enormous hamper of fruit, a white sheet, and a print of Botticelli's *Venus,* and told to re-create the painting as best as they could by arranging the fruit on the sheet. An art historian would decide whether they had passed or failed. Jeffrey and I looked at each other. Why had our daughter subjected herself to this circus?

At least it turned out that her art A-level had not been wasted. Under the flickering light of replica candles, she had the sensible idea of positioning herself on the sheet in the Venus pose while Phil, the Peter Andre impersonator, drew around her in crayon, to give them an outline to work from. I wish he hadn't stuck to her outline quite so closely. After that, everyone set to work with the fruit, and it all went fairly smoothly until a fierce argument erupted between the council worker, who felt that Venus's bosom would best be represented by a pair of grapefruits, and the lap dancer, who wanted to use melons. Peter Andre intervened in favor of melons. I was annoyed to see that Jeffrey was silently nodding along with him. The end result, I have to admit, was rather impressive, and I felt certain that they would carry the challenge until, at the very last moment, the transvestite added a most unfortunately positioned banana as a protest against "monolithic Western gender clichés" and the judge shook his head in disgust. There was to be no daylight; and they would eat gruel for dinner. At least Sophie has some practice for this from her grandmother's porridge.

FRIDAY, JULY 11

Dear Lord. The tabloids today are full of photos of Phil, the Peter Andre impersonator, with his crayon next to Sophie's thigh and headlines like BOTTY-CELLI'S VEN-ARSE. Even the *Daily Mail* had the same picture, though its caption was the slightly less objectionable "The art of love?"

Once again, I handed my change over to Niral from a clammy palm, hardly daring to raise my eyes to his. He must know. Everyone must know.

As if to confirm this impression, as soon as I'd left the news-agent my mobile rang. It was Bridget.

"God, Constance, are you okay? That is your Sophie, isn't it?" she said. For a moment I was tempted to lie, to delude her, and myself, that the pierced adolescent in that narcissists' madhouse bore no relation whatsoever to my cherished daughter.

"Yes, it's my Sophie," I said in a defeated voice instead. It was futile. I listened to Bridget try to cheer me up for a few minutes, then ended the conversation and put my mobile back in my pocket. It rang again, almost immediately. Tanya.

"Flippin' 'eck Connie, have you seen the papers today?" she said, before inviting me over for a coffee and a chat. Craving dis-traction of any sort, I agreed.

It was my first trip to her new flat, which is a big step down from their old house but nevertheless rather smart. Tanya has taken over the open-plan living room and dining area for Idle Hands, leaving Mark to run the administrative side from the storage room. Next to the vials of varnish and pots of sequins, Tanya had a copy of the *Sun* open to a *Dungeon* double spread. I took a gulp of my coffee. My jaw dropped in horror, partly from the Nescafé, partly from the sight of Sophie admiring Peter Andre's tattoos in the dim glow of a Bic cigarette lighter. Tanya tried to convince me that it was all okay, that she'd be able to make twenty grand "just like that" from talking to the magazines afterward. She is probably right, but it is not for this that Jeffrey has been putting 5 percent of his salary into a trust fund every year.

10 P.M.

Jeffrey and I have just finished watching *Dungeon*. The circumstances are far from ideal, but it's the first time for as long as I can remember that we've shared a pastime in this way. Jeffrey poured himself a whiskey and me a sherry, and we settled companionably on the sofa as the opening sequence of dark corridors lit by fake electric candelabras, with a soundtrack of thumping beats and demonic cackling, began. It was Sophie's turn to cook for the group. Her chili con carne was a modest success; if it hadn't been for the council worker being a vegetarian, and for the dwarf finding a mustache hair in his serving, it would have been a triumph.

SATURDAY, JULY 12

Today I ventured onto Facebook and searched for Sophie's name. I wish I hadn't. There were 193 results, including many fan clubs, a hate club, and a group called "I would cut off my own balls with a rusty spoon for the pleasure of having Sophie Harding make me chili con carne."

I logged back off quickly.

SUNDAY, JULY 13

Church today, and Mother, both of whom were thoroughly oblivious to *Dungeon*.

The *Sunday Telegraph,* sadly, was not. There were no lurid photos or suggestive headlines, but there was a substantial article in the comment section by some professor of sociology, which claimed:

"The reality television genre has reached its apotheosis in *Dungeon:* the contestants strut through its gaudily lit corridors, they are both manipulated and manipulating; they are the commodities and consumers of voyeurism; their much-vaunted eccentricities are what make them uniform. In her complete unawareness that the only real prison cell she inhabits is one of her own making, Sophie Harding is the new Emma Bovary."

I showed it to Jeffrey, and he didn't know what it meant either.

MONDAY, JULY 14

10 P.M.

Once again, Jeffrey and I have just watched *Dungeon*. The housemates were set another challenge: to learn how to ride a monocycle, then perform a relay race down the gloomy corridor, with an electric light made to look like a candle (presumably a real one would breach health and safety regulations) serving as a baton. Jeffrey's hand reached out to mine, and our eyes met, fearfully. We both knew that Sophie would struggle.

And she did. Even with the Peter Andre impersonator holding her hand, she could not bring herself to make that leap of faith, to peddle on ahead and keep her hands at her sides. "Go on, Sophie!" bellowed Jeffrey, rising from the sofa on her sixth attempt. But it was in vain. All the other contestants managed it, even the dwarf, on a custom-made "minicycle," but not poor Sophie. And because of her, the housemates failed the challenge, and had to face a week without wine.

Afterward, there was footage of Sophie with her scrawny ankles clasped in plastic replica stocks, weeping mascara down her cheeks, wailing, "It's all Dad's fault. He wouldn't buy me training wheels and I never learned to ride a bike properly and I hate him and you and everyone, it's not fair!"

Jeffrey had to physically restrain me from calling the producer again; then he poured us both a double scotch, neat.

TUESDAY, JULY 15

It was with a heavy tread that I approached the belfry last night. Was it too much to hope that no one caught a glimpse of Sophie on *Dungeon,* in one way or another? Alas, it was. No sooner had I put down my handbag and taken up my usual position at my rope than Miss Hughes turned to me and said, "I saw that daughter of yours in the newspaper today."

"Oh," I said, not knowing how else to reply. At that moment I noticed Gerald standing quietly next to his bell rope, his hair neatly combed, listening.

"I never thought I'd see the day when someone from this village would be caught cavorting on television like that."

Just as I was struggling to formulate a response, Gerald intervened.

"Isn't it about time we got going?" he said quietly; and we did. The lovely clanging of the bells, and the regular reaching and pulling on my rope, soon managed to erase all thoughts of Sophie, minidresses, monocycles, dwarfs, and Peter Andre impersonators.

I left feeling calmer, and gave Gerald a grateful smile on the way out.

The feeling did not last, however. When I got home Jeffrey was sitting in front of the television watching *Dungeon,* gripping his glass of scotch so tightly his fingers were white; on the screen our daughter was having a screaming match with the Brazilian lap dancer. He explained to me that Renita had accused Sophie of stealing her eyeliner. I would like to have thought her innocent, but my mascara did make a mysterious disappearance at the same time as Sophie, suggesting a certain predilection for helping herself to other people's cosmetics. I told Jeffrey, and he shook his head, then went to his decanter for a top-up.

WEDNESDAY, JULY 16

Once more to the newsagent's. This time I could no longer avoid Niral's eye as I paid for my tabloids. "This is your Sophie, isn't it?" he said, gesturing to the cover of the *Sun,* which had a close-up of Sophie and Renita screeching at each other with the headline MAKE UP, GIRLS!

"She has spirit. That Renita girl is a nasty piece of work," he said in his gentle, undulating voice. "I hope that she will be out on her ear when it comes to parole time."

Parole! Of course. Rupert had explained how it worked over the phone only yesterday, but I was too distracted to pay attention. The cell mates must be due to nominate someone soon. I realize it's unkind to hope that one's own daughter will be socially ostracized and summarily booted out, and yet I long for it to be so. Our ordeal could be almost over.

10 P.M.

Sophie is up for parole! How I hoped I would be writing those words; and how much trouble they have brought. I have had a most alarming sort of surprise.

Jeffrey and I were settled, as usual, to watch *Dungeon*. I had told him that I suspected a parole notice was imminent, and he perched on the edge of his sofa, so precariously that I feared he would spill his whiskey onto the carpet. Sure enough, one by one the housemates filed into the "interrogation chamber," that ludicrous room with medieval implements of torture on the wall, pimp's furniture, and a voice-over of a young girl pretending to be a George Orwell character. (I never liked Orwell much. Why slum it in Paris and London when he had a perfectly respectable array of relatives to stay with? But I digress.)

Each cell mate had to say whom they wanted to send home, and things were not looking good for our daughter. Though she had the physics teacher and the Peter Andre impersonator on her side, she seemed to have alienated the entire female contingent, including the transsexual, who said that she had stolen his moisturizer. Once the votes were in, the results were clear: Sophie and Renita were up for eviction. The result would be decided by a public telephone vote. As soon as the numbers to text flashed on the screen, Jeffrey put down his glass and grabbed his BlackBerry from his pocket. I was impressed that he was taking matters into his own hands. Sophie clearly needs to be out of that house for her own good, and the British public cannot be relied on to vote the right way; how else would you explain more than a decade of Labour government?

I looked over his shoulder as he typed in "RENITA."

"You've got it the wrong way!" I said. "You have to put in the one you want to send home, not the one you want to stay." Perhaps, after all, it was similar confusion that accounted for Gordon Brown's presence at No. 10 Downing Street.

"What are you talking about, you silly woman?" Jeffrey exclaimed. "Why would I want Sophie to go? This is the most fun I've had in years."

He hit SEND.

 THURSDAY, JULY 17

How could he? How could he?

A phone call from the twelve-year-old *Dungeon* producer with the oscillating accent. Did we want to go to the television studio this evening as VIP guests to cheer Sophie on and meet her if she is given parole? No, we did not. I told her that we had other plans. If Sophie could find her own way into the house, she could find her own way out. My anger overwhelmed me. Then as soon as I had hung up I called back to make sure that she would be put up somewhere safe for the night and looked after. Then I said, "Good, I should think so too," and hung up again.

FRIDAY, JULY 18

A phone call from Harriet. News of *Dungeon* has finally percolated through to Weybridge. She was shocked, and appalled.

"My niece, Constance, my niece," she kept repeating, a little insensitively. Lowering my voice to a hiss, I told her about Jeffrey's vote. She went silent, then hissed back conspiratorially, "How could he? How could he?" In such moments, I can forgive all her bragging over her beautiful baby granddaughter.

A phone call from Tanya. "Hiya, Connie, how about we bring some pizzas around to your house for parole night, make a party of it?" I didn't have the energy to refuse. She and Mark will be here at nine. Feeling too fraught to fight the current, I decided to swim along with it, and texted Rupert to invite him too.

10:30 P.M.

It's over. She's out. What a spectacle; what an evening.

Mark, Tanya, and Rupert all arrived around nine o'clock, Rupert giving me a hug and a bottle of Chilean red wine, which I hoped Jeffrey would be able to discreetly lose somewhere in the wine rack.

Mark and Tanya brought take-out pizza; Tanya ate directly from the box, which she balanced on her bump, but I made sure everyone else had plates. The smell was enough to coax Natalia out of her room to join us. She looked a little like a *Dungeon* contestant herself with her tracksuit bottoms and tiny vest top showing a good few inches of Slavic stomach. As the opening music played, Jeffrey leaped up and started pacing back and forth across the rug. I told him to stop or he would erase the paisley.

The scene that opened up on the television screen was flabbergasting. I felt like an anthropologist who had stumbled on some mysterious tribe in a clearing in the middle of a rain forest, leaping about in incomprehensible ritual. There were hundreds, thousands of people, crammed around a walkway screaming and waving banners, some of which said "Go go SoHa!!!" It took me several minutes—and Rupert's explanation—for me to understand that they were there for my daughter. "It's okay, Mum," Rupert said, patting me on the shoulder, "they're just a bit bonkers. And if it wasn't Sophie it would be a football team or a dancing dog or someone from Girls Aloud." I nodded and looked back to the screen, where the host was interviewing a teenage girl dressed in the same purple minidress that Sophie was wearing, showing off a tongue piercing, which she'd had done "to look just like So, she's so hot." I always wanted my daughter to be a role model, but this wasn't quite what I had envisaged.

The scene cut to the dungeon, where all the cell mates—even those who openly despised one another—were holding hands in a circle. It looked like a cross between an evangelical prayer, a séance, a nightclub, and death row. Sophie had clearly made an effort for the occasion: her eyes were encrusted in emerald eye shadow and she was wearing her gold sequined halter top. The overall effect reminded me slightly of Darcy, although I'm sure this is not what she intended.

Eventually, as the crowd was whipped up into a fury, as a cacophony of shouts rose from a thousand moronic mouths, and as the camera panned over Sophie and Renita, both of whom had small tears welling in the corners of their eyes, the result was announced: Sophie had 53 percent of the public vote; she was out on her ear. Jeffrey kicked over the wastepaper basket in disgust, spilling advertisements for Norwegian fjord cruises and dentures across the floor; Rupert patted my hand and said, "There you go, it's over."

But it wasn't quite. A teary Sophie reappeared on the television to be interviewed about her experience. In such circumstances, I would have advised her to maintain a dignified silence. She did not, preferring to bad-mouth all the other contestants, grudgingly admit that the Peter Andre impersonator was "quite fit," accuse Renita of turning everyone against her, and then wail "I should still be in there in the hot tub, not that Mexican slut" and start sniveling. Luckily, the interview ended there. The music started up; her television career was over. I grabbed the phone and began calling. Would she have her mobile on yet? On the sixth attempt, I gave up, having left a long answerphone message that incorporated my shock, anger, and humiliation, but, ultimately, emotional support.

A few minutes later, she texted back, saying: *bummed, stayin with a m8.*

SATURDAY, JULY 19

Another long and eventful day. It began with a trip to the newsagent first thing to buy all the papers for what I hoped would be the last time. It can't get any worse, I thought, as I crossed the threshold into the cheerily white-lit store, the tins and cans and packets of rice neatly stacked from floor to ceiling for those too disorganized to send their housekeepers to a proper supermarket.

I was completely unprepared for what I saw next. Splashed across all the tabloids, and even some of the proper newspapers, was the headline DUNGEON RACE ROW. From the tone of the coverage, Sophie's admittedly rude and inappropriate "Mexican" comment was some kind of outrage that put her on a par with the worst perpetrators of apartheid South Africa. "But she wasn't even Mexican!" I muttered to myself, aghast, as I read that channel 4 had been deluged with complaints and that the ambassadors of both Mexico and Brazil had demanded an apology from the British government.

My fingers were shaking as I handed the change to Niral. He smiled at me sympathetically, shook his head, and tut-tutted.

"Your Sophie is not one of these racialists. I remember her playing tag on the green with Mehak when they were little ones. If these newspaper types were not too lazy to come down from London and find out what is really going on before writing their mumbo jumbo I would set the message straight."

I thanked him sincerely.

"And besides," he added, leaning toward me across the counter. "That Renita, she WAS a Mexican slut, if you will pardon me my French. I have told Mehak: do not fall for these sorts of girls! Do not fall for them." He was wagging his finger toward me like a man facing down a wild tiger. "If he dares to bring home a girl like that, he will get the flogging of his life, of that he can be sure. Now, that does not make me a racialist, does it?"

No sooner had I nodded then shaken my head in confusion and left the shop than my mobile bleeped with a text message from Sophie. It read: *yo mo at stashun can u pik me up?? xx.*

As you can imagine, it was with mixed emotions that I drove to the station. As soon as I pulled in I saw her there, waiting, one hand on her suitcase, the other punching a text message into her mobile, looking tiny, fragile, so much smaller than the angry photos emblazoned across the newspapers. I felt my anger soften. She stuck her suitcase in the trunk and then hopped in. I looked at her big open eyes, delicate, blue, and bare of makeup, and her baby-soft skin. I reached out to touch her cheek. "Oh, Sophie," I said.

"All right, Mum, wassup?" she said, before turning back to her text message.

I drove home in silence, a few stray tears blurring my vision. When I got back, there was a Sky Television van parked on the corner of our drive, one wheel crushing our rustic brick border, along with a few other unknown cars and about half a dozen journalists milling around. I gasped; Sophie waved cheerily. I put my foot to the floor and spattered the hacks with gravel as I sped to the front door.

Both Natalia and Jeffrey were there to welcome Sophie home. Natalia, clearly impressed to be in the same house as a *Dungeon* evictee, volunteered to make her a cup of tea for the first time in living memory, said how much both she and her sister Lydia had enjoyed watching over the Internet, and asked if it was true that there was a camera in the toilet. I felt too weakened to inform her that the correct word was *lavatory*. Jeffrey, for his part, gave Sophie a pat on the back, and said, "Well, well, you're home. Think tactics, girl, next time you want to form an alliance. You have to unite against a common enemy. That's the thing." And with that he went out to tidy the shed.

With Jeffrey gone, I pointedly asked Natalia to go and vacuum the landing upstairs, hoping that I could finally have a proper chat with Sophie and point out the error of her ways. I had only just poured myself a cup of tea, drawn a deep breath, and begun—"Even in this day and age, there are certain rules of thumb that a young lady"—when Sophie's mobile rang. Her end of the conversation went something like this: "Yeah? Yeah . . . no . . . yeah . . . yep . . . yeah . . . yeah . . . yeah . . . no . . . Gotcha, bye."

"Who was that?" I asked.

"This guy who wants to look after my publicity," she said, tossing her hair back with a smug look in her eyes. "He said he's had lots of practice. He told me he'd get me the best deal for my interviews as long as I didn't go through anyone else, and that if any journos call I'm to tell them that I spent my gap year working in an orphanage in Mexico."

"But Sophie, who was this man? What was his name?"

"M something or other."

"M? What's his full name?"

"He doesn't have a full name, full names went out with the dinosaurs, just like that top you're wearing. He said he was called . . . M Clo. Yeah, that was it."

SUNDAY, JULY 20

You would have thought that Sunday would be a day of rest, but sadly it is not. More journalists arrived. M—I will not, cannot, say M Clo—called Sophie's mobile and told her to stay inside. He has an exclusive interview and photo shoot set up with *Hot* magazine tomorrow. They will come here at ten. I have half a mind to keep the chain on and the door closed when they knock.

MONDAY, JULY 21

I have snapped. I have booked a remote cottage in Norfolk for the week, and I will be driving Sophie there shortly under the pretext that we are going to the orthodontist to get her teeth whitened, as M recommended. There will be no Internet, no phone, no "journos," no newspapers, no connection to the outer world.

Allow me to explain what has driven me to this point. Against my better judgment—and Rupert's warnings—I allowed the *Hot* magazine team into the house this morning. Sophie had threatened a hunger strike if I did not, and Jeffrey said, "Let her do what she wants, it'll all blow over," before leaving for work, imperiously ignoring the assembled journalists on his way out.

And so I let in a stylist, a makeup artist, an interviewer, and a photographer, who all, except the latter, looked about fifteen, while Sophie received last-minute instructions from M Clo on her mobile. The interview took place in the kitchen, from which I was debarred. Nevertheless, by putting a glass to the door, I was able to catch snatches of Sophie rattling on, a newly confident inflection in her voice, about how much she admired the physics teacher because he worked with children, which reminded her of her gap year at the orphanage in Mexico, which was so, you know, tragic, yet rewarding, and so on and so forth. When she was questioned on the infamous argument, she went quiet and then said, "I've always had a problem with my temper. It's something I'm going to get therapy for. I think it's because sometimes, when I was little, my mum used to lock me in the laundry room if I misbehaved and I've not yet, you know, resolved my anger issues." There was a pause, then a sniff.

I dropped my glass in disgust. How could she? This must be M Clo's doing. I only ever used the laundry room as a last recourse, like for the time she put dead beetles in her grandmother's shampoo. Still, aware that by bursting in I would only confirm the impression that I was some kind of unmaternal ogre, I kept quiet. Soon enough, the interview concluded, and Sophie was "styled" for her photo shoot. This took place in the garden, and it was the most horrifying sight I have witnessed there since Darcy's escape. Sophie posed in front of my hydrangea wrapped in a Mexican flag of sadly inadequate proportions. Randolph, who was turning over the flower beds nearby, wolf-whistled. Next she was dressed up like some kind of Mardi Gras dancer, with a towering feather headdress and a minuscule sequined costume. I could hardly bear to watch.

Once the ghastly charade was finally over and the *Hot* impostors had left, I shut the door, fastened the chain, and turned to Sophie (whose face was smeared with bronzing powder to the point that she had started to resemble a chimney sweep). "Well? What do you have to say for yourself?" I asked, arms crossed.

Her mobile rang.

"Yeah? Yeah . . . yeah . . . yep . . . yeah . . . yeah . . . bye."

"That was M Clo," she said, beaming. "He wants me to write a children's book and I'm going to launch my own perfume, called Tongue Tied. Get it?"

You will not hear from me for some days.

SATURDAY, JULY 26

I am back. The scratches on my left arm are healing. As soon as Sophie realized that we were not, in fact, going to the orthodontist, or anywhere else acceptable to her, she lashed out like a feral cat. Luckily I had put the child's lock on the doors and hidden her mobile.

When we eventually got there, the cottage was perfect, just what I had hoped for: small, faintly moldy, no mobile reception, no main roads, nothing. Sophie said she wanted to die. However, her hunger strike lasted only a day and a half before she succumbed to a plate of sausages and mash, made from ingredients bought at the local farm. She stared down fixedly at her plate as she ate; I like to think she was dwelling on the superiority of fresh wholesome food versus her preferred diet of orange-flavored Kit Kats. By the end of the week she was going for long walks on the beach, picking up shells, drawing in the sand with sticks, and sometimes forgetting that she wasn't speaking to me.

Now that we are home, however, the histrionics have begun again. M isn't returning her calls. She got hold of last week's *Hot* magazine, and the first paragraph began:

"After being broadcast to the nation hurling racial abuse at her cell mate, you would have thought that SoHa would be feeling a touch ashamed of herself. Not a bit of it. We caught up with her at her parents' luxury five-bedroom mansion in Surrey, where the tiny blonde was happy to talk about the REAL reasons for her feud with Renita, her harrowing time at an orphanage in Mexico, her old-fashioned upbringing, and what REALLY went on behind the cameras with Phil."

I didn't want to read any further. If they could turn my perfectly normal house into a "mansion," Lord only knows what they did to Sophie's stories.

6 P.M.

I heard crying coming from Sophie's room. I knocked gently, and went in. She was curled up on the bed, back against the wall, wearing her purple minidress, with another issue of *Hot* magazine and her mobile by her side. I moved them gingerly aside and sat down. I put my arm around her. She leaned her head on my shoulder. "Tell me what's the matter," I said quietly. She gulped and sniffed onto my cappuccino-colored cardigan. No matter.

"It's M Clo," she said, and sniffed again. "He finally answered." Another sniff, and a stifled sob.

"He called me Sophie, not SoHa. That's when I knew something was wrong. Then he told me I was last week's news. And I am! Look at this!"

And she held up her new copy of *Hot* in a limp hand as she turned her face away and buried it in my cardigan. I looked. On the cover was a picture of Renita, who wore a tiny black bikini and a huge pout, with the headline MY ORPHANAGE HELL! "'Only Phil could take my mind off my tragic past,' says *Dungeon*'s new star."

As she sobbed, I stroked her hair, and told her that she was my wonderful daughter, that she could be anything she wanted to be in the world, that she was a million times more precious than this tacky world of five-minute fame and fickle headlines and silly abbreviations.

"Whatever, MoHa," she said, and sniffed.

SUNDAY, JULY 27

When sorrows come, they come not single spies but in battalions. No sooner have I patched up my distraught, misguided daughter than Jeffrey drops another bombshell on me. Over breakfast this morning, he cracked the head off his boiled egg with one bold, surgical swipe of the teaspoon, uttered a self-congratulatory "Ha!" then calmly told me that Ivan the Terrible would be coming to stay. Today. For an indefinite period. He has split up with Ivanka. He is, apparently, devastated; I imagine in the same way that a hawk feels sad after losing its grip on a water vole midair. It is just as well that Natalia is off for a couple of days visiting a cousin in London. Heaven only knows how she will take the news. I called Rupert to tell him just how thoughtless his father was, but he sounded distracted and asked me who I was talking about when I was halfway through. He has been a bit off for the past few weeks; I might pop a few back issues of *Crossword Weekly* in the mail for him to improve his powers of concentration.

MONDAY, JULY 28

Ivan is here, smoking in the conservatory; his odious presence pervades the house more thoroughly than the foul stench of his Russian cigars. And it is all my fault. To my dismay, I learned last night that I had a role to play in his unwanted presence in my house. It made me want to sit down with Reginald and discuss the concept of Divine Retribution.

Ivan arrived around seven o'clock, roaring up the drive in his show-off Alfa Romeo sports car and only just missing my terra-cotta pots of geraniums. I had prepared a casserole for dinner. Jeffrey poured the wine. Ivan poured the wine directly down his gullet, stared at me through his hooded eyes, and began telling the tale of how he has come to be divorced from his fourth wife, Ivanka.

I did not think it a suitable conversation in the company of Sophie, who is still in a fragile emotional state, but he persisted despite my attempts at changing the subject to the disgraceful and neglected state of this country's bell towers. It transpires that, although Ivan and Ivanka presented a smiling, united front when our paths crossed on holiday in the Bahamas, in reality a rift had already opened up between them.

Ivan suspected her of caring more about beauty parlors and designer dress shops than attending to his needs, leaving a horrible silence as to the question of what precisely those needs might be. Ivanka, meanwhile, suspected that he had sent her to a second-rate surgeon for her boob job, which had started to go askew.

With a small catch in his cigarette-ravaged voice, he explained that the final straw came when her failure to ensure that he was properly coated in sunscreen led to a severe bout of sunstroke. He said he still bore the scars from the blisters. He took another gulp of wine. Sophie's blue eyes were darkened with tears.

God may just as well have peeled back our roof tiles and smited me with a thunderbolt.

TUESDAY, JULY 29

Natalia got back last night, and she couldn't have returned at a worse moment. She must have heard our voices, because she wandered into the dining room to say hello, with her duffel bag still in her hand, just as Ivan was banging his fist on the table and telling Jeffrey that Russia had every right to bomb Georgia to smithereens.

Natalia dropped her bag and called Ivan a Russian pig. I had no idea that her vocabulary extended to porcine insults. It appears that, along with politics and religion, the borders of South Ossetia should not be discussed at the dinner table. Ivan looked part bemused, part amused, while Jeffrey just looked like he wanted to slip between the cracks in the floorboards and disappear.

Natalia put her hands on her hips. "I cannot live with this Russian prison-keeper of nations," she said, decidedly. She turned to Jeffrey. "You must choose. He go, or I go."

I don't know why she asked Jeffrey when I normally handle all matters relating to her employment; it must have been her sense of deference to the man of the house. In any case, there she stood, defiant, her head held high, her streaky chestnut ponytail tickling her bare shoulders. Jeffrey's eyes swiveled from her to Ivan and back again. Ivan raised one eyebrow, looked at Jeffrey, and said sardonically, "Vell, my friend?"

Jeffrey's naturally ruddy complexion had darkened to a violent shade of puce. He picked up his cheese knife, then put it back down. He looked up.

"Natalia, you must be awfully tired," he said finally, in a flat voice. "You work too hard. Why don't you take a break for a few weeks?"

She stood perfectly still for a few seconds, then picked up her duffel bag, placed the straps delicately across her shoulder, and walked right out of the room without saying another word.

And just like that, Jeffrey had stripped me of my housekeeper. Ivan guffawed, then smeared a piece of Stilton onto a cracker, placed a grape on top, and rammed it down his throat. He picked up his glass of port. "To us," he said, looking at Jeffrey.

"To us," Jeffrey weakly replied.

From the kitchen came the sound of a muffled smash and foreign words screeched in anger.

Afterward, I lay awake for a long time waiting for Jeffrey to come to bed so that I could ask him pointedly what his plan was for cleaning the windows and ironing his socks, but after I had rehearsed the question over and over again in my head, including the exact way that I would smile sadly and shake my head, I heard the familiar caterwauling of Led Zeppelin start up and noticed that the bedside clock showed two A.M. I gave up and fell into an uneasy slumber, during which I dreamed that the house had fallen into disrepair and I was trapped in labyrinths of rubbish until the blond woman with the pink rubber gloves from *How Clean Is Your House?* tunneled through to release me.

When I woke up, Natalia had already gone, leaving no indication of when—or if—she plans to return. I went down to the kitchen to find Ivan and Jeffrey breakfasting on fried eggs, Tabasco, and Belgian beer. I asked Jeffrey if he was going to be late for work and he just shrugged.

WEDNESDAY, JULY 30

Bell ringing last night. With just two weeks to go until the competition, there is a new edge to the group. Could we, can we, will we, challenge St. Albans, that ruthlessly efficient group of ringers who have been the reigning champions for the past three years? We will certainly give it our best shot.

Reginald wore red Nike sweatbands around his wrists. When Gerald rang his bell half a second too soon during the Reverse St. Sylvester Miss Hughes sucked in her breath and muttered, "Stupid little man," putting me and several others off our stroke. During the tea and biscuit break, Reginald sipped from a bottle of Lucozade, and gave us all a little pep talk.

"Friends, Christians, ringers," he said. "We gather here because we have chosen hope over fear, unity of purpose over conflict and discord. St. Albans is a fearsome enemy, but by standing together, as our forefathers have stood together for generations, we *can* overcome—and I tell you, ringers, we *shall* overcome."

"Hear, hear," said Gerald politely.

"Now is not the time to descend into petty disputes, to let the old divides weaken our sense of purpose," he said, glancing hesitantly at Miss Hughes, who was noisily eating a chocolate biscuit and ignoring him.

"We must toil until our hands are raw, we must look at our adversaries without fear, we must, above all, have the audacity of hope."

He stopped. Daphne, the postmistress, wiped a tear from her eye. I clapped, to show my support.

"On another matter," I said, as Reginald mopped his brow with his handkerchief, "does anyone know a good housekeeper?"

No one did, unfortunately; although when I had explained my predicament, Gerald at least made very sympathetic noises, which is more than can be said for Jeffrey. I've not heard a word from Natalia, but every time I ask Jeffrey where he thinks she went, he just shrugs and changes the subject.

THURSDAY, JULY 31

You would have thought that a decent housekeeper was as rare as a three-toed alpine ibex or a lump of frankincense. Try as I might, I have made no inroads in finding a Natalia substitute. It doesn't help matters that I have no idea whether I am seeking a temporary, or permanent, replacement. I asked at Church Flowers, and was met with the same blank silence I encountered at bell ringing. I am loath to go down the same road I used to hire Natalia in the first place, which was namely to use Ivan the Terrible's shadowy "Eastern Star Recruitment Solutions" business.

Sophie is of little help. I finally persuaded her to dust all the bedrooms yesterday, but in doing so she managed to knock the pottery hedgehog that Rupert made for me when he was in prep school off the windowsill, breaking off several of its prickles. In despair, I dropped the following note at Reginald's, to include in the parish newsletter:

Help required.

Respectable family seeks diligent housekeeper with high standards, clean fingernails, a good grasp of the English language, and a natural affinity with parrots. Must show forbearance to guests, regardless of nationality, at all times. Must be able to make a roux sauce from scratch, buff silver, cross-stitch hems, and pour whiskey from a decanter without spillage. No hair dye, no piercings, no insolence. Lodgings provided.

Ironically, Natalia herself would fail to meet the requisite standard.

FRIDAY, AUGUST 1

Where did July go? I have been so preoccupied with Sophie's escapades, Ivan the Terrible's arrival, and Natalia's departure that I have hardly noticed the time pass by. And now, according to my Cottages of the Cotswolds wall calendar, it is already August, and just one week before my fifty-fourth birthday.

I am still none the wiser as to what Jeffrey may, or may not, be planning. He certainly doesn't act like a man struggling under the strain of an extravagant and covert present-buying initiative. In the morning he eats his toast with his usual calm concentration, occasionally supplementing it with one of Ivan's pickles, then either drives to the station or, if Ivan is going into town to look after his mysterious business affairs, shares a lift in that horrible man's tacky ego extension of a car. In the evenings he takes Ivan to The Plucked Pheasant or sits in his usual chair with *The Economist* and a glass of scotch. There is no indication in any of this as to what sort of present he will buy me.

Not that I am obsessed with gifts, you understand—I am quite capable of buying myself whatever odds and ends I fancy—and yet I find that, to a certain extent, birthday presents are a useful bellwether as to the state of one's marriage. I still have the hand-carved wooden lovespoon that Jeffrey brought back from a rugby tour to Wales the first year we were married. It has an anchor to represent stability, a horseshoe for luck, and entwined leaves for growing love. I suppose the Welsh need their symbols as they still don't seem to have mastered the alphabet. In any case, given the eventful nature of the past few months, I can't help but wonder what Friday morning will bring.

I will organize a simple family dinner in our local French restaurant for the evening; given the current lack of domestic staff I can't even begin to think about organizing something at home. All I need to do is call Rupert and Harriet, and forewarn Mother. Jeffrey has many fine qualities, but planning social gatherings is not one of them. I still haven't entirely forgiven him for booking that belly dancer for my fortieth.

SATURDAY, AUGUST 2

Today I picked the first apricots from our tree—Randolph has been tending it well—and baked a tart to take to Tanya. I tried to get Sophie to help, but she was too busy trying to tan her tummy. I will give her one more week before I raise the subject of Cats in Need.

When I got to Tanya's, she was a little out of spirits. At almost eight months pregnant, she opened the door wearing a vast stretchy red maternity dress, with a good five inches of cleavage protruding from the top.

"I'm fed up now, Connie!" she said, sitting amid the Idle Hands boxes in her open-plan living room, which was looking markedly less slick than when they first moved in. Mark has taken over most of the day-to-day running of the business. "My back hurts, my feet hurt," she said, sighing. "I'm too hot all the time and I look like John Prescott, with Jordan's tits."

I comforted her as best as I could, reassuring her that I had started to resemble a beached porpoise by the time I had Sophie. She picked at her fingernails, which, for once, were unpolished.

I decided to distract her by asking if she and Mark had decided on a name. She said that if the baby was a boy it would be called Mark Junior, and if it was a girl it would be Pinot, Shariah, Coleen, Tiffany, or Ivanka. I successfully suppressed a shriek of horror by pretending that I was choking on an apricot kernel. Then, to change the subject, I invited her to my birthday dinner. I know it was supposed to be a family-only gathering, but she looked like she needed something to look forward to. I'm sure everyone will get along fine, as long as Mother doesn't drop anything in Tanya's cleavage or ask about baby names.

SUNDAY, AUGUST 3

Wonderful news! Oh, wonderful news! How long I have waited for this day. To think that only a few months ago I was desperate enough to consider putting him on *Telegraph* dating.

Rupert paid a visit today.

"So, you know your birthday dinner?" he began. "It's just a small thing, isn't it, family only? Low-key?"

I reassured him that it was, deciding to see where he was going before I mentioned Mark and Tanya. Then he said the words that I have been waiting a good six years to hear.

"Is it okay if I bring someone?"

Of course it was. Absolutely. Oh, yes. Feel free. Was it a friend that he wanted to bring along, I asked searchingly.

"A partner," he said, after a pause. "Called Alex."

Not just a friend, or a girlfriend, but a partner! It has such a formal ring to it that I wonder if a ring of a different sort might soon be in the reckoning. John Lewis currently stocks some very elegant hats. I think puce would be a suitable color.

I told Jeffrey, clutching my hands together with glee and staring deep into his eyes to see his own surprise and joy register. He said, "Mmm," then went upstairs.

Still no word from Natalia, nor sign of a replacement, but frankly I am too excited about Rupert's news to care about the cobweb I spotted just above Jeffrey's paper shredder.

MONDAY, AUGUST 4

I wonder if Alex is short for Alexandra, which is a lovely, regal-sounding name. Alexandra Harding rolls off the tongue rather nicely. Or could it be Alexis? I think that's Greek. I hope she shaves her armpits, at the very least for her wedding day.

TUESDAY, AUGUST 5

Just back from bell ringing. When I got to church, I found Reginald limbering up outside, swiveling his arms like a windmill, stretching out his legs by placing first one foot and then the other on top of a gravestone. He is taking the contest rather seriously.

During the break, after Reginald had delivered another rousing speech on change we could believe in, I invited everyone along to my birthday dinner on Friday. I couldn't help myself. The prospect of finally seeing my son's new girlfriend was too much to resist. Gerald took me to one side and asked if I was sure he was invited, if it might not be a little awkward after last time, but I reassured him that he was more than welcome. Three days to go!

WEDNESDAY, AUGUST 6

What, I wonder, should one wear when one is meeting one's son's girlfriend for the first time? I would like to appear elegant yet approachable, attractive but not fussy, sophisticated but not pretentious, chic but not French—ideally, a cross between Helen Mirren and Jodie Foster, with just a hint of Catherine-Zeta Jones. I will try the John Lewis in Kingston upon Thames.

6 P.M.

I'm back, and I think I have the perfect outfit: a navy silk dress with cream polka dots, from Joseph. It fits snugly around the cleavage, with just the right degree of décolletage (about a twentieth of Tanya's), then skims flatteringly down to the hemline, which is just below the knee. With low heels and a cream cardigan it will be perfectly smart, but not too formal. I do hope it will make Jeffrey say "phwoar," just once. I walked in front of the sofa to ask Sophie what she thought, and she said, "Yeah," then I turned the television off and asked her again. She stared at me for a few seconds and then said it made me look like Samantha Cameron, which I took as a compliment.

THURSDAY, AUGUST 7

One day to go! I got my hair done—a trim and recolor— then went to Church Flowers, where I invited everyone along. I just called the restaurant and luckily they were able to extend the booking—luckily it's the holiday season and they're quiet.

I wonder if she's blond or brunette. Plump or skinny. I wonder how old she is. I do hope she'll be wearing a dress too. I've told Sophie to be nice and friendly to Alex when she meets her—who knows, one day they might be sisters—but she just laughed and went to her room. She had better buck up tomorrow.

FRIDAY, AUGUST 8

Fifty-four today. Jeffrey left early this morning without so much as mentioning my birthday. I do not know what, if anything, he is playing at. It is not as if I were holding out for a breakfast tray bearing smoked salmon, freshly squeezed orange juice, and an orchid in a miniature vase: a simple acknowledgment would have sufficed. He can hardly have forgotten, given the number of times I have reiterated the arrangements for dinner tonight.

I suppose I must draw consolation, of sorts, from the other members of my household. Ivan surprised me with a mink muffler: an extravagant gift, though one of limited use during the average Surrey summer. Still, I found myself mollified to the extent of ignoring the empty pickle jars he left strewn in the conservatory this morning. Sophie gave me a set of shot glasses. Heaven only knows why.

A satisfying bundle of cards arrived on the doormat, including one from Rupert. It was a typically tasteful design, a sketch of irises—my favorite flower—on thick cream card, though the message inside was more emotive than usual: "Happy birthday, Mum, and remember I will always be your loving son, Rupert." Perhaps it is Alex's feminine influence exerting itself!

3 P.M.

Good Lord. Once more, I must ask myself: what is Jeffrey playing at?

A few moments ago, there was a knock at the door. By the time I opened it, I could hear the scrunch of a large vehicle easing off the driveway, and there on the porch stood a cage, entwined with ribbons, containing a large and scrofulous mynah bird.

There was a gift tag attached. It read: "An old bird for an old bird. Love, Jeffrey."

To think that only hours ago I was yearning for some signal that he had remembered my birthday.

I carted the creature into the conservatory. Its rheumy eyes, wizened talons, and hunched, malevolent demeanor remind me of Miss Hughes. Darcy is puffing up his feathers and fluttering his wings in an unnecessary display of superiority.

SATURDAY, AUGUST 9

I feel sick. And not just from the brine pickle juice that Ivan insisted I drink as a time-honored Russian hangover remedy.

No, it is the events that prompted me to turn to Jeffrey's brandy last night that account for my current nausea, palpitations, inner darkness, and distress.

I can't bring myself to tell you what happened. I just can't.

For all my faults, I do not think I am a bad person, or a negligent mother. What did I do? What didn't I do?

If only I had let Jeffrey buy him that model battleship.

SUNDAY, AUGUST 10

This is not an easy blog to write. It has taken eighteen hours of lying in a darkened room, twelve vials of Bach Rescue Remedy, and three hours of counting the feathers on Darcy's left wing to feel composed enough to start.

Little did I know when I began my little online diary on a frosty New Year's Day that I would eventually be using it to announce that my son, my very own Rupert, was—enough. I'm getting ahead of myself.

Friday evening began well. I put on my new dress and took more than usual care with my hair and makeup, borrowing a raspberry-colored "lip stain" from Sophie. Ivan wolf-whistled as I came downstairs, even if Jeffrey was too busy tying his tie in the hall mirror to notice my appearance.

Jeffrey, Ivan, Sophie, and I arrived at the restaurant in good time. The bell-ringing contingent was already there. Gerald presented me with a lovely bunch of delicate yellow roses; Miss Hughes, a tin of lemon sours. Edward and Harriet gave me a pretty set of gardening tools with an old-fashioned floral pattern on the handles. Pru from Church Flowers gave me a hardcover edition of the new Queen Victoria biography, no doubt a token of her appreciation for the fact that I set Ruth up with David, thus ridding her house of patchouli oil.

Jeffrey ordered champagne for all. A happy hubbub of voices mingled over the candlelight. The only thing missing was Rupert.

He arrived. With a nondescript young man whom he introduced as Alex. I simply did not understand. At first, I thought that I had made a mistake all along, and that his partner really was a business partner, or simply an acquaintance. My heart fell as the prospect of a family wedding once more receded into a distant, indistinct future.

And then Rupert was sitting next to me, with an earnest look in his eyes, and Alex was sitting next to him. At this point, the realization probably began to crystallize somewhere in my brain; but I ignored it and poured them both champagne, hastily introducing Alex to everyone as Rupert's friend and calling the waiter over to order starters. Rupert knocked his champagne flute back in one gulp, while Alex sipped his shyly and told me in a quiet voice with a light northern accent how nice it was to meet me, how I was just as Rupert described, and that he loved the vintage pearl brooch that I had pinned to the front of my cardigan on my way out as an afterthought. "It was my mother's," I muttered, poking my spoon through the cheesy crust of my French onion soup, concentrating on not splashing it, nothing else. Everyone else was chatting, no one seemed suspicious. Jeffrey was smearing pâté on little triangles of toast and loudly telling Edward how he had knocked two points off his golf handicap, while Ivan stole his pickles and ate them whole. I looked at Rupert. Rupert looked back at me. Then he placed his hand on my arm, and said he couldn't wait anymore. Alex was staring straight ahead, a flush of color rising on his clean-shaven cheeks. Rupert explained, with something of his childhood stutter returning, that Alex was not just a friend, and that he had to tell me something important about himself, that he was fundamentally the same person but with one vital difference that I finally had to grasp. Sophie leaned in and said: "Mum, he's gay. G-A-Y. Get it?"

In one moment, it all made sense. I may not be a spring chicken, but I am nevertheless not quite ancient enough to labor under the delusion that *gay* still means "jolly" or "frolicsome." Sophie had just articulated my own, newly formed suspicion. But how to reconcile this bombshell with my son? All I know about gay people is what I gleaned when I watched *Brokeback Mountain* in the mistaken belief that all the nice horses would bring back fond memories of Pony Club. It just doesn't fit. Rupert is not anguished and filled with brooding, explosive menace. He is a quiet, studious IT consultant who lives in Milton Keynes. I looked at him, I looked at Alex. I realized they were holding hands under the table. The room had fallen silent.

Overwhelmed by a mixture of shock, confusion, and Moët, I ran out of the restaurant. Jeffrey followed and drove me home in silence.

As soon as we got in, and I had shut the door behind us, I asked him if he was okay. "Of course, old bird," he said. "Bit of a shock, but that's life, eh?" He hugged me, but he wouldn't look me in the eye. He left the following morning for a shooting trip with Ivan.

I do not know what to think. Every time I consider the implications of this news my head throbs as if Jeffrey were playing his Pink Floyd album. All I can think of is the image I had formed in my head of Alex: a sweet girl, petite, with dark blond hair, a green summer dress. Someone who would have complimented me on my hair and asked about Darcy and said that the restaurant was lovely. Someone who would have realized the importance of coordinating the wedding invites with the floral decorations.

As I went to retrieve a packet of tissues from my handbag this morning, I found the birthday present that Rupert must have tucked into it when he arrived at the restaurant.

It was a beautiful embroidered silk scarf, in puce.

MONDAY, AUGUST 11

Sophie is silent and sulky. She must share my distress at Rupert's revelation. Ivan and Jeffrey are still shooting ptarmigan in Yorkshire.

I almost wish they would spare their shot for the wretched, dyspeptic mynah bird that squats in the conservatory emitting strange sounds and foul odors.

When it gets too much, I shroud its cage with a towel, which seems to send it into a stupor. I wish someone would do the same for me.

TUESDAY, AUGUST 12

Rupert sent me a text message. It read: *Mum, I hope you're ok. I'm still me. Love, Rupert.*

Not that this in any way mitigates his unfortunate choice of sexual orientation, but I was gratified to see that he hadn't written "ur."

 WEDNESDAY, AUGUST 13

Last night I went to bell ringing. How could I not? The championship is this Sunday; whatever my sense of humiliation as I made my way across the churchyard, eyes down on the luxuriant green weeds sprawling between the paving stones, whatever the sense of dread as I entered the belfry and faced my fellow ringers for the first time since Rupert's disclosure, whatever the fearsome obstacles, I knew I had to nail the Reverse St. Sylvester if we were to have any hope of thrashing St. Albans.

In the end, it was not so bad. Reginald stopped his warm-up routine of jumping jacks to pat my arm, Gerald smiled kindly, and even Miss Hughes attempted a smile, though it looked more like a sneer. And then the ringing itself began, and in concentrating on the rhythm, on the exact disconnect between pulling downward and hearing that rich clang up above, in feeling the alternate weight and lightness of the rope between my fingers, I felt calm for the first time since Friday.

Unfortunately, the sensation didn't last long. When practice finished, I saw that I had a text message from Jeffrey, which read: *Great weather, plenty of birds. Will stay another week or so. J x.*

THURSDAY, AUGUST 14

2 A.M.

Do you think homosexuality is a phase that one grows out of?

11 A.M.

After a fitful night's sleep, I was standing in the conservatory staring at Darcy, in case he held any answers in his intense, black eyes, when the doorbell rang. It was a young man, with a mop.

"I'm here about the job," he said.

"What job?"

"Housekeeper. The agency sent me. They said you advertised."

And that, I suppose, sums things up. Of course, the new house-keeper might be a man, your son's new girlfriend might be a man; you can't be sure of anything anymore.

"Um, is everything okay?" he said. I realized I had been staring at him in silence for some time.

"Yes, yes, sorry, I'm just a bit tired today. Come in."

He had kind eyes, an accent a touch like Natalia's but much lighter, and long arms that would be useful for getting the cob-webs off the chandelier. His name is Boris. After a few calls to check his references, I agreed to a two-week trial, starting imme-diately. It won't take me long to clear out Natalia's old room for him. His first task is to clean out the mynah bird's cage.

FRIDAY, AUGUST 15

Tanya stopped by today. I spotted her from my bed-room window as she pulled up the drive in her cartoonish Smart car, squeaking to an abrupt stop, then easing her huge, pregnant form slowly out of the driver's seat. Rupert will never put a woman into this state. There will be no pregnancies; no books of little boys' and little girls' names; no panicky call from him in the middle of the night to say that our grandchild is on its way; no trying to see his features in a tiny, new, reddened face; no cots, no blankets, no booties, no cuddly toys or alphabet mobiles. None of that.

There was a hammering at the door. I had forgotten to let Tanya in. When I did she ran straight for the bathroom, swear-ing. She is finding the final stages of pregnancy hard. "My bladder is the size of a ****ing pea, Connie!" she said afterward, over a glass of sparkling mineral water. She is avoiding all caffeine, alcohol, tuna fish, soft cheese, pâté, steak, and salad, and taking daily folic acid supplements. How times have changed. I told her that when I was pregnant, I had a glass of sherry most evenings and ate whatever I felt like. Mother was halfway through making a vat of her signature plum chutney the day she gave birth to me. She often used to tell me that the whole pan had curdled and had to be thrown away when she got back from hospital, with a resentful tone to her voice. Tanya shuddered. Her back aches, her ankles are swollen, and every time she tries to sleep the kicking starts.

I would happily have spent the entire morning talking about pregnancy and reminiscing fondly, but Tanya had other ideas.

"So, what's the score with Rupert? Have you seen him yet? That Alex seemed like a nice guy."

I was silent. Perhaps Tanya noticed my puffy eyes, the line on my cheek still visible from where I had ground my jaw fretfully into my pillow in my sleep.

"Oh, Connie," she said. "Don't take it so badly! It's the twenty-first century. I mean, have you seen *Brokeback Mountain*? Come on, it's not like he's just told you he's a pimp or a smack-head or"—she rolled her eyes—"a banker or something."

I nodded numbly, nibbling at the edges of my Waitrose ginger nut biscuit—I have not had the energy to bake for some days. At that point Sophie wandered in, went to the fridge, and started swigging straight from a carton of Tropicana. I felt too weary to tell her off. Tanya continued trying to reconcile me to Rupert's news.

Sophie wiped her mouth with the back of her hand and said, "Yeah, Mum, get over it. He's waiting for you to get in touch. He doesn't want to put pressure on you so he's not going to call."

Tanya and Sophie both looked at me with expectant eyes. In the background, Boris was quietly wiping down the work surfaces.

"What do you think?" Tanya said, addressing him. "Shouldn't Constance get in touch with her son, who's just come out?"

Sophie added, "As in, he's gay."

Boris put down his cloth and said thoughtfully, "In Poland it is very hard for men who are gay if they are not in the big cities. Life can be cruel for them, sometimes their family want nothing to do with them. Here, no. Britain is better in this way, people are people. Your son is your son. It is the person what counts." Then he went back to cleaning.

Once again, Tanya and Sophie stared at me. "Just do it," Tanya said, handing me my mobile. I said I would send him a text, and started to key it in. I hit SEND. They both sighed happily, and exchanged smug glances.

But they hadn't seen what I had sent, which was: *Rupert, pls remember to send a card for grandma's birthday, august 24.*

 SATURDAY, AUGUST 16

7 A.M.

I have just woken from a terrible dream. It was the day of the competition and somehow Rupert was meant to be ringing with us, next to Gerald, but when we got to the belfry to take up our positions for our turn he wasn't there; we looked and looked and finally we found him outside, standing with the St. Albans group, whose numbers had also been swelled by Graham Norton. Rupert had switched to the wrong team. He was wearing leather trousers and smiling.

Even afterward, when I was awake and knew it had just been a bad dream, I couldn't shake off that image. I sent him a text saying: *Rupert, do you own any leather trousers?*

He replied: *No. 2 jeans, 2 chinos, 2 suit trousers. That's it.*

I suppose I must draw comfort where I can. I don't want you to think that I'm a hideous bigot, the sort of person who would harbor an unquenchable hatred for someone just because of their choice of trouser material. It's just that when you spend years and years thinking that you know someone so well, when even the way the muscles in their cheeks dip when they smile has been familiar to you for more than two decades, and then you suddenly find out that for all of their adult life they have been hiding something from you and you don't really know everything about them at all, that they have never shared their hopes and heartbreaks with you—well. It isn't easy, suffice it to say.

I wonder if Jeffrey is also suffering from sleepless nights and sorrow-filled days, or if he has sublimated all his anxiety into shooting birds.

 SUNDAY, AUGUST 17

8 A.M.

A text from Rupert: *Good luck today. Let me know when yr ready to talk.*

I must rush off. Gerald will be waiting with the minibus at the village green. Despite my nerves, I have had a full breakfast—two boiled eggs, toast, tea, and juice—to sustain me through the day. I wouldn't want to fall into a malnourished trance and find myself distracted by Graham Norton hallucinations at a key moment.

7 P.M.

What a day! Never again will I trust in the shared values that bind all ringers together.

We arrived at St. Albans at ten-thirty, a little later than

expected after having to go back once for Daphne's reading glasses
and once for Reginald's sweatbands. It was a pleasant, almost
idyllic scene that awaited us: the church spires sweeping
elegantly up into a pale blue sky, merry (not gay—I will not say
gay) bunting fluttering in the breeze, twenty teams of ringers
from the South and South East milling about with flasks of
tea and picnic hampers, awaiting their turn to show off their
skills. We gathered our sashes and name tags—every team is
assigned a different color, and ours was a fetching turquoise—
then huddled together in a corner of the churchyard for a
pep talk. After we had carefully arranged our sashes over our
safety harnesses, Reginald shouted, "Can we do it?" and made us
reply, "Yes, we can!" while punching the air. Gerald obeyed with
particular vigor and then winced, as if he had pulled his shoulder
joint.

Our adversaries, the St. Albans team, were on the opposite side
of the churchyard, sitting quietly in their red sashes and praying.
I was sure that one of them, a thin woman with gray-striped hair
like a badger, kept staring at us with a strange look on her face,
but just as I was about to mention it to the others I was swept
into another rousing chorus of "Yes, we can."

It was when we were eating our bananas, as Reginald had suggested we do for energy twenty minutes before our performance,
that we first noticed something was amiss. My sash had been
chafing. I presumed it was the heat, and the scratchy material,
but the itching sensation kept increasing in intensity until I
could hardly bear it. I suddenly realized that Reginald was
scratching, and Gerald, and Miss Hughes, and in fact the whole
team of ringers. There were small bumps on the skin of my shoulder. Sabotage! I called the team together and explained my sus-
picions.

"Who gave you the sashes?" I asked Gerald. "Was it one of the officials?"

"No, actually," he said, jiggling his shoulders up and down. "It was the lady from St. Albans with the funny hair. I thought she was just being helpful."

I had another theory. Itching powder. But what to do? Even if we all rinsed off in the rather inadequate bathroom facilities, we would still be too uncomfortable to perform unhindered. What we needed was chamomile lotion, and fast. I asked an official where the nearest chemist was, but she just shook her head and said that the one in the village was shut. It was Sunday. Where could I turn?

I suddenly had a thought. Rupert. Whenever I mention a place I'd like to go to—a National Trust house, a restaurant—he has the annoying habit of tapping it into his mobile or his LapTop and telling me exactly how many miles away it is and how to get there. Perhaps he could do the same thing for open chemists in the St. Albans area. I got out my mobile and scrolled through to his number. It rang twice, then he answered: "Mum! I'm so happy you called! This means so much to me."

"Rupert, I need chamomile. Urgently. Where is the nearest open chemist to St. Albans Church?"

"Uh, what? Uh, hang on, I'll go on Google Maps."

And he did. He found one and, while Reginald drove, called out the directions. I ran in, grabbed a bottle, threw some money at the baffled-looking girl behind the counter, jumped back in the car, and then Reginald sped us back to the church at five miles over the speed limit, apologizing loudly to God and any hidden speed cameras as we went.

We arrived with six minutes to spare, and slathered the lotion all over our red, bumpy, uncomfortable shoulders. The relief was sweet. When we were summoned into the belfry, we felt abuzz, united, determined to perform. We rang our bells as we had never rung them before. We had precision, we had passion. Even Gerald didn't peak prematurely. At the end of the afternoon, none of us was surprised when we won; and the look on the faces of the St. Albans team as the results were read out made me forget, for a few glorious moments, that my son had recently announced he was gay. Instead of shaking our hands, Reginald rolled his into a fist, which he bumped against each of our hands in turn. The chamomile lotion must have gone to his head.

We drove home singing along to Radio 2, Miss Hughes tapping her long, yellow fingernails rhythmically against our trophy. And now I have just enough time to chivvy Sophie out of the bathroom so that I can have a quick shower before we all meet in The Plucked Pheasant for a celebratory drink.

 MONDAY, AUGUST 18

The light hurts my eyes. I feel sick.

Why did I not stop after two glasses of champagne? Why?

I dimly remember calling Jeffrey, and his phone rang and rang to answerphone before I hung up, and then I remember calling Rupert, who picked up straightaway, and I told him that I loved him and that he would still be my son even if he went to live in Brighton to start a shop selling stick-on handlebar mustaches. I am mortified. English people do not articulate their feelings.

I think I will ask Boris for a glass of ice water and then go back to bed.

10 P.M.

My hangover is forgotten. I feel so much better. Rupert has just left. At about four o'clock he called to say that he needed one of his old programming books that Jeffrey had stored away in the attic, and asked if it was okay if he came around after work. It was quite a long drive for a weeknight, so I said he had better stay for dinner, and I would make one of his favorites, chicken surprise with potato rissoles. As soon as I got off the phone, Sophie said she was glad I was sorting things out with Rupert because he was doing her head in calling her up to ask about me all the time, and then announced that she was off to meet a "mate" in the Italian café because chicken surprise was "lame"—the only surprise was that "it was chicken breasts stuffed with cheese and green stuff." I told her that the green stuff was chopped sage and that I varied the cheese between Cheddar and Gloucestershire, so there was indeed an element of suspense. Then as I heard the door clink shut I thought of Rupert, and wondered what it would be like to look into his hazel eyes, which have just the same mix of green and gold flecks as Jeffrey's.

A couple of hours later, I found out. After hearing him clunk the knocker three times, in exactly the same way he has done since childhood, I opened the door and saw him standing there, looking so handsome and shy in a light gray polo shirt and blue jeans, holding a small bunch of freesias in a cellophane wrapper. As I looked into his eyes I felt a familiar rush of affection, with a new edge to it. I am not normally the hugging type, but I hugged him. The spicy scent of his aftershave for some reason made me want to cry. Then I ushered him into the kitchen and gave him a cold beer from the fridge, which he sipped as I finished off dinner and chattered away about the bell-ringing championship and the size of Tanya's bump.

It was only when he was halfway through the chicken surprise (Rupert agreed that the name was entirely appropriate) that he put down his knife and fork and looked at me, with a frown making a tiny dent in his forehead. "I'm sorry I didn't tell you sooner, Mum, I really am," he said, speaking quickly. "I felt awful keeping it from you and it was just like there was never a good time. I thought about doing it when I was in university, which was the first time I felt like I could really be myself, but it was still so fresh, then I just kept putting it off and putting it off. . . . I did try to mention it once, but when I said that I had something to tell you, you said, 'You haven't been smoking that whacky baccy, have you?' and went on about how you'd read in the paper that it was much stronger now than it used to be and it would poison my fine mind . . ."

I stared at him. He was right; I had completely forgotten that episode. Why hadn't I listened to my son?

"And then I met Alex, and . . . I'm just really happy. I hope you'll get to know him, Mum. I really think you'll like him. He's repotted that spider plant you got me at Christmas, and he loves reading, just like you."

I didn't know what to say. I was happy to see Rupert so transparently happy; but to have the image of Alexandra—who I felt sure would have made a wonderful mother for my grandchildren, had she existed—so abruptly replaced by a man, albeit a green-fingered, book-loving man, still felt like an almighty wrench. But as I looked into Rupert's hopeful eyes, I couldn't bear to risk upsetting him, or making him choke on his rissole. "He sounds wonderful," I said, and I hoped that one day I would really mean it.

It was half an hour after Rupert left before I realized that he had never collected his book.

TUESDAY, AUGUST 19

I can't write for long. I must go back to the hospital. Ivan has been shot in the foot. Tanya has given birth.

WEDNESDAY, AUGUST 20

First, the good news. Tanya and Mark are the proud parents of a lovely little girl. Although a few weeks premature, she is in good health, weighing in at five pounds eight ounces. Mother and baby will be kept in for observation for a couple of days, but should be back home by the end of the week.

Second, the not-so-good news. The baby has been named Shariah. Mark claimed it had a "nice, eastern ring to it." I wondered if he had been on Tanya's gas and air, but I bit my tongue. I went to see them a few hours after the birth; Tanya was sleeping, but Mark pointed with a trembling hand to the incubator where little Shariah was curled up. Her tiny, perfectly formed fingers and toes provided a sharp contrast to Ivan's obliterated digit, which was the other reason for my visit to the hospital.

At this point I feel I should explain that Jeffrey is a fine sportsman, but I suppose that in marksmanship, as in stewardship of the Rotary Club's finances, his confident insouciance can occasionally lead him astray. It appears that, having spotted a particularly alluring bird, he fired off too soon, thus relieving Ivan the Terrible of the little toe of his left foot. Ivan received emergency treatment in Yorkshire before being transferred to a private room at our local hospital yesterday. It was with great trepidation that Jeffrey and I went to see him in his hospital suite, painted a tasteful shade of lavender. As soon as we opened the door, he stubbed a cigarette out in the pot of his peace lily before realizing it was us and explained that he thought for a moment we were one of those "do-good nurses." In Russia, the nurses are beautiful, he added. Not here. We approached him with caution. I asked him how he was, and he simply said, "How do you think?" and scowled. Jeffrey, however, patted him on the shoulder, and Ivan grasped his hand and shook it manfully.

I do not understand the Russian temperament. Ivan is a man

of foul moods, of tempestuous rages, of black, glowering discontent. And yet, having had a significant and lifelong wound inflicted upon him by my husband, he shows less resentment than he did when Jeffrey once inadvertently polished off his glass of vodka. I have to say, I do not fully understand the temperament of my husband either. This is the first time I have seen him since Rupert's life-changing announcement, and I had hoped to be able to read instantly how much he had suffered. Yet the only thing I could tell from looking at his face was that he had been out in the sun for too long without his hat.

THURSDAY, AUGUST 21

Ivan the Terrible is back, wounded, groggy, and petulant. He blunders through the house like a bear with its foot caught in a trap, scattering all in his path. Jeffrey has lost his favorite port glass, and Sophie, one of the crystal ponies she used to collect as a child. She has borne the loss remarkably well. If anything, her mood seems to have improved in the past couple of days. She has taken to locking herself in the bathroom for long periods of time, trying out a bewildering array of cosmetics and singing. Luckily, Boris is always on hand to clean the iridescent eye shadow off the sink.

When I finally got Jeffrey to myself for the first time, I thought he would be bursting to share his feelings about Rupert. "I've seen him," I told him, almost triumphantly. "I've seen him, and, darling, it really isn't so bad. I know this must be hard for you too but he really is the same old Rupert. We can get through this."

Jeffrey muttered, "Of course, old girl," and just for a moment, before he started vigorously stuffing his rubber boots with rolled-up pages of yesterday's *FT* to dry them out, I caught a lost look in his eye.

FRIDAY, AUGUST 22

11 A.M.

I've invited Rupert and Alex for dinner. It was Sophie's idea, and I followed it on the spur of the moment last night. Rupert sounded so happy when I called that I swallowed any doubts about how Jeffrey would react, and whether Ivan would make a suitable dining partner in a delicate family situation. The most important thing is to show Rupert that we support him. I'm sure that Jeffrey would agree, though, as ever, his feelings are difficult to read. When I told him about the plan over breakfast this morning he lowered his paper by about a quarter of an inch and said, "Fine."

Perhaps it really will be fine. Perhaps, over the course of the next seven hours, Jeffrey will reconcile himself to our son's situation and I'll be able to persuade Darcy to stop saying "Who's a pretty boy, then."

11:30 P.M.

It wasn't entirely fine. Of course it was good to see Rupert again, and Alex does indeed seem a very eligible young man, but I couldn't stifle a small wish that this soft-spoken, handsome young geography teacher, with his neat dark hair and short-sleeved checked shirt, had been brought home by my daughter and not my son. He would be the perfect boyfriend for Sophie, I thought, calm and steady but with a throaty laugh, which suggested a lively sense of humor. I caught Rupert looking at me as these thoughts ran through my head, and I jumped up anxiously to pass the stuffed olives around.

It was an awkward meal. Boris prepared a wonderful rack of lamb with new potatoes—his culinary skills are far superior to Natalia's—but there was nonetheless a background tension that made conversation difficult. It didn't help that Ivan the Terrible punctuated the first long pause at the dinner table by saying "There are not so many gay men in Russia, you know. In England, they are here and they are there and they are everywhere, but Russia, no. Men are men in Russia," before devouring an enormous chunk of lamb by jamming it into his mouth and then rotating his fork.

Rupert asked, "What about this year's Eurovision act?" but Ivan replied that that was a Latvian nancy boy masquerading as a Russian, who had no real manly Russian blood in his veins. I changed the subject quickly to last Sunday and Rupert's role in our victory, going on to describe the competition in such detail that Ivan was soon silent and rapt, as was everyone else at the table.

Then Ivan took over the topic of competition and started to describe the wrestling contests held between the youths of his village that he said he used to win every summer. Apparently all that was needed was a mud pit, a few straw bales for the spectators, and some low-grade vodka to wash off the blood. I saw Rupert and Alex exchange glances and roll their eyes. At least Sophie remembered her manners and listened intently, staring at his face—perhaps counting the fine lines that crinkle out from his eyes when he guffaws—while he spoke.

Jeffrey said hardly two words throughout the whole meal, but managed to drink a bottle and a quarter of wine and two glasses of claret. I wish Darcy had shared his reticence. Just as Rupert and Alex were getting their coats to leave and we were all assembled awkwardly in the hall, wondering whether to say anything of significance, to hug or not, my parrot let out a piercing cry of "Jolly Roger."

SATURDAY, AUGUST 23

A letter arrived today, addressed to Jeffrey, written in the spidery scrawl familiar from Natalia's shopping lists. It was post-marked London. Why is she writing to him and not to me? Perhaps she thinks he is a softer touch. I do hope she's not peti-tioning for her job back. Boris is so much more efficient, and is doing a wonderful job of keeping the bathroom spick-and-span despite the ever-increasing array of new makeup that Sophie is cluttering it with.

I must content myself with not knowing. Just as I was boiling the kettle—for a cup of tea, you understand, not to misuse the steam, which was quite profuse and would have had it open in a jiffy—Jeffrey appeared, collected his mail, patted me on the bot-tom, then left for a game of golf, leaving Ivan to sit in the con-servatory and smoke with only Sophie for company.

SUNDAY, AUGUST 24

Mother's birthday, and a special lunch at The Copse to celebrate. Jeffrey came, along with Sophie, although Rupert couldn't make it because he had to prepare for a work project. I suspect this may have been a front—he is usually so reliable at attending family gatherings, but it must be difficult for him to face his grandmother at the moment. Mother was in her usual form: she told all the residents who were gathered around the large oval dining room table for lunch that there was never this fuss and nonsense about birthdays in the old days, then com-plained that there was no cheese course, then said loudly that it was far too hot and stuffy, but on closer inspection was found to be wearing a flannel vest under her blouse.

After lunch, Jeffrey took Sophie home and I went to visit Mark and Tanya, who are now at home with little Shariah. Tanya, who has taken to motherhood quite naturally, cooed and jiggled her, while Mark sat watching them both with an equal measure of awe and fear in his eyes. I bit the inside of my cheek to stop myself from thinking that I would never catch Rupert with that look on his face.

After this scene of domestic bliss, I went back home to find that Ivan had singed the edges of my parlor palm with his cigar.

MONDAY, AUGUST 25

Just now, I popped into the kitchen for a glass of elder-flower cordial and was accosted by a very strange sight: Sophie changing the dressing on Ivan's foot. It made me realize that one silver lining to the raging cumulonimbus of Ivan the Terrible's visit is that it has revealed a new and admirable side to Sophie's character.

To be quite frank, I have been worried about Sophie. Very worried. Maternal pride has no place here. Her behavior this summer—the impromptu trip to Ibiza, the tongue piercing, the misguided foray into reality television—shows her to be irresponsible, inconsiderate, and easily led astray.

And yet, since Ivan arrived back, hobbling and swearing, Sophie has transformed into a veritable ministering angel. She bathes his wounded foot (without a face mask!); she listens to his endless turgid tales about bear hunting and yacht buying. The man is as loud-mouthed, foul-breathed, egotistical, and repellent as ever, so Lord only knows how much she suffers. And yet she puts on such a brave, cheerful face. I am impressed.

TUESDAY, AUGUST 26

Sophie has christened the mynah bird—whose presence I have largely ignored—Fergie. When I said, "After Sarah, how nice," she just looked at me and shrugged. Earlier, I caught her in the conservatory trying to teach the wretched creature some sort of inane ditty that went "My humps, my humps, my humps, my humps, my humps." I really should arrange some charity work to fill the remaining month before she goes off to Bristol. Just not on any literacy projects; I'm not sure that she would be a positive influence.

No bell ringing tonight; we're taking a short summer break. I miss the adrenaline rush of competition, the camaraderie, the uplifting sound. I persuaded Jeffrey to play backgammon while an old recording of *Songs of Praise* played in the background, but it wasn't the same, and after I had beaten him for the second time I wasn't too disappointed when he retreated abruptly behind *The Economist*.

WEDNESDAY, AUGUST 27

I don't know how much more of this I can take. Sophie has run away with Ivan.

THURSDAY, AUGUST 28

Once more, I find myself sitting at my keyboard, my palms sweating and my head pounding. Once more, my own flesh and blood has dealt me a devastating blow.

Yesterday, Sophie failed to appear for breakfast. So did Ivan. Both of them are late risers, so this didn't alarm me to start with. I saw Jeffrey off to work, making sure he took an apple with him, then decided to empty out the kitchen drawers and give them a good clean. This absorbed me for several hours—how had a receipt for twelve pink-frosted Krispy Kreme doughnuts got there? Why was there a glittery My Little Pony sticker still clinging to the back of the drawer behind the teaspoons?—until I suddenly realized that it was almost midday and the house was strangely silent.

I called out to Sophie. There was no reply. I went up to her room and tentatively pushed open the door. It jammed on a pile of clothes, but once I had wedged it open I saw that her room was empty, and in a typical mess. I even noticed, with a catch in my breath, half a bottle of Ivan's red-label vodka on the floor. But there was no sign of Sophie. I told myself she must have gone out, and went downstairs to start on the dining room drawers.

And then I heard the familiar sound of Jeffrey's tires on the gravel, followed almost immediately by the sound of his key in the lock. I rushed to the hall to meet him. He had a funny look on his face, which reminded me of Mother in her doughtier days, when she used to raise a rolling pin above her head in anger. He handed me his BlackBerry and said, "Read this."

It was an e-mail from Ivan—sent from his BlackBerry, Jeffrey said—but the subject line read *from soph!!!* What followed was clearly her hand. It read:

Hiya mum & dad, cant stop larfin when i think of you looking about the house 4 me today. Im not there!! me and ivan are going away together!!! im so happy, hes lush, and he's dads best m8 I know ull be happy for me in the end. dunno bout going to school. mum always said finding the right man was just as important as getting a dugree and the only boys who do sociology are gay (no offense to rupert!!) in a cab, dunno where we're going, its like a film or sumthing, cant stop larfin!! Luv soph :) Ps ive got fergie.

Ivan's BlackBerry had subsequently been switched off. I have never seen Jeffrey so furious. His normal calm, composed expression had slipped away like a mask being taken off; his cheeks were magenta, his eyes wide, his pupils tiny. His shock made me suppress my own. I said I should make us some tea and led him into the kitchen, but as soon as we were there he noticed one of Ivan's shot glasses, picked it up, and then hurled it across the kitchen with a roar. It narrowly missed the carved wooden cockerel that Harriet gave me for my birthday last year.

And now he has gone to London, to track down Ivan's acquaintances and try to find some clues as to where they are hiding. I don't know if he's taken his hunting rifle.

FRIDAY, AUGUST 29

Why me? Why?

SATURDAY, AUGUST 30

Forgive me for yesterday's outburst. Jeffrey still has no leads, but I realize I must try to get a grip. I can't continue to wallow in this muted hinterland of drawn curtains, soporific novels (I find Maeve Binchy works best), crumpled tissues, and cups of tea.

To strengthen my resolve, I decided to compose a short list of people trapped in situations worse than my own.

King Lear. Neither of my children, as far as I am aware, is entangled in a plot to kill me.

The woman in Lionel Shriver's book *We Need to Talk About Kevin*. Rupert may be gay, but to the best of my knowledge he has not committed mass murder with a crossbow.

That's as far as I have gotten.

SUNDAY, AUGUST 31

2 A.M.

I can't bear it. Where is she? What is she doing with that man? When is she coming home? How can she stand his halitosis? Why has she not called, or e-mailed, or sent me a text message? Perhaps he has drugged her and smuggled her to somewhere even more treacherous than the outskirts of London. Perhaps they are in Moscow, or Chechnya.

2 P.M.

I woke early this morning, cold, with the sheets pushed off over the side of the bed. I noticed once again that I had small red crescents imprinted into the palms of my hands from where I had dug my nails in my sleep. This was hardly surprising, given that I could clearly remember dreaming that Ivan and Jeffrey were fighting a duel with old-fashioned pistols, while Sophie looked on wearing a wedding dress (one of those horrible strapless, tarty ones) and a publicist in dark glasses filmed it all on his mobile phone with a grin on his face. When the shots rang out, Darcy, my beloved Darcy, suddenly fell from the sky and I woke up with tears in my eyes.

I went to church and knelt until my legs hurt and prayed. Then Rupert came around with a new copy of *Hello!* magazine and a box of Belgian chocolates, and although he was clearly worried too, he sat and chatted about this and that, so I almost forgot to worry about Sophie for half an hour. As soon as he left, however, I found myself staring at the framed photo of Sophie that was taken on her twelfth birthday: her hair is platinum blond and she is squinting a little in the sun, standing in front of the glossy petals of the magnolia tree with her hands jammed in the little pockets of her pink checked birthday dress.

Where is she now?

5 P.M.

Just as I thought today could not get any worse, Natalia showed up on the doorstep. It took me a few moments to recognize her: she's bleached her long brown hair a peculiar shade of yellowish white and lost quite a bit of weight. She was wearing a denim miniskirt to show off her scrawny, orange legs. "Can I coming in?" she said, and as soon as I remembered my manners I said, "Yes, of course, how lovely to see you again," all the while hoping that she wasn't going to demand her job back and frighten off Boris, who is such a thorough cleaner that he has formed an almost emotional bond with the vacuum cleaner. I needn't have worried. She had come to collect some things she had left behind, which I had packed into her peeling gold-colored suitcase and left in the spare room. Once I had handed this over to her, she asked if Jeffrey was home—I suppose she wanted to say hello to him as a courtesy. When I said he was away and wouldn't be home that evening, she left without even saying good-bye. Thank heavens I have a replacement with better manners.

MONDAY, SEPTEMBER 1

Bank holiday Monday. There is rain dribbling down the windowpane, and the wind is lashing the magnolia tree, scattering the last dead petals across the lawn like dirty confetti. On the television, the news shows footage of a six-mile traffic jam on the M5, caravans stacked behind cars with bikes and boats on the back, families who thought they would be building sand castles staring at the windshield wipers scraping back and forth.

Why should I pity them? At least those gridlocked parents don't have a daughter who has absconded with a middle-aged nine-toed semialcoholic Russian. At least they haven't had to suffer a visit from Harriet, who took my hand, smiled, and shook her head slowly in pity, then asked if there hadn't been something amiss with Sophie's character right from the beginning, as evidenced when she stole a fairy cake from Laura's sixth birthday party.

TUESDAY, SEPTEMBER 2

A new month, a new school year. I remember how much Sophie used to love choosing a new pencil case and sharpening all her coloring pencils before the first day back. She would test them out by drawing colorful mustaches on the serious men in Jeffrey's newspaper. Once she gave John Major red and green dreadlocks. Where did that little girl go?

That is the question that poor Jeffrey, in the most literal sense, is desperately trying to resolve. Every day he calls, and every day his voice sounds more dull and mechanical. He says that at least work is so quiet he's hardly missing anything—I suppose that's one advantage to this seemingly endless recession. He's managed to glean from Ivan's business contacts that the unspeakable man is still in London, and probably staying somewhere in the West. Jeffrey spends his days driving in circles, asking at hotels, loitering in vodka bars.

And if he finds her, what then? I know Sophie's temper, and her stubborn streak. How will he persuade her to come home? I should have given him a Topshop voucher to take with him as bait.

It seems my best hope is that Ivan will grow bored of her. This is a terrible thing for a mother to say, but I want my daughter to have her heart broken in two.

WEDNESDAY, SEPTEMBER 3

Jeffrey came home this morning. He did not bring our daughter, but he did bring Fergie. For a while, I felt too bitter to report this. He has now left again. He spoke as little as possible, and drank only two sips of the iced tea I handed him.

He discovered the ill-fated mynah in a bus shelter in Shepherd's Bush, on the same street as a dry-cleaning business where, according to a tip-off, Ivan was meeting a business contact. Both cage and bird were daubed with graffiti. It has taken Boris two hours of work with a prewash Vanish stick to clean her feathers. Inside the cage was a note: "Pls sum1 look after Fergie! She doeznt bite! Xx" and a half-open packet of dry-roasted peanuts, which had been pecked at. When I recognized Sophie's handwriting, I cried.

Fergie is now recovering in the conservatory. Darcy is cagey, as I suppose is a parrot's prerogative, but he will just have to learn to cope with the cruel realities of life, like the rest of us. Jeffrey has gone back to London.

Earlier, as I was towel drying Fergie, I looked into her dark eyes and recognized a fellow victim of Ivan's callousness and Sophie's fecklessness. She blinked. With her eyes shut, she is not quite so ugly. I have fed her some linseed to improve her plumage.

THURSDAY, SEPTEMBER 4

Does anyone else get the feeling that Armageddon is upon us? Glaciers are melting, wildfires are rampaging through California, my son is gay, my daughter has run off with a Russian, and now, to top it all, Fergie the mynah bird has begun to speak.

It is an eerie sound, and an eerie sight. Every few minutes she scrunches up her wings (which still bear traces of spray paint), shuts her eyes, opens her beak, and belches out a few hoarse, indistinct syllables. It sounds a little like "Nothing, kill, hate."

I had no idea mynah birds could be so nihilistic. I'm not the superstitious type, as you well know, but my nerves are frayed at the moment and Fergie's horrible utterances are adding to my sense of foreboding and dread.

I have covered her up with a tea towel. I hope she finds the scenes of rural Kent soothing.

11 P.M.

At last, another clue! I was on the phone earlier with Bridget, who, unlike Harriet, can always be relied on to keep calm and say the right thing. She made sympathetic noises as I told her everything that had happened, mixed with just the occasional muted gasp, but when I got to Fergie and her grim pronouncements, she went suddenly quiet. Then she said, "Constance, perhaps she's trying to say Notting Hill Gate."

I've alerted Jeffrey.

FRIDAY, SEPTEMBER 5

Another breakthrough! Rupert called. He has finally managed to access Sophie's Facebook page, by setting up a false account in the name of one of her distant school friends, with a kitten as the profile picture, and asking her to add him as a friend. She did so today. He can confirm that her status is *in london, baby!!* More important, she had added a photo of the pool at the hotel where she and Ivan are staying, to show off to her friends. Rupert managed to zoom in on a monogrammed towel, which read "Abbey Court." He had checked online; there is indeed a hotel of this name in Notting Hill Gate. He has called Jeffrey, who is driving there as I type.

SATURDAY, SEPTEMBER 6

Sophie is back home. It is with giddy relief, once again tempered by lingering anger, that I write this.

Jeffrey called yesterday afternoon to inform me that Sophie was in the back of the car and that he was driving her home. I still do not know all the details of how this came about.

I paced back and forth as I waited for them to get back, trying to work out whether I would feel more like hugging her or throttling her. First I asked Boris to tidy her room and put a vase of fresh-cut flowers from the garden on her desk, then I took it away and replaced it with an unopened letter from the Bristol University accommodation office. Then I took this away and put the flowers back.

My stomach tightened when I heard the sound of Jeffrey's car. I rushed to the door. Jeffrey got out. He opened the door for Sophie. She got out. She was wearing a gem-encrusted green silk minidress, which I could tell with one glance was extortionately expensive, but in all other respects she was clearly the same old Sophie: slight, pale, and tetchy.

She stumbled in her new high heels as she walked up the drive, avoided my outstretched arms (which was perhaps prudent given that I was still undecided on the hug/throttle dilemma), and dashed to her room, kicking the shoes off behind her. I followed. I heard the dragging sound of furniture being moved toward the door, the crash and tinkle of a vase falling and smashing, then a series of swear words that do not bear repetition.

At the time of this writing, she has not left her room, with the exception of one furtive midnight raid on the last of Ivan's pickle jars. If only we had not given her a bathroom. I have tried gently knocking and cajoling, and I have tried hammering in anger, but all attempts are in vain. She refuses to open the door and declares herself, once again, on a hunger strike. I called Rupert to ask his advice and he said to give her time. I hope it doesn't take much longer.

Jeffrey has been more approachable, but only just. Once it was clear that Sophie would not be venturing out anytime soon, I made Jeffrey a cup of tea and urged him to tell me exactly how he had succeeded in extricating our daughter. He was more than usually evasive. He simply said that he had gone to the hotel, found their room, and dealt with the situation. He reassured me that Ivan would be unlikely to trouble us again; then he opened the newspaper to catch up with the weekend's rugby union results.

Good Lord. A terrible thought has just occurred to me. You don't think he's killed him, do you?

 SUNDAY, SEPTEMBER 7

Sophie is out. Much like her brother, I suppose you could say, except that I had been waiting for this to happen. Last night, I was just drying my hair after a bath when I heard the television. I went downstairs to find Sophie sitting on the sofa, her feet tucked up underneath her, gorging herself on a plate of cheese and crackers, with *America's Next Top Model* on in the background.

"Sophie!" I said.

"All right, Mo," she replied, hardly looking away from the screen.

"Do you want to talk?"

"Nah."

This morning I skipped church to keep an eye on her. She spent a long time feeding Fergie and talking to her. When I went into the conservatory to top up Darcy's water bowl, she told me, while staring at the floor, that she'd left Fergie at that bus stop only because they were going to be thrown out of the hotel if they kept her, and that Ivan had made her do it. Then she went quiet for a few moments, before saying "Mum, did you ever notice that Ivan's breath was really minging?"

Guessing what the word *minging* meant, I smiled and said that I had.

 MONDAY, SEPTEMBER 8

10 A.M.

Jeffrey's PA just called. He has been arrested. I am shaking. Should I hide his hunting rifle?

4 P.M.

The good: Jeffrey has not, it would transpire, shot Ivan the Terrible with his hunting rifle.

The bad: He has been arrested on suspicion of fraud.

I cannot say any more. I must go at once to the police station.

TUESDAY, SEPTEMBER 9

How to describe the trauma of yesterday's events, the stomach-knotting shame?

The phone call from Jeffrey's PA was followed shortly afterward by the low rumble of an engine and the sight of a police car pulling into the drive, in full view of the neighbors. I do not think I possess the necessary sangfroid to be a successful accomplice. I would have made a poor Bonnie to Jeffrey's Clyde.

I shouted to Boris to deal with the visitors, then I ran upstairs. I knew I had to hide the hunting rifle. I did not know where. I took it from the cabinet in Jeffrey's study, holding it in a sport sock so as to avoid leaving fingerprints. I hurried from room to room in search of inspiration, knowing that at any moment the police would be upon me. The only relevant image I could summon was of some dreary gangster film Jeffrey had once subjected me to in which the criminals hurled their murder weapons from a bridge into a raging torrent. There were neither bridges nor torrents at hand.

Finally, with the sound of voices in the hall, I seized upon the idea of burying it in the newspaper at the bottom of Darcy's cage. I opened the cage. A policeman opened the door to the conservatory. I paused. Darcy, who is not the sort of bird to spurn a spontaneous opportunity to stretch his majestic wings, launched himself out of his cage like a cruise missile and swooped across the conservatory, narrowly missing the police officer's head. He swore. I stood aghast, gun in one hand, extra-large men's tennis sock in the other.

I expected the officer to grab the weapon and inspect it for blood. I imagined that at any moment I would feel the cool metal of handcuffs against my wrists. Instead, the officer—who looked only about Rupert's age—merely showed me his search warrant and said he needed to look through all of Jeffrey's business documents. I was confused, and then relieved, and then angry. What on earth has Jeffrey been up to?

That, of course, is the question which dictates our fate, and which kept me awake, trembling, all last night. He is being held on suspicion of making false passports and driver's licenses and submitting inaccurate tax returns. I do not understand. He insists that he is innocent; of course he is innocent. As soon as I saw him yesterday, my anger dissipated. His eyes were red, his skin white, his tie loosened about his neck. He was the only man in the police station—aside from the policemen—who was not dressed in polyester sportswear. He told me in a small, quiet voice that he hadn't done anything wrong, that this was all some horrible misunderstanding.

He should be charged within days. Needless to say, he is being represented by the best possible lawyer: a business acquaintance named Simon, who resembles some strange hybrid of hyena and bald eagle. I can only hope that he gets a result before the world, and in particular Miss Hughes, finds out what's going on.

 WEDNESDAY, SEPTEMBER 10

6 A.M.

I've woken up and I can't get back to sleep. It's pointless trying. If I do, I'll slip back into my horrible dream that Jeffrey has been jailed for life and Sophie and I forced to visit him on a public bus wearing velour tracksuits, having to press the button for our stop without any antiseptic hand gel. Why me? What have I done to deserve this annus horribilus? The most distressing thing that is meant to happen to a woman in my position in the fifty-fourth year of her life is the advance of a few more wrinkles. Not all this. Dear God, not this. What if he really is jailed? What if we lose the house? What if I have to start buying discount tins of baked beans?

4 P.M.

Shame upon shame. The police officer on Jeffrey's case, a soft-featured young man who looks only about Sophie's age, took me to the station for questioning this morning. My only comfort was that I really do know diddly-squat about Jeffrey's financial affairs, and could assure him as such with no hesitation. It was a short interview. Afterward, I saw Jeffrey. He had missed his morning shave for the first time since he was under general anesthesia for a hernia operation in 2001. He didn't have much to say. Neither did I.

I declined a lift home from the kind officer, who has a boyish cleft in his chin and a disconcertingly high-pitched voice. One police car sighting in our village in the space of a day is more than adequate.

Rupert is coming around this evening to have dinner with me and Sophie. I am going to bake a large and elaborate fish pie, thus hopefully engrossing myself for at least an hour and a half. I have told Boris to take a few days' holiday. As quiet and discreet as he may be, I cannot bear anyone else in the house right now.

What will become of us? And where on earth has Boris hidden my hand whisk?

Gerald visited today. I was polishing the silverware in a futile attempt to alleviate my stress through monotonous labor when the doorbell rang.

I opened it, and there he stood, my fellow ringer and onetime admirer, dressed soberly in dark trousers and a blue shirt, with neither low-grade milk chocolates nor petrol station flowers in his hands. I was taken aback. He said, "Hello, Constance."

I said, "Come in."

I made the tea myself while he waited in the sitting room, then I brought it in on a tray with some of his favorite currant biscuits laid out. He didn't touch them. He took a few sips of his tea, knitting his gray-streaked eyebrows together, then said that if the feelings he'd mentioned once before were still disgusting to me I should tell him, and he would never trouble me again. He said he'd tried everything to distract himself from them—gardening, Sudoku, teaching Poppy to walk backward—but nothing had worked. He said that he had heard what had happened to Jeffrey (How? How had the news got out?), and that he couldn't bear the fact that I'd been put in this distressing position by a man who was not worth a single one of the glossy auburn hairs on my head. He said that, in short, he had come to assure me of his deep, his sincere, and his passionate love. Then he spilled a little tea onto his lap and looked away.

I am sure you will spare me your harshest judgments if I tell you that I was not unmoved. I value loyalty above all—bar cleanliness—but my patience with Jeffrey has been sorely tested. I think it was only at this moment, with someone else insisting that I had been badly treated, that I truly began to feel it. And it wasn't just because of Jeffrey's arrest. Through all the distressing events of this year—Sophie's escapades, Rupert's revelation—he has not exactly been my rock. If I am to be honest—really, ruthlessly honest—I would have to say that he has been more gravel than rock. He spends more time talking to his BlackBerry, or to Ivan, whose name I shudder to type, than to me. He has stopped noticing things: a new dress, a haircut, a few pounds shifted for summer—all these pass him by. Of course I still love him—almost in the same way I love the children, or the garden, even, as part of the fabric of my life, a constant—but our relationship is not quite what I imagined when I studied the Debrett's guide to homemaking thirty-four years ago.

And there sat Gerald, staring fixedly at my curtains, rigid. In the beginning I was shocked, and rather horrified, when I found out what those notes meant. But after his outburst at Sophie's birthday party, I admired the way he withdrew, became quiet, dignified, yet always concerned about my feelings. The clock ticked. I studied the pale floral pattern on Gerald's chair. In the background, Fergie squawked "humps humps humps." I knew what I had to do. I am not entirely lost. I told Gerald in a gentle voice that I thought he should leave, and escorted him to the door. He paused on the doorstep and said: "Constance, can I still hope?"

I met his eye for a long moment before shutting the door.

FRIDAY, SEPTEMBER 12

Wonderful news! Jeffrey is free. Simon the hyena-eagle has pulled it off: there is insufficient evidence to press charges, and I can collect him this very afternoon.

Our future is secure, our reputation restored.

Why, then, do I feel a certain heaviness to my tread?

SATURDAY, SEPTEMBER 13

Jeffrey is back. He is a changed man. Patient readers, I have turned to you again and again in times of crisis and you have not let me down. Please do not abandon me now. This is my darkest moment.

When I went to collect Jeffrey, I wasn't immediately troubled by his altered appearance. He may have been pale, rumpled, and dejected, but this could easily be explained away as the strain of an unexpected stint behind bars without hot baths or brandy.

We said little on the way home, beyond a few remarks on the slight chill in the air and the first few autumn leaves on the road. He asked after Sophie and I told him that she was well. Then I said that I had bought steak, his favorite, for dinner.

When we got home, I made him a cup of tea and expected him to slowly resume his old ways: fending off my questions, flicking through the *Financial Times,* sauntering off to his study. Instead, he sat me down, looked me in the eye, and said the words that no man or woman can hear with equanimity, even after thirty-three years of relatively harmonious marriage.

"Constance," he said, in a quiet voice. "We need to talk."

He began by apologizing, unreservedly yet unemotionally, for the ordeal he had put me through.

He explained that Ivan had always dabbled in risky business ventures, and that he had long suspected that his latest venture, the "Recruitment Solutions" initiative, had been something of a front for smuggling young eastern Europeans into London. I was shocked. I hadn't imagined that there were any further available depths for Ivan the Terrible's execrable character to plumb, or that Jeffrey could possibly have condoned such activities.

Jeffrey apologized, again, for his lack of judgment. He explained that he felt such a deep loyalty toward Ivan, one of his oldest friends, that he had always willingly turned a blind eye to his faults. He said that spending time with Ivan made him feel young and adventurous again.

This changed when Ivan eloped with Sophie. Jeffrey said that when he finally tracked them down to their hotel in Notting Hill Gate, Ivan refused to let Sophie go. Jeffrey suspects this was due more to Ivan's stubborn pride than to any sort of genuine affection. The situation was mortifying. Jeffrey pleaded with them to part. Sophie threatened to stab herself with her new stiletto heels.

Jeffrey said that he had no choice but to threaten Ivan with informing the police of his dubious business practices. It had the desired effect. Ivan bundled Sophie, who was bewildered and upset, out of the hotel and into Jeffrey's car, then sauntered away. Jeffrey is convinced that Ivan, in a staggering display of audacity, turned the tables and went to the police to accuse Jeffrey of exactly the sort of crimes that he himself was implicated in. The police even found incriminating documents in the guest room that belonged to Ivan, but helped to keep Jeffrey in his prison cell until the hyena-eagle persuaded them that the evidence was flawed and insufficient. I could barely believe that we had been so close to disaster.

Despite the shock, I was relieved that Jeffrey had finally decided to open up. It was the longest conversation we had had since he last attempted to explain the rules of cricket to me. I made another cup of tea and sat back down. Jeffrey looked at me with his bloodshot, baleful eyes. He said that his time in his cell had finally given him time to think, alone, without distraction.

He said that he had cried over Rupert, because he would never see him marrying a pretty girl in a white dress, because he would never get to watch him hold his grandchild.

He said that it was all his fault that Sophie had run off with Ivan. He said that he felt that he had failed as a father.

He said he was tired of his job and disillusioned with the endless quest for wealth, the slow accumulation of more and more things that he didn't need. He said that when he was a boy he read a book about the first European settlers in Latin America, and that he used to dream of galloping across the pampas with the wind in his hair.

He said that he thought he would rather be a gaucho than a corporate lawyer.

He said that he wasn't sure of anything anymore.

He said that that included me.

SUNDAY, SEPTEMBER 14

Jeffrey and I leave tomorrow at 6:25 A.M. for Buenos Aires. We may be gone for some time. I have signed a hasty agreement with the cleaning agency so that Boris will be paid a small retainer to look after the house. Sophie will just have to grow up and look after herself. If she doesn't, then the combined forces of Harriet, Edward, and Rupert should get her to Bristol for the start of term.

I have packed sunblock, insect spray, water-purification tablets, a first aid kit, clean needles, a guide to poisonous snakes, E45 cream, a warm hat, sturdy boots, a travel iron, a book of crosswords, a compass, and Bach Rescue Remedy. Jeffrey has packed a lasso. He has not packed his BlackBerry.

I have considerable reservations about this journey, but it may well be the only chance we get to save our marriage.

I do hope they have flush lavatories throughout Argentina.

WEDNESDAY, SEPTEMBER 17

We are here. Physically, we are safe. Psychologically, I am not so sure. Jeffrey has bought himself a leather cowboy hat, which he insists on wearing at a silly angle that he considers "rakish."

We are, at least, staying in the Hilton, which has a very smart bank of computers in the lobby. Jeffrey wanted to find some "scruffy local place, somewhere with character and geckos on the walls," but frankly I felt I had indulged his midlife crisis quite enough already by hauling myself abruptly into the southern hemisphere. For once, I stood firm, although I did compromise a little by settling for a standard double and not a deluxe.

Buenos Aires is sprawling, dirty, chaotic, crowded, and suffused with hotheaded Latin spirit. As we took a stroll in the historical Sal Telmo district yesterday we heard the beating of drums, and before we could duck for cover a colorful, clamorous street parade was upon us. Jeffrey attempted to dance, but his lead-footed shuffling bore little resemblance to the lithe elasticity of the Argentinean girls, who were dressed in shorts as tiny as Sophie's. I hid in a lace shop. The Latin spirit also shows up in the quick temper of Argentinean waiters. Who would have thought that, after twenty-six years, they would still be so tetchy at a passing mention of the Falklands?

With all the sights and sounds, bustle and business, of the capital, Jeffrey and I have hardly had time to think, or talk, let alone decide anything about the future of our marriage. This will change. In two days we leave for the sierras, and who knows what.

FRIDAY, SEPTEMBER 19

I am alone in Argentina. I am alone. Jeffrey has gone.

If only I hadn't refused to take a tango lesson with him. If only my attempts to sympathize with his midlife crisis—for such it no doubt is—had not been overpowered by an aversion to kicking my heels about like a Latina strumpet.

As it is, my refusal to accompany him to a Buenos Aires "milonga" proved the final straw. He has left for the estancia

without me. He said he needed time alone. He did not say when—
or whether—he wanted me to join him. He has taken his cowboy hat.

So here I am, alone in front of a glowing computer screen in
the lobby of the Hilton, marooned on this marble-clad island of
civilization amid the great, seething, dusty unknown. When I
think of home—my favorite wicker chair in the conservatory, my
daily walk past the village pond—my chest tightens. But I cannot face the long flight back alone. I cannot accept that this is
the end.

9 P.M.

Feeling stronger after a salade Niçoise from room service
with half a bottle of Argentinean white from Mendoza. It was
surprisingly good. Over dinner, I watched an American program
called *Frasier* on the gigantic flat-screen TV and found myself
laughing; then I remembered where I was and why and I cried.
The lobby is full of people on their way out for the evening;
women in skirts and heels, men in jackets, children being told
off for dipping their fingers in the ornamental fountain. There is
an elderly couple in front of me now; they could be Argentinean
or perhaps Spanish, both immaculately dressed in cream, with
creased, nut-brown skin. Her hair is pure white, scooped back in
a chignon held with a tortoiseshell clip. He has stopped and leaned
his cane against the wall to help her put her cardigan on. I've got
to go. I think I'm going to cry again.

SATURDAY, SEPTEMBER 20

I've not told anyone at home what has happened. How can
I, when I'm not even sure myself? Perhaps Jeffrey will call in the
next day or so and he'll be back to his usual jaunty, unruffled self.

I jumped in expectation when my phone bleeped this morning, as I was eating breakfast. It was a text message, which read: *Hi Mum, hope yr ok and enjoying Argentina. Have a steak for me! Love Rupert.*

Like the rest of the family, he doesn't know the real reason for this trip.

I sat there, alone, in front of a little glass bowl of grapefruit compote and a plate of sausages and tomatoes, and I did not know what to reply. In the end I fell back on: *Hello Rupert, weather good, food good, take care, love Mum x.*

It wasn't a lie, but it didn't really tell the truth either.

I wonder if I can make it to the Argentinean national museum and back on my own without getting lost or mugged.

6 P.M.

I could, and I did. They have some very beautiful artifacts for such a wild country.

SUNDAY, SEPTEMBER 21

Last night I went to the Hilton bar, alone. I realize that in usual circumstances a woman should not drink by herself, but I think the fact that after thirty-three years of marriage my husband has abandoned me in favor of a herd of cattle should be taken as a mitigating factor. The bar in question is very plush, with dark oak fittings, a sweeping view across the city, and no men in baggy T-shirts eating crisps in dark corners. It is certainly a contrast to The Plucked Pheasant.

I perched myself delicately on a bar stool, opened my copy of Joanna Trollope's *The Spanish Lover,* and waited to be served. When she came over, the barmaid took one look at me—my novel, my white blouse which I had pressed with the traveling iron—and gave me a broad, sympathetic smile. She looked about thirty, with pretty features and one tiny streak of gray in her thick black hair. As she poured a gin and tonic she made small talk, and it was so nice to have a fellow human being to chat with—not that this blog isn't a great relief too, of course, but sometimes one pines for an actual voice—that I could almost overlook her dreadful lisping accent. I expect I will see her again this evening.

 MONDAY, SEPTEMBER 22

1 A.M.

readers ive learned a word in spanish and that word is *cabrón*. Adriana the barmaid says that is what heffrey is and she is right. *Cabrón cabrón cabrón cabrón!*

3 P.M.

I am embarrassed to see my earlier outpouring. Please understand that I am in a situation of peculiar stress. Thirty laps in the hotel pool and an iced Perrier have helped to clear my head.

Still no text message from Jeffrey. No e-mail, nothing. I could have been run over by a mad Latino driver or trampled to death by a samba street parade for all he knows, or cares. *Cabrón.*

I did, however, receive the following:

yo mo, hope ur havin a wicked time in argentina. has dad fallen off his horse yet?!! lol
do u have a spare credit card? wanna buy darcy more nutz :)
luv soph xx

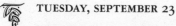 **TUESDAY, SEPTEMBER 23**

This morning, with the help of Adriana the barmaid's map, I made it to the national art gallery and back. On the way, I stopped off to buy Rupert a leather belt and Sophie a purse. Jeffrey would no doubt have tried haggling, but I was happy to accept that such an activity is inimical to an Englishwoman's soul and hand over five dollars apiece.

4 P.M.

Is this it? Is this what it feels like when a marriage is over? Empty, anonymous, dislocated, dizzy, alone? I'm eating well, I'm sleeping well. Every night when I go to bed, I read my book propped up on four plump white pillows and luxuriate in the space.

Is this it?

 WEDNESDAY, SEPTEMBER 24

Two e-mails arrived today. The first read:

Connie,
Sorry to scarper, old bird. Feel much better up here in the fresh air. Getting a grip on things—including a polo mallet! Think I'm a natural. Next time I try, the horse will be moving!! We'll talk soon, I promise. Just need to clear the head.
Hope the Hilton's okay. The credit card's in your handbag if you need anything.
Love,
Jeffrey

I did not feel that it merited a reply.
The second read:

Dear Constance,
You are gone, and I don't know why. Rumor has it that you're in Colombia. Perhaps you always wanted to go there, and Jeffrey has taken you off on a spontaneous, romantic holiday. But I worry this

is not the case. I can't help but think that Tuscany would be more to your tastes. Constance, if you don't want to be there, if you have traipsed after that man for no good reason and are regretting it, if you want someone to come and see you and bring you home, just say the word and I will book my flight. (I am presuming Jeffrey did not get his shotgun through security.)

Love,

Gerald

I didn't reply to that one either.

THURSDAY, SEPTEMBER 25

Today is my thirty-fourth wedding anniversary, and the fourth anniversary that Jeffrey has apparently forgotten. My bags are packed. I am not going home. I am not going to find Jeffrey.

I am going "traveling."

Over the course of several evenings, Adriana, who is a native of Patagonia, the mountainous territory in the south, has described the rugged splendor of her country. Her voice is mellow and hypnotic, once you get used to the lisp. After a while I could almost smell the cold, clean wind blowing off the glaciers. I felt a strange yearning. I wanted to go. Why should Jeffrey be the only one to disappear when he feels like it? Why should I languish here, breaking the paper hygienic seal on my own lavatory day after day?

Because, I know you are thinking, I am not the sort of person to indulge in flights of fancy. Because my feet are firmly on the ground, encased in L.K.Bennett court shoes. Because, to be frank, strange places, strange people, and strange food scare me. And yet Adriana swept all these worries and more away with the quiet determination of a glacier displacing moraine. She wrote down some essential phrases in Spanish, including "No, thank you," "Yes, please," "Leave me alone, you son of a she-dog," and "One steak, medium-well." I felt light-headed, and free.

I am taking a taxi to Buenos Aires airport, followed by a short flight to El Calafate. Once there, I have the address written down of a hotel that Adriana assures me is modern, comfortable, and an excellent base for booking a trip to the glaciers.

Jeffrey tried to call me earlier, and I pressed the BUSY button. *Hasta luego, amigos.*

FRIDAY, SEPTEMBER 26

I've made it to Hotel Sierra Nevada in El Calafate, and it certainly is not the Hilton. The carpet is threadbare, my room is small, and the walls are flimsy. There is a conspicuous lack of fluffy white pillows. But it will do.

I shudder to think of the cost, but I called Harriet from my room to check that she had gotten Sophie to Bristol without mishap. Apparently, Sophie had cried when Harriet refused to let her put Fergie in Edward's Land Rover along with a case of 1998 champagne, but then perked up again when the student union reps greeted her at the halls of residence with a welcome pack containing paracetamol, Red Bull, and a tub of pasta sauce. How different it was in my day, when the best you could hope for was a library card.

Harriet asked me if Jeffrey and I were enjoying ourselves on our little jaunt, with a sarcastic edge to her voice. I said that we were, very much, thank you, then eased the telephone cable out of the socket while exclaiming loudly about the dreadful foreign phone networks. After that I went to the tourist information office, just a few minutes from my hotel, and booked a trip to the Perito Moreno Glacier for tomorrow. I will be picked up by minibus at eight, then driven up to the mountains and given crampons and a training session before a five-hour trek across the ice. It will make quite a difference from my usual stroll to the village to buy the newspaper. My only regret is that I left my thermal underwear at home.

SATURDAY, SEPTEMBER 27

I am alive. I have walked on a glacier, and survived. It was "awesome," in the parlance of the American youths who also took part in the expedition.

Black rocks reared up into the sky; the cold air scoured my lungs. The ice—twisted and ancient, veined with bitter blue—reminded me of Jeffrey's heart. I trampled on it.

SUNDAY, SEPTEMBER 28

I was woken up early this morning by a phone call from Rupert. It was strange to hear his voice, tinny and distant, as I lay in my narrow little bed with the swirly pink and purple polyester cover, looking out the window at gray peaks and gathering storm clouds.

"Dad called. He's worried about you. How come you aren't with him? What's going on?"

I told him he should ask his father that.

"I did! You know what he's like. He said he was learning polo and he thought you were holed up in the Hilton. But when I called the hotel they said you left two days ago. I've been so worried!"

I told him that I was in Patagonia and rather enjoying myself.

"Patagonia?! What about Dad? What's going on? What are you going to do?"

"Penguins," I said, my eye drifting over to the cover of the guidebook by the side of my bed, which I'd picked up from the airport. "I think I'll go and see the penguins."

Then I told him to take care, and pressed the little red button to cut him off.

TUESDAY, SEPTEMBER 30

Readers, I have traveled by bus! Bus! I, who had always agreed with Margaret Thatcher's view that you were one of life's failures if you set foot in one of them after the age of twenty-five. It seems that you can't get anywhere without them here, and that Lady Thatcher's opinions are not generally held in high esteem. Fortunately, a friendly French girl at the Sierra Nevada explained how the system worked, and even helped me to buy a ticket. The journey wasn't nearly as ghastly as I had imagined. I booked the most expensive seat, which reclined to almost business-class flatness and came equipped with a cushion, a curtain, and a box of biscuits. If it wasn't for the woman next to me snoring, I would have been quite comfortable. Who would have thought that the Argentineans would succeed where National Express (so I am led to believe by occasional sightings on the M25) has failed?

And so here I am, in a snug hotel in Rawson, with the tang of the Atlantic reaching through to the rather threadbare lobby every time the door opens to let in another group of young men from New Zealand wearing superfluous woolen hats.

WEDNESDAY, OCTOBER 1

Today I saw penguins, real penguins, honking and wad-dling in a seething mass of black and white as the wind buffeted the smell of seaweed across the beach. It was like I had walked right through the television screen and into a nature documentary—I almost expected to see David Attenborough hunkering down to explain the feeding patterns of these wonderful creatures, and Jeffrey sitting on a rock scowling at the remote control. The penguins themselves, with their neat little mono-chrome costumes, clumsy movements, and jovial expressions, reminded me a little of Reginald. The thought made me homesick for a moment, but then I distracted myself by asking a courteous fellow tourist from South Korea to take a photo of me with the camera I'd bought especially for the trip. On the credit card, of course.

When I got back to the hotel, I sent Sophie a text message to ask how it was going at Bristol. She replied, several hours later, with one word: *wikid*.

Then I texted Boris to check that the house was okay, and he replied immediately: *All in order, boss*.

THURSDAY, OCTOBER 2

Have spent the day walking on the beach and reflecting. Argentina is not entirely what I had expected. In fact, I'm not sure what I did expect, in the sudden whirl of booking our tick-ets and packing our bags, but I believe it featured dirt, cacti, shacks, and a dearth of civilized things such as breakfast cereal. Instead, I find that even relatively small towns like Rawson have skyscrapers, office workers in suits and ties, neat pavements, cash machines, supermarkets, and pharmacies that glow green and white in the evening. Of course, this pattern is not uniform, and some of the things I had vaguely imagined do indeed crop up. I snagged two cardigans on flowering cacti in the botanical gardens of Buenos Aires. On the bus over here, as soon as we pulled out of the center of El Calafate you could see the buildings deteriorate into ramshackle tower blocks with patchy lighting and groups of boys playing football in dirt clearings.

I expect I shall see more tomorrow, as I start a twenty-hour trip back up to the center of the country and a warmly recom-mended estancia near Cordoba. I wonder what Miss Hughes would say if she could see me now? I suppose that would very much depend on whether she managed, for once, to locate her spectacles.

MONDAY, OCTOBER 6

This is the life. The air is clear and crisp, the terrain rolls away in gentle, undulating hills; it reminds me a little of a holiday in the Welsh valleys, except with better weather and food, and more thorn trees. I am staying at a small estancia, or working ranch, which is also very comfortably decorated for guests. I have a lovely little bedroom with a wrought-iron bed frame, smooth creamy walls, dried lavender standing in iron pots, and a beautiful French window with blue curtains sweeping down to the floor and a view out onto grazing cattle, trees, and, at night, millions of undimmed stars. There is a sense of space here that quite eludes one in the Cotswolds. We are one hour on a dirt road from the nearest village. There is no human settlement as far as the eye can see, no noise; just green hills, and the fluctuation between silence and birdsong. I am going to rest, read, and think. Then perhaps darn the hole in my hiking socks.

TUESDAY, OCTOBER 7

How much do I miss Jeffrey? This is the question I have been pondering all day, as I went for a brisk walk around the perimeter of the estancia in the morning chill, and as I eased myself slowly into the swimming pool this afternoon. It is a question that is hard to dissociate from routine. If I was at home, and it was seven P.M., and I was waiting for him to come home so that I could tell him all about some squabble with Natalia or show him the cushion covers I had bought for the spare room, then I know the answer would have been a great deal. Here I am not so sure.

I swam length after length in the small turquoise pool as the spring sun warmed my hair, feeling the heat of my body over-power the cold of the water, asking myself again and again: "How much do I miss him?" Even after I had gotten out, lain on my lounger, and counted all my goose bumps, I wasn't sure of the answer.

Now I am sitting in front of the computer in the "ranch house," a snug lounge lit up with candles and decorated with leather bridles, horseshoes, and old black-and-white photos of gauchos looking stern in their traditional floppy hats and wide trousers. I can still feel a glow from the sun, which brought the freckles out across my shoulders. Or perhaps it is just the excellent Argentin-ean red that I'm sipping from a glass as wide as a goldfish bowl. In any case, as I thought in Buenos Aires—which already seems like an age ago—I feel strangely detached.

Jeffrey called when I was en route here, staring out at the inky night. I picked up out of instinct, partly because I haven't figured out whether I'm "talking to" my own husband or not, and partly just to stop the ringing, which had woken up a fierce-looking fel-low bus passenger with a prodigious black beard. Jeffrey said, "Hello, old bird," in a familiar voice, confident, slightly ironic; I made a small cocoon out of my cardigan and traveling blanket and said hello back. He asked if I was okay; I said yes. Then he proceeded to tell me in great detail how he had roped his first calf that day. I told him I was on a bus, waited long enough to register the shocked silence, then hung up. He did not call back.

So you will see that we are in limbo. I don't know what Jeffrey has told work; I don't know how long the credit card will last. But while I am here I will make the most of it. I think I shall order steak for dinner, again.

I only hope I don't end up eating one of the creatures that helps to make the view from my room so picturesque.

WEDNESDAY, OCTOBER 8

I have been riding! It was quite a different experience from the last time I sat on a horse, which would have been at a Pony Club gymkhana in 1970. There are no dumpy skewbalds named Daisy, no weaving between stripy poles or jumping over barrels. The horses here are slender but tough, with Roman noses and dense coats. Carlos, one of the gauchos, took me on a trip out from the estancia and across the meadows to a small, limpid river. Those years of Saturday morning lessons have paid off; I still have a secure seat, managing to remain in place when my horse spooked at one of the small hawks that are as commonplace here as pigeons. I think Carlos was impressed. What's more, I managed this feat in spite of some very unfamiliar equipment: the saddles here are huge and well padded, almost forcing you to slouch with your legs out straight in front, in flagrant contradiction to the diagram in my Pony Club manual, which showed a straight line passing from shoulder to elbow to heel. I can almost hear Mrs. Hough, the riding mistress, bellowing "Toes up, heels down" in vain. When Carlos nudged his horse into a trot and mine followed, I instinctively began rising up and down to the rhythm in the correct style, but it felt most unnatural with the Argentinean saddle. I saw Carlos laughing, then covering his mouth with his hand when he saw that I had seen. By the end of the trip I'd gotten used to a sitting trot and holding two sets of reign in one hand, and was quite convinced that I could give Jeffrey a run for his money.

THURSDAY, OCTOBER 9

A most unusual occurrence today: Sophie called, and she did not ask for money. Instead, she asked me if I was okay. I thought for a moment, and then I said that I was. Then she asked what was going on with me and Dad. I thought for another moment, then said: "I don't know." This did not seem to satisfy her, but then I suddenly remembered something I had inadvertently read in the problem pages of a trashy magazine while tidying her room, and I said, "We just need a bit of time and space." She said, "Oh." Then she said, "****, I'm out of credit," and we were cut off. I called her back and asked her about Bristol, and she said it was "awesome" and she was having a "wicked" time and she'd made tons of friends and last night was eighties night at the union and they all wore pink leg warmers and sweatbands and they got home at four A.M. and decided to make a fry-up out of everything in their cupboards, which was "sick." Then I asked her how the course was going, and she said, "All right."

After the call, I swam thirty-four lengths, and tried not to think about Jeffrey.

FRIDAY, OCTOBER 10

This morning I woke up with tears in my eyes. I had dreamed that Sophie, Rupert, and Jeffrey were all on a cruise liner, and I had cast myself off in a little dinghy with seventeen cans of baked beans and a camping stove, and the waves between us were growing bigger and bigger so that their faces peering over the deck of the ship were getting obscured, and then I couldn't see them at all, and ten of my cans fell overboard, and I suddenly remembered I'd forgotten my moisturizer. Just as I was rummaging about the boat to see if I could find it after all, everything suddenly shifted and I was peering into the cupboard in the belfry, at the Tupperware tub of biscuits and the half-empty bottle of Dettol and the dead spider. I was suddenly aware of a leaden silence. I turned and all the bell ringers were standing in a line, looking at me and shaking their heads, even Reginald, with his lips pursed, even Gerald.

It took a long ride out with Carlos to clear my head. Luckily he is easy company, his English being almost as nonexistent as my Spanish. Occasionally, he will point to something—a bird, or a cow—and say what I presume the word for it is in Spanish, and I'll repeat it, then I'll say it in English and he'll repeat it. If he wasn't so tall and serious-looking, with his molten black eyes and muscular shoulders, his lisp would remind me of Manuel from *Fawlty Towers*. We tried a canter on a lovely little uphill stretch, but I felt so torn between sitting back as the saddle dictated and leaning forward as I had been taught years ago that it was rather bumpy.

SATURDAY, OCTOBER 11

Although I came here, I suppose, to be by myself, I find that I've struck up a few friendships. It is off-peak season, and the only other guests at the estancia are an American couple a few years older than me. They're called Bob and Rosa, and both have that deep, even honey tan that marks them out as hailing from far sunnier climes than Surrey. It turns out that they live in Miami, where Bob recently retired as a software specialist and Rosa as a dental nurse. At first I thought they were a normal married couple, who had gone through their lives together comfortably clocking up the years, the children and grandchildren, but it transpired that the truth was a little more complicated. After a few brief poolside chats, then some longer conversations over wine in the ranch house, I learned that this was in fact a second marriage, for both of them, and that they had a bewildering array of descendants and divided loyalties between them. "We're like a walking *Jerry Springer Show*," said Rosa, laughing and holding her glass of wine in front of her with a perfect pink lipstick mark on the rim. "Except without the trailers or the sex changes," added Bob, a touch too quickly.

I found myself warming to them immediately, and they, I think, to me. They must have noticed my wedding ring, but they are sensitive enough not to ask any questions. I wonder what they think. They already appear to view me as a typical English eccentric simply because I insist on swimming every afternoon, even though the pool is still rather chilly. I told them that I spent every summer as a child playing in the sea in Cornwall and building sand castles in the rain, but this appeared only to reinforce their opinion.

Carlos too seems to find my daily swim an entertaining spectacle. Only today, when I stood on the fourth step down, the cold water lapping around my thighs, I looked up and saw him leaning on a fence post, watching me and smiling incredulously. The Argentineans must have a weaker constitution. No wonder we won the war.

SUNDAY, OCTOBER 12

Today, I galloped. I'm still buzzing. Rosa thinks I'm incredibly brave. I can still hear the thud of hooves beneath me, the rush of speed. Carlos and I had not been making great progress in our daily rides; I enjoyed the views, and our limited conversation, but every time we broke into a canter I tried to lean forward, the saddle stopped me, and I would have to slow down. Today, however, was different. We had just walked the horses through the river, where mine dropped his noble head and drank with a great slurping noise, which made Carlos laugh. It was late afternoon, the sun was throwing long shadows from the thorn trees, the earth smelled warm and mellow. I felt peculiarly relaxed.

We came to a large, open, grassy meadow. Carlos looked at me and smiled, then urged his horse into a trot, then a canter. Mine followed, and I felt the usual imbalance. Carlos kicked his horse on faster, turned around and looked me in the eyes, and gestured for me to sit back. For the first time, I did. He smiled, and urged his horse on faster still. Mine sped up too. I sat back, my hips swaying and absorbing the motion, the ground reeling away beneath me. I felt incredibly free. When we stopped, I was grinning like a lunatic. Miss Hough would have been horrified by my technique, but Carlos looked at me with a broad smile across his tanned, handsome, thirtysomething face, and said, *"Muy bien."*

MONDAY, OCTOBER 13

I've just been on Facebook for the first time in months. As I was sipping my wine and talking to Bob and Rosa about absent friends, I suddenly felt the urge to find out what my own little online circle had been up to. Once I had logged on, the first thing I saw was a status update from Bridget, which read *is wondering if Dita von Teese is an appropriate role model for a 53-year-old publisher.* I pondered this for a while. On the one hand, from what I once read in a magazine, she would appear to take her clothes off for money; but on the other hand, it is very artfully done, and the clothes in question are beautiful and vintage. I imagined what Jeffrey would say if I asked him. It would probably be "A tart's a tart." I took another sip of wine and typed in the word *yes.*

Then I saw that Tanya had posted pictures of little Shariah, and I forgot all about the ethics of burlesque stripping. She is indescribably gorgeous. In one photo, she is curled up in a little ball, clutching a white teddy bear, her eyes creased shut and her dark little lashes fanning out onto plump pink cheeks. In another she is looking straight at the camera as if she wants to take it apart and chew it, her eyes blue and wide, a few curls of brown sticking straight up from her head. In the least dignified of the pictures, Tanya has dressed her in a rabbit jumpsuit complete with ears. The bonnet I knitted her, however, is conspicuously absent. She must have outgrown it already.

After a few minutes staring at these pictures and sipping my wine, all the thoughts that had been pushed to the back of my mind by Sophie's disappearing act, Jeffrey's arrest, and our sudden trip over here began to gather and loom. I thought about Harriet's grandchildren, and Rupert, and how he will never hold his own baby in a soft pink blanket in his arms, and then before I knew it there were tears rolling down my cheeks and Bob and Rosa were by my side asking if everything was all right.

I felt incapable of lying. I blurted out everything about Rupert, and then this led to Sophie and Ivan and, finally, Jeffrey. Rosa put a sympathetic arm around my shoulders and said that Jeffrey sounded like a schmuck, which Bob translated for me as "idiot." Sensing that I wanted to be alone, they got up and quietly left, leaving me free to close down Facebook and pick up a real coffee table book on the history of Argentina's estancias, immersing myself in a simple world in which women cooked and men rode horses and that was about that.

TUESDAY, OCTOBER 14

Is Jeffrey a schmuck? The word has a more satisfying resonance than its British counterpart. Schmuck, schmuck, schmuck. Is he, indeed, a *cabrón*? I am visualizing Jeffrey, sitting in a deck chair in the garden with a gin and tonic and the Sunday paper while I visit Mother, alone.

Rupert called this afternoon, so I asked him: "Do you think your father's a schmuck?" He asked me if I had been out in the sun without a hat, which did not move things forward one way or the other. We moved on to other matters, and he reassured me that Darcy and Fergie were both well, and that Boris was keeping the house tidy and developing, in his boredom, an unhealthy fixation with vacuum cleaners. He has taken apart both of my models, cleaned them thoroughly, and put them back together again. He asked Rupert for permission to spend some of the housekeeping budget on additional nozzles.

Just then, I noticed the time, and said I had to dash to go riding with Carlos.

"Who's Carlos?" I heard Rupert ask just as I was hanging up.

WEDNESDAY, OCTOBER 15

Today I looked in the mirror for a long time. Matters have improved slightly since the last time I did so. The fresh air is good for my complexion; either that, or it's the Crème de la Mer face cream I bought from duty-free on Jeffrey's credit card. I have lost a little weight, probably due to a combination of exercise and the lack of facilities to whip up a quick coffee cake or batch of flapjacks. My stomach is a little flatter, my legs feel more toned. My hair has grown out of its usual gently layered bob, and I'm beginning to think it suits me longer. There are wisps of gray appearing at the roots, but the sun has streaked my auburn color through with caramel, so they don't stand out too much. All in all, I'm in reasonably good shape, should anyone happen to look at me.

THURSDAY, OCTOBER 16

Jeffrey called this afternoon as I was lying by the pool reading a crinkled copy of U.S. *Vogue* and wondering if I should buy myself a new Versace lipstick. The line was bad, but I could just make out that he was asking me to be a bit careful with money before it cut out. I ordered a Sex on the Beach and went back to the magazine. I think Drenched Damson would be just my shade.

MONDAY, OCTOBER 20

Dear God. What will you think of me? What have I done?

Looking back over previous postings, if you don't already know, you are two currants short of a tea cake, as Mother used to say. I feel like I'm drowning in shame, guilt, excitement, and life.

This has been going on for three days and only now have I plucked up the courage to tell you. Except I'm not telling you, because you already know.

I shouldn't have. I never should have. I have been married faithfully for thirty-four years. We have two children. For thirty-four years I have never allowed myself to seriously consider another man. It would have been ridiculous, the sort of thing I read about in Sophie's magazines or watched on reality television until Jeffrey switched to the news. That, and the dandruff, is why I shut the door on Gerald. Thirty-four years together, thirty-four years of being a good wife, thirty-four years of breakfasts and dinners and holidays and family and sleeping with my face ten inches from his.

And those thirty-four years counted for nothing when Carlos took my wineglass from me, drank from it, then gently, knowingly, brushed his fingers against my thigh.

I hate myself. I'm loving this. What am I going to do?

TUESDAY, OCTOBER 21

I still don't know what to do, but I have made a start by calling Bridget. As she lives in London, where standards of behavior are considerably more lax than in east Surrey, she is unlikely to choke on her own tongue with outrage. I felt strangely nervous about talking to her, even though, as students, we used to spend hours in each other's rooms, sitting on the floor with our backs to the narrow bed, talking about boys when we were meant to be studying Byron. After eight rings, just as I was about to give up, almost with a feeling of relief, she picked up. It was early evening for her, midday with a piercing sun for me; I tried to imagine her curled up on the chair by the phone in her flat wearing her black-ribboned cardigan with the autumn night already darkening around her. "Constance!" she said. "I've been wondering what's happened to you. How come you've not been in touch? I was beginning to think you'd been taken hostage by that new Polish housekeeper or something." And she laughed, her husky laugh that hasn't changed since she was nineteen.

I cleared my own throat. Needless to say, it took a little while to apprise her of the fact that I was marooned on a cattle ranch in the middle of Argentina, without Jeffrey, or even an adequate supply of linen blouses. Once we had gotten past her shock, and once she had asked ten times if I was okay and I had said, without conviction, yes, she seemed to sense that there was something else. So I told her about Carlos. As I was midway through—I think I was telling her about the other day, when he took me to the river and we went skinny-dipping and rode home dripping wet—I noticed that I was looping the telephone cable round my finger so tightly that it had turned white. I dropped it, and carried through to the end, and my current dilemma.

"Oh, Constance," she said softly after I had finished.

"What on earth am I supposed to do now?" I asked, resisting a strong urge to form another telephone cable tourniquet.

She did not, of course, have the answer. Instead, she told me a little of her life now. She said she has had quite a few "flings," as she called them, which involve dresses, and dancing, and dinner— a certain retro "scene" that has little to do with antique furniture— and that they were nothing to be ashamed of. She said that I had to get over my hang-ups; she could tell from the tone of my voice that I was imagining my mother standing in front of me tut-tutting and wagging her finger and calling me a hussy. This image has indeed stalked my dreams.

Then she went off on a different tack.

"Do you know what though?" she asked. "I still miss Philip." This was her ex-husband, whom she had divorced because he had once "economized" by canceling her subscription to the *London Review of Books* and because he clacked his fork against his teeth when he ate. "I still have one of his shirts in my wardrobe. I like the sight of the sleeves. I miss knowing—or thinking that I know—that another life revolves around mine, even if it just means someone knowing that you've been to shop to buy the milk or booked the train tickets for the weekend in Bath."

This was not what I had expected. "What are you saying?" I asked. "That it was a mistake to split up?"

"No," she said confidently. "It wasn't a mistake. It's just sad, that's all."

"Where does that leave me? What do I do?" I asked, hearing the note of desperation in my voice.

"That, Constance, is what you and only you can decide."

Then I heard a suppressed sneeze just to my left, caught a glimpse of cerise-colored chiffon, and realized that Rosa had been listening to the entire conversation, tucked out of sight behind an ornamental nineteenth-century saddle.

 WEDNESDAY, OCTOBER 22

Oh, God. An e-mail, from Jeffrey:

conmie peqase come, ive broken my arm my righr one no good typong with left. youre not answering your phone. god I hope youre cjecking your emqil. you need to fly tyo santa rosa, then bus to chacharamendi, then taci to estancia. i am so sorry. i am a cad anq a fool. i miss you. my arm jurts like buggery. can you forhive me?

What am I going to do?

11:05 A.M.

Carlos has resolved the dilemma for me. He has been learning English. Before, he would just look at me and smolder. Today, he opened his mouth and said, "I . . . like . . . Britney Shpearsh," then beamed proudly.

My taxi will arrive in twenty minutes.

FRIDAY, OCTOBER 24

I am with Jeffrey. He is in a poor state. I found him lying on his bed in his small room, the curtains closed, his arm encased in white, his face the color of corned beef. Why are men congenitally incapable of applying their own sunscreen? When he saw me, he jumped up, then yelped with pain.

He sat back down again, and I perched on the side of the bed, not touching him, just looking at those achingly familiar features turned burgundy under the Argentinean sun. I felt a rush of relief and, I think, love. He told me I looked amazing, that there was something different about me. I blushed. I don't think I have blushed in front of Jeffrey for more than thirty years.

I changed the topic to the estancia, which had a certain rugged beauty, though it did not compare favorably to the one I had just left. There is no swimming pool here, no dried flower arrangements in the room, no gently rolling hills and whispering streams. In fact, the surest sign of civilization is the large, clunky computer I'm typing on in the lobby right now. Rupert would probably laugh and call it prehistoric. I miss Rupert.

I have come a long way north, and the climate is different. Jeffrey took me for a stroll around the grounds, his arm cradled in a sling, and pointed out the acres of stretching, red, dry soil. The Andes loomed up behind a haze of heat to the west. I felt almost sick and disorientated by the scale.

We have talked about this and that, about food and horses and weather, but we both know we're skirting the issues that count.

I'm booked into a separate room. Jeffrey didn't argue; he just gave me one of his long, hard looks.

SATURDAY, OCTOBER 25

Should I tell him? How can I? How can I not?

Every moment I'm with him, helping him put on his sling, making sympathetic noises as he winces, smearing SPF 30 onto his neck, I feel like a fraud. The guilt has settled in the pit of my stomach. I have the same feeling of nausea that I had when Jeffrey once made me eat oysters.

SUNDAY, OCTOBER 26

I A.M.

you knew about natalia, I bet you all knew about natalia, I bet everyone knew except me. How could he? in our own house under our own roof and she has such tacky dyed hair sometimes it looks almost purple how could he? It started last new years eve, the murder mystery I organized just for him, just to cheer him up, she cheered him up in the dark when everyone was looking for clues seeing nothing. its worse than what I did, at least carlos was never in the same room as jeffrey smiling and asking hiim if he wanted a cup of tea like a two-face scheming little snake. and you know what the worst thing is because there is a worst thing, even though its bad enough already, the worst things is that he said he thought it was just natalia but he didnt know, he wanted to be honest and get it all out in the open to start again afresh, and he didnt know and couldnt say for sure that one night it was natalia and not her twin sister lydia

11 A.M.

I have calmed down, and sobered up. As you will have gathered, last night Jeffrey and I finally had the conversation. It was over dinner, which was served inside the tiny "restaurant," which is really just the ranch lounge with the wooden sofas pushed back and a few simple tables dragged onto the cold flagstone floor. We ate steak that was so fresh it melted and drank the best part of two bottles of strong, heady local red. Then I looked at him and said the words that he had said to me six long, long weeks ago: "We need to talk."

I had planned to tell him how much he had upset, frustrated, and disappointed me, then tell him about Carlos and apologize profoundly. I didn't get the chance. Before I could begin, he took my hand and said, "I want to start again. I want to make things right. But first I've got to tell you something and I don't know if you will forgive me. I should have told you last time, before we came out here, but I couldn't, I just couldn't."

I squeezed his hand back, and waited nervously. Then he told me. It only ended the day she left the house after that row with Ivan. Looking back, I don't know how I missed all the signs, but last night I felt so shocked it was as if he'd stood up and slapped me across the face—with his good arm. For the first time in my life, I felt overwhelmed with anger, with pure, sheer rage, a million times stronger than the fury I once felt when Sophie came home drunk and vomited into my Le Creuset skillet pan. I stood up, tipped Jeffrey's plate onto his lap, and swiped his wineglass over onto the floor. The waiter gasped and rushed over, which surprised me, because I thought these Latino types were accustomed to histrionic outbursts.

I can clearly remember the sight of Jeffrey, his mouth gaping open, a salad garnish nestled on his shirt, before I marched out and walked, for a long time, under the black sky. The stars, spread out in a vast, glittering array, offered no consolation. I haven't seen him since.

Last night, I waited until the lounge was empty, then went back in, helped myself to the remains of a bottle of wine from behind the open bar, and wrote my blog. I don't think Jeffrey has left his room today. His curtains are still drawn.

It had been going on for the best part of a year. How could he? How could he, in our own house, in a room in which I had chosen the curtains, chosen the exact shade of apricot cream for the walls? How can I forgive him?

3 P.M.

Still no sign of Jeffrey. I called Bridget, but to my shame, as soon as she picked up I began crying. It took about ten minutes to get the story out, and when I did she said, "Oh, Constance," and I could feel the sympathy radiating out across the distance, feel the care in her voice, but it made no difference to me, absolutely none.

How could he?

MONDAY, OCTOBER 27

Last night, we had the conversation, round two. He came and tapped on my door at six in the evening, as I was lying propped up on the bed, trying to read my novel and sniffing. When I opened the door and saw him standing there, utter dejection in his eyes, and one small, wilted purple flower clutched in his hand, I didn't know what to feel. I let him in. He came and sat on a small stool, I sat on the edge of the bed. He could see the pathetic knots of used tissues on the bedside table. "God, Connie, I'm so sorry, you've got to believe me," he said, and I could see in his eyes that he was, and that, at that moment, he saw me as an object of pity, of helplessness. Something within me rebelled.

"I'm sorry, too," I said, stiffening my back. And then, without dwelling on the details, I told him about Carlos.

Now, as you will have gathered, I am not what you would call a feminist. The traditional arrangements between man and wife have always suited me just fine. I have never exactly been a firebrand defender of gender equality. And yet, after Jeffrey's reaction to my disclosure, I'm beginning to feel a little differently. We have both done wrong. I know this. But our situations, I am sure you will agree, are not morally comparable. He cheated on me continuously, for many months, under our own roof, calmly buttering his toast in the morning as if he had not just committed an atrocious act of adultery in the cleaning cupboard. I cheated on him for less than a week, with a strange man, in a strange country in which I had been summarily abandoned. Our situations—our sins, as Reginald would have it—are patently not symmetrical. So why, then, was he quite so outraged? Why did he leap up from his stool and kick it over? Why did he shout that he thought he knew me but didn't know me at all before running out and slamming the door behind him, then swearing as, presumably, the effort jolted his bad arm?

Why has he not come around today, with a flower, seeking forgiveness?

Why is it so much worse if a woman does what a man does with routine cruelty?

TUESDAY, OCTOBER 28

Stalemate. I am ignoring Jeffrey; Jeffrey is ignoring me.

WEDNESDAY, OCTOBER 29

Today I finally dug out my adapter and charger and plugged in my phone for the first time since getting here. I had two concerned answerphone messages from Sophie and Rupert, one from Tanya, who said that Shariah sent her love, and one from Harriet, who asked me if everything was all right in a worried voice and then told me that there was a rumor going around that Jeffrey and I had been thrown in jail in Costa Rica for drug smuggling. I deleted that message, but listened to the ones from Sophie and Rupert several times. Their voices made me cry. Perhaps I should go home. Perhaps this is it. For the first time, the strange heat and dust and vast blue sky oppress me. I miss home, I miss my children, I miss drizzle and narrow country lanes and the smell of cakes rising in the oven. Perhaps I should give up on Jeffrey and fly home alone and sell the house and buy a flat and throw myself into whatever divorced women do—take up pottery or stained glass or something, lend Miss Hughes a hand at Cats in Need, start embroidering. Is that what my future holds?

I knew I should call Sophie and Rupert back but I couldn't face it. Instead I wrote a text message, and sent it to them both: *With Dad, still alive, love Mum x.*

THURSDAY, OCTOBER 30

Today Jeffrey smiled at me over breakfast, a weak, flickering, uncertain smile. I smiled back, involuntarily. Then I scowled and went back to picking the burned bits off my bread roll.

FRIDAY, OCTOBER 31

I checked my e-mail earlier and found this message from Reginald amid the usual unsolicited junk offering me cheap train tickets or free knitting patterns:

Dear Constance,

I don't know where you are, but I hope you are well. We are all worried about you. There are all sorts of wild rumors flying around that we're doing our best to ignore. I pray to God every day that you're sunning yourself on an exotic island and not being used as an unwitting drug mule or anything dreadful like that. If you get this, please let me know that you are safe. I can't bear the thought of you festering in a prison cell. I know that you would sooner starve than eat a rat. Remember the face you pulled when Miss Hughes brought her homemade savory scones to church and the cheese was a bit off?

Well, wherever you are, I'm sure that some news from home will cheer you up. Rosemary has come back! Apparently she ditched her acrobat when they were on tour in Estonia and he tried to make her put her head in a lion's mouth. As I have often observed, dear Constance, the Lord moves in mysterious ways. She has had her hair cut and thrown away the leotards and is back to her good old self. Gerald is delighted. He was a bit shocked at first but then he came to me for a quiet talk and I advised him on the importance of Christian forgiveness.

I think that is the only news to speak of. The roof continues to leak in the corner, but we're only £143.76 away from being able to afford the repairs, and I'm hoping to raise that at next month's cake bake. If only you and your walnut slices were here we'd be home and dry, in more ways than one!

Warmest wishes,
Reginald

The message made me smile. I wrote back to tell him that I was well, but kept the details vague. Then I went for a long walk, and as the dry grass scratched my legs, I thought of Gerald and Rosemary rebuilding their life together, and I wondered.

SATURDAY, NOVEMBER 1

I actually feel happy. The guilt in my stomach has gone, a heavy sadness has lifted off my shoulders. Things are not perfect—I don't think they will ever really be perfect—but oh, they are better.

Last night Jeffrey knocked on my door at about six. I threw the tissues in the bin, ran my fingers through my hair, and let him in. He had a picnic hamper and a bottle of wine.

Once again, he said the words "Constance, we need to talk." Then he asked if I would come out with him. I agreed, on the condition that I could put on some insect repellent first.

He led me on a winding path toward the perimeter of the estancia, past cacti and bushes filled with small birds, up onto a little hillock with a view stretching out to the Andes on one side and to the plains melting into a flat horizon on the other. He spread out a blanket, which I noticed from a monogram must have been stolen from Lufthansa on our flight over. I decided not to reprimand him for his lack of morals. Instead I took off my sandals and sat down. He unpacked the food—empanadas, which are a surprisingly edible foreign version of the Cornish pasty; hunks of cheese; and big, rosy apples—and unwrapped two wineglasses from a hand towel. When he opened the bottle, the pop echoed for miles. Then there was silence. I looked down, at the evening sun lighting up the fine hairs on my arms, then I looked up, and I saw that he was watching me with damp, serious eyes.

"Connie, I am an arse," he said.

"I know," I replied, and smiled. We clinked our glasses; they bumped together, loudly. We drank, and ate, and once we had done that and we were stretched out among the crumbs he told me again that he was sorry, for everything he had done, for how he had reacted, that he wanted to start again.

He told me that he'd hated himself when he was sleeping with Natalia, but that he'd felt cut off from me, from home life, from his feelings. He said it was like living in a sort of bubble; he had been contented enough but somehow insulated, nothing had really mattered, nothing had felt real. And then it had been pricked. I raised my eyebrow at his choice of wording, and he laughed. I remembered how much I used to enjoy making him laugh in the old days, when we were first together, and I would describe elaborate caricatures of my English tutors. When had I stopped trying to entertain him? When had he stopped listening?

He told me that he'd thought he'd already been through his crisis when he was locked in his cell, but it turned out that it was only when he was out here, alone and hurt, that he truly realized what mattered and what didn't. Then he took my chin between his thumb and forefinger and told me that I mattered.

SUNDAY, NOVEMBER 2

A new month, a new beginning. Jeffrey and I are going traveling together. I think we'll start by heading to the tropical Iguazu waterfalls, and then see where our fancy takes us.

Do not be alarmed. I'm not naïve enough to think that one picnic has saved our marriage. The hurt runs deeper than that; it will take more. But I am willing to try, and so is Jeffrey: we will be striving together against the odds toward a common goal, for the first time since we lost the remote control for three days and eventually hunted it down to the pocket of Sophie's dressing gown. Also for the first time in recent memory, we are going on an adventure together. And it will be an adventure in more ways than one: we are on a strict budget. Alpha & Omega has stopped paying Jeffrey's salary. Before he left, he told them that he needed to take time off for a family emergency, but he has not been in contact since. He says that he has developed a sort of phobia at the thought of his old job, a little like how he used to feel whenever his mother would mention the dentist, except that in this case there are no sticky badges or cups of pink water to coax him back. We have investments, of course, but apparently the accursed recession has taken its toll. No matter. We will cope. I remember a Girl Guide camping trip when I was a child: sleeping on a paper-thin foam mattress, washing in cold water, eating baked beans warmed over a stove. I'm sure two-star hotels can be no worse.

I must go back and help Jeffrey pack; we leave in an hour. You may not hear from me for some time.

FRIDAY, NOVEMBER 7

A tropical beetle has eaten right through the leather of my sandals! I've had to replace them with flip-flops, the sort of rubber things that Sophie would wear, in bright turquoise. Jeffrey says I look "cool." We're at the Iguazu falls, in the steamy northeast. Yesterday we took a boat trip that wove so close to the waterfall we could feel the spray in our faces. Jeffrey rocked the boat on purpose and made me shriek, then grabbed me and gave me one of his bear hugs. It may be twenty-three years since he played club rugby, but he still has a powerful grasp.

Anyway, I can't write anymore because I need to e-mail Rupert and Sophie, check Facebook for new photos of Shariah, and use the phone booth next door to check in with Harriet and Mother, who thinks that Jeffrey and I are on an extended watercolor course in Andalucia. There is no free Internet where we are staying (although there is, thank heavens, a flush lavatory). This cybercafé connection is expensive, and the keys, as ever in such haunts, are grubby.

SATURDAY, NOVEMBER 15

We're in Rio de Janeiro. We've rented a moped. Earlier this evening, I clutched Jeffrey's waist as we zoomed along the seafront at a full seventeen miles per hour, with music from a teenager's ghetto blaster pounding in the background, skyscrapers rising up behind us and the setting sun turning the sea the color of sherbet. As Jeffrey valiantly steered the bike around some teenage girls dancing in the street, I thought that he reminded me of Che Guevera, except without the head scarf or the extrajudiciary killings.

SUNDAY, NOVEMBER 23

We're in Lima. I have walked the Inca trail, and encountered French-style lavatories, and survived both challenges. The lowest point of the trip came when Jeffrey and I had our first proper argument since beginning our adventure: studying the map, he was convinced that we had to follow a path leading up the left, but I was sure I could discern a bumbag hovering above a pair of broad American buttocks through the mist on a trail leading off to the right. Neither of us would give in, and our difference of opinion segued inexplicably into an argument about Natalia and Carlos. Eventually, the mist cleared, and we were distracted by the majestic crags of rock rising up ahead of us, and by another American, who appeared from behind a bend wearing a yellow waterproof poncho, tapped Jeffrey on the shoulder, and said, "The housekeeper? Man, that's low." I took this as a moral victory and the argument was soon forgotten.

Did you know they eat guinea pigs here? From the window of a bus (the quality of which has sadly deteriorated since Argentina) I saw a lady with a makeshift barbecue and a whole row of the hairless, roasted creatures, their expressions still bearing the indelible cheeriness of a family pet. I should tell Sophie. Perhaps it would stem the frequent complaints she puts in her e-mails about the quality of food in her hall of residence.

FRIDAY, DECEMBER 5

News, real news! Late last night my mobile—which I had just managed to recharge—rang. It was Rupert. After I had picked up with a sleepy hello, he said that he was sorry, he'd lost track of which time zone we were in. Then, with an uncharacteristic peeved tone in his voice, he asked, "Where are you, Mum? How long are you going to go on like this? Whenever I go home to check on the house, it freaks me out. It's spotlessly clean but so empty; the pile of mail in the hall is as tall as the hat stand. And I think Boris is starting to go nuts all by himself—he's buying second-hand vacuum cleaners on eBay and hand-washing the carpet."

I gave a small, sad laugh, and sighed. I do miss home. Today is the fifth of December, the fifth day of Advent, and here I am sitting in an Internet café in Bogotá, sweating in a Hello Kitty vest top that I bought in a market stall near the bus stop after the jungle moths got to my blouses. I had a sudden vision of cold, crisp mornings, of sitting down to write my Christmas cards, studying my list from last year with all the people who failed to send me a card neatly crossed out in red, and I sighed again. Every time I mention going home, Jeffrey gets the same pale, twitchy expression he acquires whenever he checks his bank account online, and he changes the subject. Our daily budget has been getting ever smaller, and I have started to yearn for life's little daily luxuries, the clean, warm towel on the towel rack, the cold apple juice in the fridge.

But I digress. Rupert had not finished. After I had told him that of course I missed home and that I was sure we would be coming back at some point in the not too distant future, and Jeffrey had woken up beside me with a jolt, Rupert said again: "But when? Will you be home by Christmas? By New Year? Oh, Mum, please say you'll be back by the New Year."

And it turned out that the reason he was so keen for us to be home by then was that he had something planned: a civil partnership ceremony with Alex.

Oh, readers, I had a mixed surge of emotion: sadness, I suppose at the finality, at the fact that Rupert's gayness wasn't a passing phase, like the time he got into "grunge" as a teenager, but most of all happiness, that he had found someone he wanted to be with for the rest of his life and whom he wanted to commit to in the eye of the law. As he told me of the plans—just a small, low-key gathering, family and a few close friends, perhaps dinner afterward—I could hear the contentedness in his voice, and I shared it. After all, a gay wedding is just as valid an excuse for the purchase of a new hat as a heterosexual one. Jeffrey agreed, but it took him a long time to get back to sleep.

SATURDAY, DECEMBER 6

My head hurts. The whir of the electric fan in this cyber-café is making it worse. My own hands are as clammy as the keys. Do not be alarmed: I am not suffering from some virulent South American disease, but from the aftereffects of too much aguardiente, a spirit that is quite the thing over here and that Jeffrey tells me is a little like Sambuca.

Last night we talked about our future. Jeffrey took me to a little bar with dark alcoves and coffee-scented candles and ordered a bottle of the spirit, which came with two squat little glasses. After he'd drunk three in quick succession, he admitted that he'd been desperate to avoid thinking about how things were going to work out when we got back home. Up until Rupert's call, he said he'd had his head in the sand. And now he was going to try to pull it out.

"I'm scared, Connie," he said. "I think I've lost my job. You don't just go AWOL for three months and expect to get away with it. God knows what kind of messages are sitting on my BlackBerry back home. I told them I was having a personal crisis and that was that. But you can't have a personal crisis when you're a senior partner. You can't have any kind of personal life at all," he said, as he poured himself another glass of the clear, fragrant liquid.

I squeezed his hand. "But darling, I thought you didn't want to be a lawyer anymore. I thought that was what this was all about."

"I didn't!" he replied. "Back home, I was sick of it, sick of the alarm in the morning, the train, the meetings, the routine. I was sick of watching my nearest colleague wipe his keyboard clean with a disinfectant wipe every day. He used to do his mouse too, and his phone. All I wanted was a bit of adventure. But now . . ." His voice trailed off.

"Aren't you a bit fed up of this too?" he picked up again. "Fed up of being able to go anywhere and do anything?"

I admitted that I was. I have started to have dreams—clear, vivid dreams—in which I am walking along the green to the church to bell ringing, but then suddenly I'm lost, and the familiar path has twisted and turned into something I don't recognize, and I'm walking faster and faster but getting nowhere. Either that or I dream I'm in the kitchen, cooking a big roast for Rupert and Sophie—I can hear them laughing and chatting in the dining room, but just as I walk through the adjoining door with a tray of Yorkshire puddings in my hands they're gone, the room is empty, even the familiar oak table has vanished. On one occasion I found myself in the Lima bus station instead; on another, in the haberdashery department of John Lewis.

I told Jeffrey all this as I swallowed a few glasses of aguardiente, which tasted more like sherry the more I drank it. Jeffrey squeezed my hand back, and as I looked at him I realized that there were tears in his eyes, and in mine.

"I miss the kids too," he said. "I expected that. But the oddest thing is, I even miss work. I miss putting on my tie and cuff links in the morning and coming home at the end of the day feeling like I've accomplished something, like I've earned the right to relax. Whereas with all this drifting, it's fun, but. . . ."

I told him I knew exactly what he meant. Adventures, I have decided, are like shortbread biscuits. When you can't have any, you crave them, but given a whole tin and no restraints, you soon start to sicken of them.

"So we're agreed," I said. "We're going back."

"We're going back," he said. "But I don't think it's going to be the same."

Then he explained why he was so worried about money. While I have largely remained blissfully ignorant of whatever has been going on in the news, Jeffrey has kept a weather eye on the Reuters Web site. All our investments have been clobbered.

"I'm not sure what we're going to live on, or how we're going to live," he said, swallowing his sixth, or seventh, glass of liquor.

Perhaps it was the insulating effect of the aguardiente, perhaps the fact that a month ago I thought I was going to lose Jeffrey and end my days a lone, embittered divorcée, but these words did not have the devastating effect that they once would have.

"We'll manage," I said. "Don't you worry, we'll find a way, even if I have to start buying cheap cuts of meat and doing the Christmas shopping at Woolworths."

"Woolworths has gone, remember?" he said. "It'll have to be TK Maxx."

I looked at him, and I realized that he was right: everything had changed.

SATURDAY, DECEMBER 13

I am home, and it feels like I'm in a different world. No more sweaty cybercafés and sticky heat: I am wearing a woolen jumper, sitting in Jeffrey's study in a leather-clad swivel chair, LapTop balanced on a solid oak desk, shelves of old legal textbooks and tennis trophies stretching up on either side. Out the window it is winter, and I realize just how long I've been away. When I left the garden was still lush with the final throes of summer; now it is bare, trimmed back, bleak. Randolph did a good job before returning to America.

My own reflection in the bathroom mirror gave me a shock. I was accustomed to seeing a pale, neat image of myself looking out against the backdrop of cream marble tiles. Now I am a toasty, golden brown, with freckles crowding all over my forearms, and my hair grown long and wavy, streaked through with white and gold. I wonder what the children will say when they come around tomorrow.

Jeffrey and I got back last night, worn out after the first economy flight we were able to book home. I had no idea that one was expected to eat with plastic cutlery and watch the same film as all the other passengers at the same time. I think Jeffrey struggled to adjust. He looked irritable and distracted throughout the whole of *Mamma Mia!*

Now that we're back, he has been pacing the house, opening

the doors to the rooms, closing them again. He has given Boris, who kept the house in an immaculate state, two weeks' notice. The poor man is a luxury we can no longer afford, even if he did bake us a welcome-home cake and buff every piece of furniture with beeswax while we were away. He took the news with his usual unflinching courtesy, but afterward I heard the mournful sound of one of Rupert's old Radiohead albums drifting from his room.

SUNDAY, DECEMBER 14

Bliss. Rupert and Sophie together under my roof, for Sunday lunch, and it was just like my dream, except when I walked through the door to the dining room they were both still there, Rupert with a navy turtleneck pullover and a touch of stubble, Sophie grinning despite her "monster" hangover. She took the train home this morning for the Christmas holidays, and apparently she's already missing university. All those stabs of guilt I felt for abandoning her as I woke up in a strange bed in Brazil or Bogotá were unfounded. Left to her own devices, she has flourished. She has filled out a touch—whether this is the result of a wholesome lifestyle or too much white wine I cannot tell, but it suits her; and there is something changed, more confident, in her general behavior. The tongue stud has gone ("the only other girl with a tongue stud was a goth, so it had to go," she explained). Not only did she refrain from hiding her peas under her knife, but she declared that she was no longer a vegetarian, and that I should feed the nut roast to Darcy because she would much rather tuck into some lamb—all the veggie options at halls were "minging," she said, so she'd given that up too. I met Rupert's eye, and we both smiled.

Rupert asked a lot of questions about our trip, and there was a gleam of pride in Jeffrey's eye as he got out his atlas after dessert and showed them both where we had been, the many borders we had crossed. I took out my camera and showed them some of our shots, from the hundreds of penguins huddled against the wind in Argentina to Jeffrey standing on Copacabana beach with a piña colada in his hand and a cocktail umbrella tucked behind his ear. Sophie said it looked awesome, just like a trip her other best mate, Liam, took in his gap year.

Rupert admired all the pictures, and then asked, in a tentative voice, "But are you glad to be back?"

Jeffrey and I held hands, looked into the young, smiling faces of our children, looked out at the cold December drizzle, and said that, yes, all things considered, yes, we were. I tried to hold that thought in my mind as I visited Mother, who told me that I was as brown as a farmhand.

 MONDAY, DECEMBER 15

10 A.M.

I can't sit still. I am too nervous. Jeffrey has gone in to see Andrew, the senior partner at Alpha & Omega. I had to tie his tie for him this morning; he had forgotten how. This does not bode well for a seamless return to corporate life.

3 P.M.

He is home. He is no longer a partner, I am no longer a partner's partner, as it were. And yet, as I shall explain, all is not entirely lost.

When his car crunched up the gravel on the drive and he got out, I struggled to read his expression. He had loosened his tie; he wasn't dejected and hangdog, he wasn't ecstatic with relief. It wasn't until I had made him a cup of tea and we had both sat down at the kitchen table that he told me what had happened.

"Well, my career as I knew it is over," he said, nonchalantly. He then told me how he had met up with Andrew and a severe woman from HR with a blond ponytail and metallic glasses. I did not like the sound of her. My instincts were correct. While Andrew asked him what had happened and whether he was okay, HR woman asked him if he realized how much disruption his disappearance had caused the company and its clients. Jeffrey said that he had explained as best he could that he had had some sort of personal crisis, but HR woman coldly asked him if he could supply a doctor's note to back that up. Jeffrey asked if she would accept the receipt for a leather cowboy hat in lieu, but she would not. And on it went in circles, until Andrew said that it was time to cut to the chase: sadly, Jeffrey could never have his old job back. It had already gone to Amanda (Andrew had at least had the good grace to look ashamed of himself, Jeffrey told me), and besides, in these tough economic times the company had to have 110 percent confidence in its partners. However, there was another role being offered: training the junior lawyers, on a part-time basis, and sharing the job with a woman who was just back from maternity leave. The salary would be half what he was previously on (or really a quarter, given the reduction in hours), but Jeffrey was not in a position to say no.

"Law is a small world," he said. "And most of the big firms are laying people off. Who else would take me on now? And do I even want to go back to the way I was before?"

So they had shaken hands, and he had signed the contract, and he will start work in his new, reduced capacity in the New Year. As soon as HR woman had retreated with the paperwork, Andrew took Jeffrey to lunch at The Cheddar Cheese, a musty old pub off Fleet Street—apparently the budget no longer stretches to the likes of Nobu, at least not for Jeffrey. There, he admired Jeffrey's tan, and Jeffrey told me that he caught a wistful look in Andrew's eye as he was telling him all about his prowess with the lasso and the moped.

All in all, as we finished our tea, we both agreed that things could have been a lot worse. I asked Jeffrey how we would get by with the money, and he said we would have to see. He's meeting with his financial adviser tomorrow; he said he was pretty sure we could no longer afford a financial adviser but that, just at the moment, we couldn't afford not to have one either.

TUESDAY, DECEMBER 16

We're going to have to sell the house. I can't write anymore because I'm crying and because I need to go into Boris's room to get Radiohead back.

WEDNESDAY, DECEMBER 17

For the first time in many months, I once again turned to bell ringing for comfort last night. I lay down with a slice of cucumber over each eye for half an hour first, so nobody would know that I had been crying. For a moment, I thought of recycling them for a salad, but decided we were not, yet, that desperate.

As soon as I walked across the churchyard I began to put the house to the back of my mind, savoring the anticipation of seeing my old friends. I was not disappointed. Reginald started and stared at me as if I were some sort of heavenly vision, then clasped me in a bear hug. Gerald looked a bit awkward, but gave me a small, quick hug and told me I looked very well. Rosemary was by his side, wearing a tweed skirt and a V-necked pullover looking for all the world as if she had never once fleetingly joined a traveling circus. During the coffee break, she came over and whispered, "Don't worry, he told me everything. I know that you've got nothing to be ashamed of. It was just as well he tried his luck with you, and not Miss Hughes. She'd have snapped him up, make no mistake. I know her sort: there was a bearded lady in Vilnius who had just the same glint in her eye."

What with this reflection on the universality of human nature and the need to concentrate intensely on my bell after months with no practice, I managed to spend almost the entire evening without thinking once about a stranger taking down my pictures and traipsing up my stairs with his clumpy stranger's shoes and opening the door to the bathroom with his grubby stranger's hands.

THURSDAY, DECEMBER 18

Today, Boris gave me a briefing on everything he does to look after the house, which will fall into my hands when he leaves. He will be going home for Christmas on Monday, and will be back in Britain to look for a new job in the New Year. I'm sure someone will snap him up. When I told him he could keep the vacuum nozzles he bought, tears of gratitude welled in his eyes.

As he described dusting the tops of the wardrobes in all five bedrooms, polishing the floorboards in Jeffrey's study, vacuuming the rugs, scouring clean the downstairs bathroom, the family bathroom, and the master bathroom, the prospect of moving into a new, smaller house became a little less terrible.

FRIDAY, DECEMBER 19

Last night Jeffrey said that he wanted to cook me a special dinner, so I put on a nice dress and some perfume, and took the batteries out of the smoke alarm in the kitchen. He grilled a couple of steaks, which caught fire only once, and made his own pepper sauce, splattering it across the kitchen tiles in an elaborate arc. Thank heavens Boris is with us for a little while yet.

Then he lit a candle in the dining room and put Van Morrison's "Brown Eyed Girl" on in the background. I was touched. He must have seen how upset I was about the house. As we were halfway through the steaks, which were tolerable, though nowhere near as tender as Argentinean beef, he suddenly slumped down from the table. I shrieked, fearing an angina attack, but he told me to be quiet. It was then that I noticed that he was on one knee. He took a little box from his pocket, and gave it to me.

It was simple, creamy cardboard, tied with a burgundy velvet ribbon. I opened it up. Inside was a ring, a beautiful ring—not diamond, not platinum, just a lovely, striking pear-shaped piece of turquoise flanked by two smaller pieces of coral on a thick silver band.

"Constance, will you remarry me?" he said, and smiled, the corners of his eyes crinkling upward in that lovely, familiar way.

"What on earth do you mean?" I asked.

He got up off the floor, knees creaking, and explained that after everything we'd been through together, and everything that lay ahead, he wanted to renew our vows, to make an official fresh start. He was sure that my friend Reginald would do the business.

I was sure he would too, but could I be sure I was ready for this? Jeffrey and I had just spent some of the best weeks of our marriage together; and yet, back in the house, every time I passed Natalia's old room, or found one of her old pink hair scrunchies lurking in the back of the bathroom cupboard, I felt a surge of surprisingly sharp anger and hurt.

This was not an easy thing to do, but I closed my hand over Jeffrey's, gently pushing it down over the open ring box, and said, "Not yet."

Last night, when I woke up in the early hours, I turned over and saw that Jeffrey too was lying awake, staring at the ceiling. I nestled my head into his shoulder, and eventually we both fell asleep together, until we were woken at seven A.M. by the sound of Boris vacuuming.

SATURDAY, DECEMBER 20

One good idea at least has emerged from Jeffrey's touching but awkward proposal yesterday. The prospect of having a church service after Rupert and Alex's civil ceremony was so appealing that I called my son this morning to ask him what he thought. Rupert may not be a regular churchgoer, but he has always got on brilliantly with Reginald, and he told me that he had so many fond childhood memories of church that it would make the day feel more significant somehow if we could arrange something, provided that Alex agreed, and that—he sounded a little anxious here—Reginald thought it appropriate.

I immediately called Reginald, who was delighted with the idea. "Of course, we'll have to fudge the wording a little, but I'm sure I can manage a blessing—I think Colossians 3:12 would do the trick. And what's the good of being a CofE vicar if I'm not allowed to fudge?"

No sooner had I thanked him and put the phone down than Rupert called back to say that Alex was "chuffed" with the idea too. "He said we'd get lovely photos, Mum, and he's right. The town hall may have more enlightened politics but it's still an eyesore."

And so we're all set. Jeffrey has just booked the cars to take us from the town hall to church, and then back here to see in the New Year all together. The plan would be perfect, if only I could find at short notice a wedding cake with two men on it.

MONDAY, DECEMBER 22

A sad farewell at the airport to Boris, who had asked permission to take one of Darcy's tail feathers to remember him. Then I spent the rest of the day making mince pies with Sophie, who told me all about university: the time they all played a joke on a girl called Stacy by sneaking into her room and turning every piece of furniture upside down and writing an upside-down message on her mirror in lipstick; the time everyone played a trick on her by sneaking into her room and taking Heidi, her cuddly giraffe, hostage; and also her course, which she said was fine.

By the time we'd gotten through all this, a veritable mountain of mince pies had formed, which is just as well—they're Rupert's favorites, and he will be here from Christmas Eve to Boxing Day. Harriet and Edward invited us to their house for Christmas Day, but I declined—I want to enjoy the last Christmas in our house, and not face any mortifying remarks as to why I have not yet had my hair recolored.

On Boxing Day, Alex and his parents will be joining us, which has already caused me to wake at two A.M. with the following questions on my lips: Should Jeffrey and I congratulate them unequivocally, or attempt to share a moment of somber solidarity on the subject of what might have been, of the grandchildren never to be born? Will a leg of ham suffice?

TUESDAY, DECEMBER 23

I can't type more than a few lines. I am exhausted in body and soul. I have been Christmas shopping on a budget. The morning—which involved meeting up with Bridget in London to buy presents—was not unalloyed hell. It was wonderful to see my dear friend, who hugged me so tightly I thought I would burst. She helped me find all sorts of quirky, inexpensive presents, including a set of "carpet golf" for Jeffrey. And yet the crowds that surged and pressed all around us gave me flashbacks to the streets of Bogotá where pickpockets relieved Jeffrey of twenty U.S. dollars and his last remaining packet of extra-strong mints.

It was the afternoon, however, that really took its toll. Food shopping for Christmas used to involve writing a list for the housekeeper (whose name I will no longer deign to mention), then taking a leisurely stroll around the broad, white, quiet aisles of Waitrose to pick up any extras. Today I went to Lidl. It was Jeffrey's idea. He said that they stocked many high-quality products at a bargain price, and that if he could only turn back the clock a year he'd have invested his savings in them rather than in U.S. property derivatives.

This may well be, but it has taken me a strong coffee and a nip of brandy to revive myself from the trip. It was a disorientating, discombobulating experience: the narrow aisles, the cluttered displays, the bargain bins stuffed with "slipper socks" (I was unaware such a hybrid existed), and chocolate Father Christmases whose foil wrappers were peeling off.

I swear that woman ran my foot over with her trolley on purpose as I reached for the last packet of ninety-nine-pence Parma ham.

WEDNESDAY, DECEMBER 24

The last of the Christmas cards arrived today, and among them was a lurid pink envelope bearing Natalia's erratic handwriting. I showed it to Jeffrey, and he threw it on the fire without saying a word. He held my hand as we watched it burn. It made a strange pop and hiss and emitted a bitter smell.

THURSDAY, DECEMBER 25

Merry Christmas, my dear readers. I hope your day has been more tranquil than my own. All I had hoped for was a quiet family meal, and that Mother would not crack her dentures on the fifty-pence piece Jeffrey always hides in the Christmas pudding. It was not to be. No sooner were we all seated around the table—a CD of carols from King's College Choir playing in the background, the plastic contents of cut-price Christmas crackers all around us, a steaming platter of Lidl sprouts in the center—than there was a knock on the door. Or rather three bold, vigorous knocks, the knocks of a self-assured and potentially violent visitor. We all exchanged glances, apart from Mother, whose hearing is not what it was, and who continued to look at the lime-green plastic comb that had come out of her cracker as if it might leap up and stab her. Jeffrey, Sophie, Rupert, and I rose from our chairs and went to the door. Jeffrey opened it. And there on the doorstep, with a poinsettia plant, a bottle of vodka, and a young woman in his arms, stood Ivan the Terrible.

"Merry Christmas!" he boomed. "It's the season for forgiveness, no? I've brought you vodka with the gold flakes in. Please meet Irania, my fifth wife. I save the best to last!"

And with that, somehow, they were over the threshold, Ivan clasping Jeffrey in a bear hug, Irania taking off a fur-lined coat to reveal a black silk minidress, scarlet tights, and over-the-knee patent leather boots.

What could I say? What could I do? You can imagine my feelings on seeing the man who had absconded with my daughter and framed my husband for fraud come crashing into our quiet family Christmas. And yet there is something about Ivan, some irrepressible force, that has you graciously accepting his crushed flowers and hanging up his coat before you can say "b***** off, you Russian b******." Jeffrey looked as if he might punch him, but Ivan clasped both his shoulders and said, "I am a new man. You must believe me, old friend."

I turned to Sophie, fearing for her reaction, but she was simply giving the pair of them a cold, appraising look, and when I got closer she whispered, "Her boots are totally last season, Mum."

And then we sat down to lunch, hastily eked out with some leftover new potatoes. Luckily, Irania did not eat much. Mother, for once, was stunned into silence, although she continued to stare at our visitors as if they posed an even greater threat to her person than the green comb did. As soon as the meal was over, she went to lie down. It was then that Ivan unscrewed the top of his vodka bottle, poured a generous measure into everyone's port glass except Sophie's, because she covered it with her fingers, and said, "Now we can talk. Now you can tell me you forgive me. I am ashamed of myself. For long nights I have lain awake. Irania here can tell you that." He winked at her, and she giggled.

Jeffrey, who has never been able to bear a grudge, picked up his vodka glass, eyed the specks of gold floating in it like celestial dandruff, and clinked his glass against Ivan's. There ensued a long catch-up—punctuated only by the Queen's Speech—in which Jeffrey regaled Ivan with the highlights of his trip, and Ivan told Jeffrey how he had cleaned up his act, closed his recruitment business, and was doing a roaring trade in corporate liquidation solutions.

Eventually, after Rupert and Sophie had retreated to the other room to play cards, the conversation turned to future plans. Banging his vodka glass down on the table, Ivan said, "I want to settle down here. Spread roots. Be an Englishman in his castle. I'm selling my Moscow flat and I want to buy a house just like yours, with the roses around the door and the village pub a stroll away. I want Irania to stand in the kitchen looking out at the green

English lawn making cakes for our children. Our many children." Another nudge, another giggle. Readers, you can guess where this conversation was heading. After another few glasses of vodka, and despite my kicking Jeffrey sharply in the ankle, he said to Ivan, "Old man, if you really like this house, you can buy it, you know. Connie and I fancy a change."

There was a silence. I stared fixedly at the Lidl paper napkins, which featured a red robin with remarkably long eyelashes, and pondered the following dilemma. Which is worse: to have Ivan the Terrible take over my house, infiltrating every room with his malodorous presence, replacing my roll-top bath with a gold-edged Jacuzzi, or to open the door to a real estate agent?

Before I could formulate an answer, I saw that Jeffrey had reached over the table to shake Ivan's hand and that Irania was staring at the French windows with a proprietary smile.

It was only afterward, when Ivan and Irania had left, and Jeffrey and I sat on the sofa together with a tube of heartburn tablets, that he told me the amount Ivan had offered was considerably more than what we could have hoped for on the open market. Revenge, he said, with a sheepish smile. "Don't worry, Connie, it's not going to go back to how things were with Ivan. No shooting trips when you need me," he said, smiling guiltily. We talked again about the money, and the sense of relief that we would not have to have strangers traipsing through our home.

"And you can buy yourself a lovely hat for Wednesday now," Jeffrey added, squeezing my hand. After thirty-four years, he has finally learned to say the right thing.

FRIDAY, DECEMBER 26

After the drama of yesterday, lunch with Alex and his parents was mercifully uneventful. It was wonderful to see Alex again, who really is a charming young man. He gave me an illustrated hardcover book on the parrots of the world as a Christmas present, and remarked on how much my hair suited me longer. His parents were equally pleasant. Rather than any mortifying heart-to-hearts on the inadvertent rearing of homosexuals, we talked about the traffic on the M25, the weather, the sad decline of rural post offices, and the sad decline of the village pub.

Alex and Rupert repaired to Jeffrey's study to watch *Casino Royale* on DVD while we chatted. I didn't think that gay people liked action films, but life, as I have discovered, is full of surprises.

SATURDAY, DECEMBER 27

Once more unto the breach: today I went sales shopping for my mother-of-the-groom outfit. It was not an easy task. Last night I had lain awake deliberating on what would be the appropriate outfit to wear as a well-preserved fifty-four-year-old woman about to witness the civil union between my son and a geography teacher. I suppose if I had been truly desperate I could have sent myself in as a case study for that reality TV program with the two hectoring women, but instead I went to John Lewis. Sophie came along to pick up a few pullovers for the cold winter in halls and to advise. After a few unsuccessful experiments with outfits that made me look like, variously, a French maid and a nun, we struck on a combination that made me smile, and Sophie gasp, as soon as I stood in front of the mirror. I will be wearing a fitted mandarin-collared dress in puce-colored silk, a cream brocade jacket that falls in a flattering line over my hips, and a broad-brimmed, elegant puce hat.

Jeffrey will wear his suit. Like with so many things, as a man he has it easy.

SUNDAY, DECEMBER 28

Jeffrey and I took Mother back to her home, where she complained that the nurses had not taken down her Christmas cards yet, and then, when she found two in the bin, complained that they had. We have decided not to tell her about Wednesday. I fear the gay civil partnership will be too bewilderingly modern for her. It was bad enough the time that Rupert tried to explain e-mail.

 MONDAY, DECEMBER 29

Jeffrey and I dedicated most of the day to carpet golf. I hope that in our new home we will have a flatter carpet; every time I got close to the overturned tennis trophy that we were using as a "hole," the deep pile interfered with the path of my ball. I don't understand why Jeffrey did not encounter the same problem.

 TUESDAY, DECEMBER 30

Sophie just presented me with the most lovely surprise: a tailor-made two-man figurine for the cake, which she had crafted herself from papier-mâché made from yesterday's paper. You can almost discern a news item about Gypsies on one of the grooms' suits, but it is a touching gift. One more shepherd's pie and twenty-seven more canapés to bake, and I'm ready for tomorrow.

 WEDNESDAY, DECEMBER 31

11 P.M.

What a day, what a wonderful, wonderful day. Even as it went along, every moment seemed to acquire the light and the stillness of a photograph in the family album. The smile on Rupert's scrubbed, glowing face; the way Alex smiled back at him; their matching lemon ties and gray suits. Harriet, who appeared to be there on sufferance, turned almost the same color as my hat during the ceremony, and Edward had a coughing fit, but I have already edited that out of my recollections. Then there was the drive across the village green, which was brushed with frost; the short walk into the church, which the Church Flowers ladies had lined with cream roses and red poinsettias. Hazy winter sun fell through the stained glass, daubing color onto the faces of my dear friends: Mark and Tanya with little Shariah bundled up in a sequined blanket, Bridget in a velvet jacket, David wearing a pink tie that matched Ruth's pink dress, Rosemary and Gerald and Miss Hughes all standing straight in a line. Alex and Rupert sat in the front-row pew, their shoulders touching. Reginald intoned a reading in his gentle voice, spoke of "love which binds everything together in perfect harmony," and Jeffrey looked at me with enough warmth in his eyes to burn through the frost, enough to cure, even, Miss Hughes's chilblains.

And then it was over, and we were walking out in clusters to the churchyard, and Rupert took my arm and said, "I'm proud of you, Mum. I know everything you've been through."

I clutched his arm back. "You've always been a sensitive boy," I said.

"No, Mum, I mean, I really do know exactly what you've been through. I know because I read it on your blog."

I nearly dropped my handbag in shock. I had presumed that you alone, strangers who I now also count as friends, were my audience. When I thought about some of the things that I have written on this blog—my initial horror at Rupert's revelation; my skulduggery with Ivan's sunscreen; Carlos, oh dear Lord, Carlos—I momentarily felt dizzy. But then Rupert tightened his grasp on me. He had finally tracked down my blog, he said, when he was worried about me after Jeffrey and I had gone AWOL somewhere in Peru. As my blog was anonymous, he'd had to Google all the things I was likely to mention to track it down—eventually, a combination of "Jeffrey Rupert Sophie Darcy bell ringing John Lewis" did the trick. He told me he'd loved it, he loved me, I had nothing to be ashamed of. I hugged him back. What is the point of dwelling on the past? What more, indeed, is there to say here?

Alex called Rupert away; Jeffrey caught up with me and I put my hand in his pocket. He clutched it, and it took him a few moments to realize that I was wearing the ring he had bought me, which on a whim I had fished out of his bedside table, where it was crammed in between *Golf Monthly* and a miniature Swiss Army knife key ring. He rubbed his thumb over the smooth, cold metal and smiled at me, and at exactly that moment a joyful note pierced the thin air as from up in the belfry the bells, the glorious bells, rang out.